Search for the Warwick II

A Novel

by

Sherry Ann Miller

Published and Distributed by:

Granite Publishing and Distribution, LLC
868 North 1430 West
Orem, Utah 84057
(801) 229-9023 • Toll Free (800) 574-5779
Fax (801) 229-1924

Page Layout & Design by Myrna Varga • The Office Connection, Inc.
Cover Design by Tammie Ingram
Cover Art by Tammie Ingram

ISBN: 1-932280-95-2
Library of Congress Control Number: 2005930374

First Printing, July 2005

1 3 5 7 9 10 8 6 4 2

Printed in the United States of America

Dedication

To Chad, the Tiger of our family,
who strives to lead us in righteous paths,
regardless of the obstacles in his way.

To Sean, who will always be Mama's Sugar Babe.
He knows my heart,
and how much I love him.

To Mike, the MysterE in our daughter's life,
and the hope in my heart forever.

To Brian, who inherited his Brown Eyes from me,
but his tenacious spirit from God.

To Big J, who faces the struggles of life with true heroism,
and conquers with every effort.

To Jeff, the Fire Starter in our daughter's heart,
and the promise in mine.

To Michael, my Minky-Monkey, who touches my soul
with his undying love for his family . . .
thousands of us!

The valiant character, John Dunton,
from the Warwick Saga, was created out of the hero
I see in each and every one of you,
my sons.

May you realize miracles can happen in your life,
and the Lord can lead you to those activities
that will uplift you
and enlighten your soul.

With all my love,

Mama

Chapter One

Endowment of Hope

*". . . be sober, putting on the breastplate of faith and love;
and for an helmet, the hope of salvation."*
~I Thessalonians 5:8

*I*t's the twenty-sixth day of January, 1638, and I'm ten and one-half years old today, thought Thomas Dunton as he scrubbed the forecastle deck with salt water and a stiff brush.

Hard, physical labor had changed Thomas in many ways. His knees had calloused over the past eighteen months, as had his young hands, which now looked more like an older seaman's than he'd ever thought possible. Stronger than the lad he'd been before his enslavement to Moorish pirates, Thomas knew his strength came from lifting heavy buckets of seawater up from the waterline day after day, and scouring the decks of *El Djazair*, a sixty-four-foot square-rigged sailing vessel upon which he was confined.

Thomas' lean body, now resilient and agile, had learned to step quickly out of the way of the taskmaster's whip or the grasp of a jealous seaman. He'd also developed a discerning mind, able to look ahead with caution and astuteness, which came from always trying to outguess what his master would want him to do next, before Captain Abu even asked. These qualities had earned him a place far better than the average pirate's slave. Good food and plenty of it, adequate rest, and a generous amount of trust had been his ever since he'd been sold to his present master, Abu Benjamin El Djazair, at Algeria a year ago.

Has it really been a year? Thomas wondered. Although each day waned along slowly, when he looked back at the accumulative hours, he was surprised at how fast his time in Algeria had passed. He'd spent most of that time slaving for Abu upon the Mediterranean Sea. Twice they'd sailed through the Strait of Gibraltar and up to the Bahia de Cadiz in Spain, where Abu traded his slaves for wine, fine linen and other marketable goods.

When not actively engaged in doing something requested by Captain Abu, Thomas forced himself to find something to do that would please his master. Whenever he found a spare moment, his thoughts turned to those slaves less fortunate than himself, and he aided them if he could. However, his first consideration was to please Captain Abu, for he knew that if he failed, he would be sold to someone less likely to appreciate his efforts.

During the past year, Thomas arose before dawn every day, offered silent prayers unto God, then began the strenuous labor of hauling buckets of saltwater and scrubbing all the exposed decks. Many times he would finish before Abu awakened. Thomas had never been assigned to clean the ship's decks. This was a task he had chosen on his own, to please his master. The first to work and the last to sleep, that was Thomas' motto. His diligence had earned him a trustworthy place among the ship's crew, and far less punishment from Master Abu than the other seamen-slaves around him.

Rumors among Master Abu's men spread quickly, and Thomas had learned there was a price on his father's head. The pirates blamed John Dunton for King Charles' invasion of Salé last year. His fellow slaves liked to taunt Thomas, telling him that John Dunton would never come for his son while the risk was so great to himself. Thomas refused to believe them. He knew that if his father was still alive, he would do whatever he had to do in order to rescue him. Thomas vowed he would be ready for the moment his father arrived to release him from bondage.

Thomas had also learned that his master's son, Benjamin, had passed away twenty years ago, when he was about Thomas' age. Sometimes Thomas thought Captain Abu looked upon Thomas as his surrogate son. This could only help Thomas by affecting his master's leniency. Thomas would give him no cause to complain. By his shrewd attention to details, without being told what to do, Thomas had already earned a favorable position aboard *El Djazair*.

This morning the air was crisp, almost cold, and Thomas wished he still had his mother's cloak to keep him warm. Then, he dismissed the thought with a shrug. Her cloak had gone to someone in greater need than he, and Thomas would keep warm by staying busy. With more vigor than normal, he pushed the brush forward, then pulled it back, over and over again, until the deck's wood had that familiar sheen to it that impressed Abu so much.

As he scrubbed the ship's decks, Thomas continued thinking about his parents. He did not know where they were, or even if they were still alive, for they had been captured by the pirates the same day as Thomas. But his heart held a perpetual prayer that they would find a way to free themselves from their own captivity. If they could, he had no doubt that they would then rescue him from his enslavement.

These secret hopes were all that sustained Thomas. Even in his darkest hours, Thomas prayed continually for his parents' escape. Only after considering John and Rebecca Dunton's needs, did Thomas' prayers turn to himself. Then, his pleas to Heaven turned to an eventual rescue from his life of toil and tyranny.

"JOHN DUNTON, YOU know I have every confidence in you," said Rebecca as she carried thirteen-month-old Jane upstairs to her bed.

"Yes, that's not what bothers me." Her husband's reply, spoken in almost a whisper, surprised her.

"Then, what is it?" Rebecca asked, turning back to face him.

John stood at the foot of the stairs, as though hesitating whether or not he wanted to come up just then. He put one foot on the first step and sighed. "I have just enough money to purchase my ship and pay for the repairs to it, then I will have nothing left with which to hire crew or barter for Thomas' life."

Rebecca turned into a child's bed chamber, placed Jane gently in the cradle, then snugly tucked the blankets around her sleeping daughter. After she kissed Jane's forehead and stroked her golden curls, she joined John as he headed toward their bedroom.

"I thought Simon said you were to use his money," she said as they dressed for bed.

"I will not use Simon's life savings. It's all he has left with which to keep himself and his sisters. It's not right."

"But Thomas is his grandson. If he has the desire to help in this way, to deny him the right to do so because of your stubborn pride is wrong, John. It's just plain wrong."

"It's not pride that stops me, Rebecca. It's concern for Naomi and Ruth. Simon isn't getting any younger, and neither are his twin sisters. Who will care for them if they have no money when Simon and I leave?"

"They can rely on me. I have the income from my father's tinsmith shop and apartment. And I'm an excellent seamstress. I will be happy to share what I have with them."

He pulled her into his arms and she went willingly, grateful for his strength and height. Not only was John tall, nearly 6'4", he had rock-hard muscles that could barely be constrained beneath his flowing cotton shirt. Rebecca tilted her head back to study his dark eyes, and whisked her fingers up through his thick brown hair. She saw no sign of surrender, but she did see in his expression the depth of his feelings for her. She hoped he could see the same emotions within her. The fervor with which she loved John Dunton always seemed to astound her, regardless how often she dwelt upon the sentiment in her heart.

How she loved this man!

"Why did the Lord ever bless me with such a fine woman?" he asked, as he tilted her head back farther, apparently so he could search her eyes with the same longing as she had studied his.

"You've changed the subject . . . again!" she reminded. "John, you must let Simon help you."

"I must do nothing of the kind," he said stubbornly, and she felt his stubborn wall of pride rising up again. Releasing her, he climbed into bed.

Rebecca followed, pulling the quilt up to her chin. "Put yourself in Simon's place," she coaxed. "Suppose Thomas was your grandson, would you love him any less?"

John leaned up on one elbow to look down at her. "No."

"Would you not give everything you had to rescue him, even if it meant you would have a more difficult life later on?"

"I would still have to think about my sisters, if I were Simon," suggested John. "They cannot be midwives forever."

"Then, if my rental income, and my seamstress income, is not enough for the four of us in your absence, I will have to become a midwife myself. Three viable ways to cover our expenses should ease your mind. Besides, we have little need for material things, only for food, which we grow most of by ourselves, already."

"You and our aunts do not grow wool, wheat, cotton or flax, all of which keep you in clothing and bread. Yes, the four of you can survive on fruits, vegetables, milk, eggs and meat. But that does not give you the other basics, and if Simon uses his funds in exchange for Thomas' life, our women will suffer in our absence."

"So, what you're really saying is that there are now two more women to consider. Had it not been for Jane and myself—"

Quickly, he put his fingers against her lips. "Do not even think such thoughts," he whispered hoarsely. "You and Jane are the only reason I'm still sane after all that I've been through."

Rebecca kissed his fingers tenderly. He slid his arm around her shoulders and held her close to him.

"I could not do what I am about to do if I did not have you and Jane here waiting for me," he insisted. "Never think that you are any kind of burden, Rebecca, for you are quite the opposite. You give me hope. Because you believe in me, I have courage to do what must be done, what any good father would do if his son were enslaved in Algeria."

Hesitating only for a moment, Rebecca finally realized what John was trying to tell her. "You would barter yourself for Thomas' freedom?" she questioned.

John nodded. She could feel his breath upon her neck as he did so. "I may have no other choice," he confessed.

A lump swelled up in her throat. "Then, we'll sell the cottage and everything we own, and I shall move in with Naomi and Ruth in your absence. That surely must be worth something."

"I wouldn't do that to you and Jane," he insisted.

"It's already been offered to us dozens of times," she argued. "Simon, Naomi, Ruth and I are one on the subject."

"No." John rolled on his side, his back to her. It was his way of saying the topic was no longer up for discussion.

Rebecca sighed. How could she convince John that there were other options open to him? If only he would learn to accept assistance from those who love him. When he'd gone to Salé, Morocco, last year with the King's armada, he'd gone with a chest of gold given him from

Lord Blackwell, to use to purchase Thomas' freedom, if the need arose. As John had explained, it was a kind gesture, but Lord Blackwell knew John would never have need of the money, not really. The King's errand was to rescue the English and Christians from their pirate captors by force, and that is exactly what they'd done. Unfortunately, Thomas had not been found among the rescued, and John had returned heavy-hearted.

It wasn't until last November, almost three months ago, that they learned Thomas wasn't at Salé, Morocco, when the armada arrived there last summer. According to Edward Blackwell III, upon whom Thomas had compassion in Algeria, Thomas had been taken to Algeria sometime before April 1636. If Thomas was still alive, they may learn of his whereabouts in Algiers.

Spooning behind her husband, Rebecca put her arm around his chest. "Do not shut me out, John. I want the same things you do."

He rolled over to face her. "I'm sorry," he whispered. "It's just . . . I will have no armada this time, no fleet of ships to help me fight the Algerians, no King's army at my command. And Simon is insistent upon going with me, when his health isn't the best, and his sisters are aging rapidly. How can I put their burden upon your shoulders when you have Jane to worry about? If I use Simon's money to ransom Thomas, I may be consigning my wife, my daughter, and my son's grandaunts to a life of poverty. I do not want that for any of you."

"Then, we shall pray," she said, snuggling toward him, "and God will bless us, as He has always done in the past. Somehow, He will help us accomplish that which will be required to rescue our son."

John kissed her forehead and pulled her closer. Acquiescing to John's wish for nearness, she continued cuddling against him. Then, choosing her words carefully, she said, "I shall also pray that God shall find a better way to bargain for Thomas' release than with your life, John. For when you rescue Thomas, you will have two children and a wife who need your life more than any pirate could."

John tilted his head back and smiled at her. "With faith like yours, nothing is impossible," he whispered, then he kissed her soundly.

HOURS LATER, JOHN paced back and forth downstairs in the kitchen. To his dismay, his sleeping habits had become erratic, and he often found himself awake long before anyone else in the house. Responsibility for Thomas' fate still fell heavily upon John's shoulders, and he could not forgive himself for failing to protect his young son when the barks, *Warwick* and *Little David*, were captured by pirates in March of 1636. Thomas had only been eight years old at the time, yet in six more months, Thomas would turn eleven.

The last memories John had of his only son were at the auction block in Salé, Morocco, twenty-one months ago. Thomas had been eight years old then, and shackled in chains and fetters, the same as John. The lad's clothes were tattered and worn, his face and body thin and frail in appearance. However, that day Thomas had shown John the heart of a true warrior, for he had tried to console John by saying, "I'll be all right, Father. Truly I will. I've been pretending that I'm really Joseph, with the coat of many colors. You know him from the Bible, don't you?"

The memory was most difficult to bury. Indeed, even if he'd wanted to forget, it would be impossible. Thomas' last words haunted John since the moment Thomas had said them. They had penetrated

John's thoughts nearly every moment since that terrible day. "I pray every morning and every night that God will somehow find a way for us."

The hope he saw on young Thomas' face overwhelmed him. The lad knew, beyond any shadow of doubt, that his father would eventually save him from a life of slavery. Thomas' thoughts and hopes shone out through his dark brown eyes, and there was no denying them.

It was the most difficult moment John had ever experienced, having to be led away from his only son in fetters and chains, not knowing where Thomas would end up, or when they would ever see each other again.

Even in his dreams, John found no peace, for every night he would awaken with a shudder, having just seen the haunting nightmare, the face of his only son, his beloved son, pale and weak, calling out to him in a hollow, echoing manner, "Find me, Father. Please . . . find me."

John tried to set aside the memory of their last meeting, knowing it would never go away completely, and concentrated, instead, on what happened after their fateful separation. John had been sold that same day to a pirate named Aligolant, along with sixteen men from the bark, *Warwick*. Aligolant had whipped John mercilessly, many times, and John's back now bore the scars to prove it. He had risked his own life countless times to ensure that his sixteen crewmen would not starve, would not suffer from the lash, or from the impulsive wrath of the pirates.

Horrible as all his experiences were, through all the trials that followed, one memory still stood out more horrific, and yet more noble, than any other. Tears came to John's eyes. The faith young Thomas had shown him displayed more courage than John thought a child could possess. Thomas never wavered in his belief that John would find him. Now, John would have to show Thomas more courage than the child should ever have to know . . . how a father would lay down his life for his son.

Other disturbing memories flooded over him. His enslavement in Salé, Morocco, had brought him terrible experiences: serving a vicious, heartless pirate, striving to keep his men alive by smuggling raw shellfish to them, mutinying against Aligolant, recapturing the *Warwick*, and delivering the pirates to the English, then standing trial for piracy himself.

After John was acquitted, thanks to Simon Harris' and Lord Henry Vaine's valiant efforts on his behalf, he was allowed to return to his beloved Rebecca. It had been his thoughts of her love that had kept him sane in the months that followed. He wasn't much of a praying man, but when he did pray, he always remembered to thank God for Rebecca. Without her, he doubted he would have retained his sanity throughout the past two years.

John heard Rebecca stirring upstairs, and quickly put away his thoughts. He scooped some ground oats and barley into a pan of water and prepared their breakfast.

A little later, as Rebecca busied herself in the kitchen, John fed his toddler daughter the last of his porridge. Jane was perfect in every way, from the generous covering of golden curls on her lovely head, to her pudgy, tiny pink feet. Her eyelashes were long, and tended to curl at the tips, like her mother's. Jane's eyes surprised him most of all because they were as turquoise as Rebecca's. The only parts of himself Jane had at all was a tiny cleft in her chin and the dimples in her cheeks when she smiled. Otherwise, she was her mother's daughter all the way through, including the special soft spot in her heart for her papa. John realized that Jane had completely captured his heart.

As John spooned small portions of the porridge he'd made into Jane's open mouth, he was amazed at how much one little child can eat. She especially liked to eat from her father's bowl, and John allowed it after he'd finished eating his portion. If he did not get the spoon into her mouth soon enough, she would pout and scold him, "Papa!" This, too, delighted him. It had become a morning ritual, and he worried how she would feel once he set sail for Algiers, leaving her far behind.

"I'm going into the boatyard this morning," he told Rebecca, who was kneading bread dough at the other end of the table.

"How soon will they have the ship ready?" she asked.

"Just a few more weeks," said John. "They seemed anxious about getting their money when I was there last week, so I thought I'd bring a portion to them today. Perhaps that will hurry them along."

John tried to give Jane another spoonful of porridge, but she refused to open her mouth. Apparently, she was full. He wiped her face with a damp cloth, then helped her down from the chair.

"Auntie Omi," Jane said, pointing to the side door.

"No, Jane. Aunt Naomi is busy this morning," said John. "Perhaps later on."

"Auntie Woof," Jane insisted, still pointing to the door.

"No, Aunt Ruth is busy, too."

"Gwam-papa?" asked Jane, this time with hesitation in her voice.

"You know your grandfather has patients until late in the afternoon."

"Uht – do?" asked his young daughter, her inquisitive eyes flashing at him in irritation.

Laughing aloud, John said, "I suppose you'll have to help your mother make bread."

Jane clapped her tiny hands together. "Bwed!" she squealed in delight.

He picked her up and put an apron around her tiny chest, tying it in the back. After wiping Jane's hands to make sure she was clean enough, John dumped some flour on the table in front of her while Rebecca pinched off a small piece of dough and placed it in the flour, rolling it around to coat it, before she gave it to Jane.

Thirteen-month-old Jane grabbed the dough and patted it into the flour, rolling it around and around in a lop-sided manner, apparently delighted to be such a big help to her mother.

With his daughter occupied, John quickly gave Rebecca a kiss on the cheek. "I shall be back by evening," he said, studying her reaction.

She gave him a smile. "I will keep the soup warm for you."

"You're still not upset about last night, are you?"

"No," she answered. "I talked things over with God for a good long time and He comforted me. Everything will be all right. You'll see."

"With your faith, how could any man fail?"

"It only takes faith the size of a mustard seed, John."

"For you," he admitted, duly chagrined. "For some of us it takes the whole tree."

JOHN'S COTTAGE, AS Rebecca had named it, sat at the edge of a hamlet near Stepney Parish on the outskirts of London, a rural area that was quite beautiful. From *John's Cottage*, Rebecca had a marvelous view. She could see far over a field, a meadow, and a narrow strip of salt marsh to the many ships of sail that passed up and down the river, Thames, which wound through the valley like a wide silver ribbon between Stepney and the rolling hills of Kent and Surrey. Today, not a ship sailed, for the air was completely becalmed. Rebecca couldn't see the dockyards from her home, for a small hill obscured that portion of the river. However, she knew that John would soon be there, tending to the affairs of the bark he was buying, which he would name the *Warwick II*.

After John left, Rebecca finished the bread kneading, cleaned Jane and the table properly, then tidied the house and washed the few articles of clothing that needed washing. She hung them over a wooden rack by the fire, then went out to the smokehouse with Jane.

Simon and his twin sisters, Naomi and Ruth, lived next door to *John's Cottage*. Though not related to Rebecca by blood, they were family to young Thomas, and they had become Rebecca's dearest friends.

Rebecca, Naomi and Ruth had helped John and Simon butcher a pig two weeks ago, the hams and shoulders of which they were now smoking, to preserve into the spring season. The fire in the smoke-house had to be stoked and fed every few hours. Volunteering to take charge of the smokehouse, herself, Rebecca was amazed at the many skills she had learned from Simon, Naomi, Ruth and John.

Who would have thought she could learn new skills so quickly, or adapt to this lifestyle with so much ease? She had grown ever stronger the more she applied herself. Gone was the genteel Rebecca Webster, a woman raised to marry a more refined man of the gentry. Now, she was Goodwife Rebecca Dunton. A mariner's wife had not been the way she had pictured her parenting years, but she was pleased to have found Master John Dunton, regardless of his lifestyle. He had enabled her to replace that spoiled child she'd once been with a woman whose strength of will and body, determination of mind and soul, matched the love she felt in her heart for her family. With that love, she had become a better person than she was before, and this pleased Rebecca immensely.

With Jane's interference, Rebecca finished stoking the fire in the smokehouse in twice the time it normally took, but Rebecca did not mind. She couldn't imagine what it would be like without Jane interrupting the order of her daily routine.

After a brief visit with Naomi, Ruth and Simon, Rebecca took Jane home for her nap. Nursing Jane until she fell asleep, Rebecca then put her daughter in bed, and went downstairs to do some mending that she'd been postponing. Whenever John was home, she let a few of the less pressing chores wait while she spent time with him. Then, she began sewing a torn pocket on an apron. When she finished, she attacked some of John's stockings. She had no idea how he wore the heels out so easily, but it was a simple matter to darn them properly so that he could wear them again for many more months.

As she set to work with her needle and thread and darning ball, Rebecca listened intently to see if Jane would stir. Jane was changing from an infant into a little girl, and her sleeping habits were also changing. The long, luxurious naps in the morning were getting shorter, and the afternoon naps were lengthening. Soon, Jane's morning nap would no longer be needed.

As she estimated how many more stitches she needed to darn in the heel of John's stocking, Rebecca felt a strange tingling sensation in her heart that spread outward until she was engulfed with it. Goose bumps raised up on her arms and chest, and she sensed that she was no longer alone in the little parlor. She looked up from her darning and saw, if only for a moment, the brief expression of love on her father's face, as he stood near the mantle. Since her father had died almost two years earlier, his appearance quite startled her. Rebecca gasped and quickly stood up, dropping her sewing onto the floor.

He appeared for only a few seconds, but he had such a smile of content that she was not afraid. In her heart, she heard his voice plant words of encouragement that she pondered long after he'd gone. "You must learn to trust those whom you do not, Rebecca. If you cannot, then you must, at least, trust me."

"I do trust you, Father," she whispered, but before she'd finished, Jeremiah Webster had vanished into thin air as though he'd never been there at all.

Rebecca blinked as the full realization of her father's appearance settled into her heart. Tears filled her eyes and she sank back into the chair. She had witnessed something for which there was no explanation, other than that her father had visited her from beyond the grave. His spirit lived on, and he was watching out for her well-being, something she had never really thought about until that very moment. Of course, the scriptures were filled with evidences of life beyond the grave. In Genesis, it was mentioned several times that the dead were gathered to their people, including Abraham, Isaac and Jacob. But she hadn't concerned herself about the eternal realm of the family. She never had any personal proof until now.

Putting the darning aside, Rebecca pulled her Bible down from the mantle and opened it to Malachi 4:5-6, where she read: *Behold, I will send you Elijah the prophet before the coming of the great and dreadful day of the Lord: And he shall turn the hearts of the fathers to the children, and the hearts of the children to their fathers, lest I come and smite the earth with a curse.* Understanding seeped into her, line upon line, as she contemplated these verses of holy scripture. Truly Malachi's words had been fulfilled by the vision Rebecca had of her father. Her heart yearned for Jeremiah Webster stronger than ever before, and apparently, his heart was turned toward his daughter, as well. Because parent and child loved one another so deeply, the veil that separates those departed souls from the living had parted, if only for a brief moment, and Rebecca was filled with knowledge and hope that surpassed all that she had ever known.

For the first time in her life, Rebecca knew that God had sent her father to watch over her, to help her with whatever trials lay upon her future path. She did not know who her father wanted her to trust, but she knew she trusted her father, Jeremiah Webster. It was one of the most comforting sensations she'd ever had, and it left her singing hymns of praise for the rest of the day.

Chapter Two

Return of the Warwick

". . . within the Parish of Stepney are the most serviceable
Men in the Nation; without which England could not be
England for they are its Strength and Wealth."
~John Strype

*W*hen John arrived at the dockyard in South Stepney Parish, he was filled first with surprise, then frustration and anger.

The ship he had contracted to purchase, slightly larger than the original bark, *Warwick*, was sixty-four feet long, twenty feet wide, with a burthen of one-hundred-two tons and twelve cannons, six to each side, had last been seen, sitting in dry-dock at the Stepney shipyard, with at least a month's worth of work to prepare it for sailing.

Now, curiously, it was floating at anchor in the River Thames, with workers aboard, as though preparing the sails for a freshening breeze.

Furious that he'd not been given the opportunity to inspect the ship before it was launched, John was certain the repairs could never have been completed so quickly, not without the laborers working both day and night to finish it.

He left his horse with a stableman and hurried over to the repair office where Goodman Beck, a burley man with balding head and stiff, dark bristles above his ears, greeted him. "Master Dunton, what brings you to the River Thames today?"

"More to the point, Beck, what is my ship doing in the water before I've inspected the repairs?" asked John, his demeanor darkening.

"Forgive me, Master Dunton, but Lord Blackwell inspected it three days ago, he did. Said the remaining repairs would be done at his docks in Chatham, so he said. They're to set sail as soon as the wind comes up."

"Lord Blackwell?" questioned John.

"Yes, sir. He paid the entire balance due on it, he did. Said to tell you when you next called that you could find the ship in Chatham." Beck wiped a bead of sweat off his brow with his shirt sleeve, and stammered, "I – I don't think he was expecting you this soon, though, not at all."

"Thank you," said John, completely puzzled by Lord Blackwell's actions. "I shall pay him a visit today."

"You do that," said Goodman Beck. "I apologize that we surprised you, Master Dunton, but Lord Blackwell insisted we oblige him, he did. And you know how convincing he can be, don't you, sire?"

John nodded. Yes, he knew well enough the persuasive powers of Lord Blackwell. "Did he mention how his son is feeling?"

"Edward was with him, he was," said Beck. "He looked right fine to me, though I didn't question him, I did not. It's not my place, now, is it?"

"Thank you, then. Good day, Beck."

"And to you, Master Dunton, good day."

What can this mean? John wondered as he walked back to the stables. Had Lord Blackwell gone mad, commandeering John's ship and ordering it sent to Chatham? When John had mounted his horse, he rode quickly back to *John's Cottage*, told Rebecca he was going to Chatham straight away, and left again without telling her why. How could he tell her why, when he did not know himself?

Arriving well after dark, John left his horse with a manservant at the gate, then went up to Blackwell Tower and knocked at the front door. Within a few moments, the head butler, an endearing man named Wilson, opened it. "Welcome, Master Dunton. Lord Blackwell is expecting you. Come in. Come in. I will let him know you've arrived."

"Thank you, Wilson." John stepped inside the massive hall, giving Wilson his cloak and hat. Afterward, he walked into the drawing room where a wall of bookshelves filled with hundreds of books stood opposite a round maple table and two impressive arm chairs. Upon another wall, John admired an antique set of pistols that his Lordship had mounted in a maple frame. A small brass plaque below them read: *1578*. The flint-lock pistols were almost sixty years old, yet they were in remarkably flawless condition.

"John, how good of you to come," said Lord Blackwell, walking into the room and shaking John's hand vigorously. "Come, sit with me. Have you eaten?"

His Lordship never seemed to age. He was still tall and wispy, with silver hair, pale blue eyes and a pointy nose, rather like a rose thorn. His severe features did not allow for his true character, however, for John had known Blackwell for several years, and found the man compassionate and genuine, yet tough when the need arose. His only blind spot was for his son, and this had been tempered over the past year or two.

"Not since breakfast," John admitted.

Turning to his servant, who was standing by the open door, his Lordship said, "Wilson, bring my friend some food and wine."

Wilson nodded and left the drawing room immediately.

"About my ship," John began as soon as he sat upon a chair opposite Lord Blackwell.

"Straight to the point," his Lordship smiled. "One of the qualities I like about you, John. Did Wilson tell you that Edward is feeling much better?" John shook his head, but before he could respond further, Lord Blackwell said, "No? I did not think so. He's a good one for keeping house secrets, that one. So tell me, John, do you plan on sailing her by yourself? Or were you planning to hire some seamen to go with you?"

"About my ship," John raised an eyebrow, refusing to answer any other questions until some of his own were explained to this satisfaction.

"It's a gift, John. A trifling thing, really. Edward and I talked about it at great length, and he's determined to help you find your son. As for myself, I owe everything I have to young Thomas, and to you.

"If Thomas hadn't preserved Edward's life in Algeria, Edward would have died there. And, if you hadn't memorized those amazing details about Salé or recaptured the bark *Warwick* and returned it to England, King Charles would never have authorized the Salé Fleet to sail to Morocco in the first place. You were the turning point in the King's decision. The success of the Salé Armada was in your hands. Without your ingenuity, Edward would have died in Salé. So you see, John, I owe everything to you and Thomas. You have given me back my son, but I have not returned the favor." He gave a wan smile, then added in a more convincing manner, "It is intolerable that the King will not send another armada for you, but I understand his reasoning. It would take every ship in his Majesty's Royal Navy to take on Algeria, and King Charles cannot leave England undefended in order to do so.

"But that leaves Thomas without any hope of rescue, and it leaves you facing a monumental task by yourself. Edward will not stand for it, and neither will I. Besides, Edward is sleeping less and less. He keeps muttering the name *El Djazair* in his dreams, although he cannot, for the life of him, remember what it means. However, he is certain that it has something to do with Thomas. We're hoping he might remember something more important if he can only see Algiers once again. It might spark his memory and bring something of value to you in rescuing your son."

"So, about my ship," John insisted for the third time, although he already had an idea about the plans that his Lordship and Edward had made in his absence.

"I completed the purchase for you," confessed Lord Blackwell.

Quickly, he added, "The *Warwick II* should be here by week's end. Then, I will have all the repairs finished and the modifications done to the sails, once you've explained that portion to my workers. Edward wants to go with you to Algeria, John. With you as Captain, and owner of the *Warwick II*, and Edward as Master. He will stop at nothing to rescue Thomas, for he cannot sleep peacefully until the lad is safe. His nightmares have been unbearable for him. But his hope for finding Thomas has eased his mind some, now that he is embarking on this voyage and—"

John stood and slammed a riding glove down upon the round table. "Forgive me, Lord Blackwell, but I cannot take Edward with me as Master, nor as midshipman or deck hand. I cannot take him at all. Have you forgotten what Edward did to Rebecca before she escaped and found me?" John could restrain his outrage no longer.

Lord Blackwell expected too much of John. He could not allow the man who whipped Rebecca and forced her father to prison, resulting in Jeremiah Webster's death, to accompany him on his voyage to Algeria. How would Rebecca react to this situation?

Lord Blackwell shook his head, stood and came towards him slowly, his blue eyes fastening on John's with an intensity born of love for his only son. "Edward knows exactly what he did to Rebecca. However, he is hopeful that she will forgive him once he explains to her what happened to him." He paused, apparently for emphasis, then said, "If Rebecca does not forgive him, the ship will still be yours, and you will sail without Edward. You must, at the least, give him the opportunity to prove to you, and to her, that he is repentant. Without Rebecca's and your forgiveness, he cannot put his life back together."

John, like Lord Blackwell, knew what it was like for a father with only one son to his name. The two men both had their sons captured by pirates and forced into slavery. *Should I acquiesce?* he wondered. Finally, he said, "Edward is planning to overcome a major obstacle, your Lordship. I can only pray that he is up to it." John shook his head. "For my own part, I forgive him. It was impossible to see his emaciated, tortured condition after his rescue, and not forgive him. He's suffered enough. But to expect Rebecca to have the same compassion as I . . . well, that must be her own decision. I will have no influence in Edward's behalf upon her. Rebecca's father's death has been hard for her to bear, and Edward is responsible for that. I can only imagine that she will find no forgiveness in her heart for your son."

"If that is the case," Lord Blackwell sighed, "Edward may not accompany you on your mission to rescue Thomas. But if she will permit it, will you accept Edward under your command?"

"I will," John nodded. As his pride caught up with him, he added, "It does not sit well with me to accept anything charitable."

"My gift is not negotiable," insisted Lord Blackwell with a fatherly smile.

John understood the man's intentions, and nodded. "You have explained your feelings well enough that I am persuaded this is an act of appreciation. If I stood in your place, I would do the same."

"Good, it is settled. Now, sit with me. Wilson will have food here shortly."

John raised an eyebrow. "Your gift of the *Warwick II* may be settled. But Edward cannot expect his problems with Rebecca settled, as well."

His Lordship nodded. "That is something only Rebecca and Edward can resolve," he agreed.

Wilson arrived with slices of smoked pork, cheese, bread and wine, as well as a tureen of hot potato and leek soup. As he placed them on the table, he said to John, "How is Goodwife Dunton these days?"

"Rebecca is quite well, Wilson. Thank you for asking. She has never forgotten your kindness to her while she stayed at Blackwell Tower."

"Thank you, Master Dunton. Please tell her we think of her often, and we miss her."

"I will, Wilson. She does the same for you, I am sure."

After pouring the wine, Wilson left them alone once again. John ate hungrily, glad for the refreshment. More importantly, he was relieved to know that he would have money with which to barter for young Thomas' life, if it came to that. He would not have to accept anything from Simon.

When he was finished, he turned his attention back to Lord Blackwell. "Where is Edward?" John asked.

"Aboard the *Warwick II*," said his Lordship. "By the way, why did you choose to rename your ship? You know that superstitions will plague her. It will be difficult to find men to crew a renamed ship."

Shrugging, John explained, "Rebecca told Thomas that should he ever escape, he should search for the *Warwick*, for I would be found aboard her. The bark was grounded at Hurst Castle, and has now been disassembled. Should he ever escape, how is Thomas to find her? Superstition or not, the *Warwick II* is the only name she will sail under while I am in command. Besides, I do not put my trust in superstitions, I put my trust in God."

Nodding, his Lordship said, "I see." Then, he changed the subject back to John's question, which he'd answered only briefly. "Edward wanted to take over as master of the *Warwick II* immediately, so he will sail with her to Chatham. He is determined to make certain, for himself, that everything is in order for you."

"Is it wise to let him get his hopes up like this?" John questioned. "He must first obtain forgiveness from Rebecca."

"John, I have finally seen hope in his eyes, and some small resemblance of the sanity he had before his fiancée, Sarah Jenkins, died. If you were his father, and had seen him go through all that he has, would you not want to give him hope?"

"You know me well," John agreed. "It is my compassion that will be my downfall. Isn't that what you once told me?"

"Perhaps, I was mistaken," said his Lordship. "For your compassion was passed on to your son, and his compassion saved Edward's life. I will be forever in your debt, John. This ship of yours, and your mission, is but a small repayment for all that you have done for me."

"It seems a large price to pay," John admitted.

"Not when you compare it to the life of a father's son," Lord Blackwell said pointedly. "There is no price a father will not pay."

Nodding, John said, "My own life, if necessary."

A stillness came over the room as Lord Blackwell whispered, "And should it take my son's life in the process, he will die doing what he wants to do most in all the world. A compassionate father cannot deny his son that opportunity, regardless how much he fears for his son's safety."

LORD BLACKWELL ORDERED a carriage for John's ride home, with John's horse tethered behind. John slept all the way back to *John's Cottage* and arrived just in time to watch dawn spread over the hillsides in varying shades of pink, lavender and red. Stopping only for a moment to inhale the crisp morning air and enjoy the sunrise, he bid the driver farewell, untethered his horse, and took it to the stable. Then, John went inside, where he found Rebecca upstairs in bed, nursing Jane.

"Oh, John," she smiled warmly. "I was hoping the carriage I heard was you. Did you have a nice visit with his Lordship?"

John sank onto the bed and propped his head up with a pillow. Looking at his wife and daughter nestled together brought such sweetness to him, and he marveled at the blessings of the Lord in his behalf.

"Your prayers were answered," he admitted, "though I did not know before now that you have such a close relationship with Deity."

"Really?" she asked. "And how were they answered?"

"Lord Blackwell made us a gift of the *Warwick II*, including its repairs and outfitting. He says it is the least he can do for the boy who saved his son's life."

Tears filled her eyes. "Yes, that is so like his Lordship. Generous to a fault when it comes to those he loves."

"How could he have done anything less, with you praying so hard for God's blessings in our behalf?"

"God watches over us more closely than we realize," she confessed. "For while you were gone, He sent my father to me."

John blinked in surprise. Had he heard her correctly. "Your father?"

"I know it sounds silly to speak of it, John, but I also know what I saw and what I heard. My father came from God's realm and spoke to me."

"I wouldn't be the least surprised," said John, reaching out to stroke young Jane's face. He was surprised, however, that he felt this way. If asked two years ago how he felt toward God, his response would have been entirely different.

After John explained to Rebecca everything Lord Blackwell had done regarding the *Warwick II*, he concluded with, "Edward wants to be master of the ship, next in command under me."

"Why?" she asked, alarm in her voice, her turquoise eyes widening.

"His sole desire is to find Thomas. I have told his Lordship that you would, at least, listen to what Edward may say to you. It is my belief that he also wants to make his peace with you."

"What does he expect from me, John? He's already taken my father, my dignity. . . ."

"His Lordship claims he's repentant. He said Edward is returning to the kinder man he was before Sarah Jenkins died."

"I will have to witness this miracle for myself," she said ruefully.

"I do not trust Edward in the least degree."

"I understand that you mistrust him. I do not blame you. But Edward is willing to help me find Thomas, and I am tempted to let him sail with me."

"Do you want him to go with you, John? Knowing what he's done?"

"I know only that our son is in Algiers. Edward has been there, and he knows details about the country that I do not. He may be instrumental in helping me locate Thomas."

"For Thomas' sake," she agreed, "I will listen to Edward, but I cannot promise to forgive the man who is responsible for my father's death."

"I understand," said John. "If you cannot resolve the issues between you, I will have to find another way."

"Then what about finding Thomas?"

"I will have a cartographer meet with Edward and draw up as many details as he can remember. However, it may break his heart if he is not allowed to sail with me."

"What of my heart?" she asked.

John shook his head and shrugged. It was a question he could not answer with any satisfaction. Finally, he whispered, "If I am willing to give my life for Thomas, will you not sacrifice your heart for him?"

🌴 🌴 🌴 🌴

FOR SEVERAL DAYS, Rebecca paced back and forth in their garden, slammed things around in their house when she thought John wasn't looking, and felt completely on edge. Edward would be arriving today, and she was supposed to sit and listen to his apology, perhaps even forgive him, as if a simple word or two could undo what he had done to her and her father. It would not be easy.

Lord Blackwell had explained more than two years ago that Edward had gone temporarily insane when his first fiancée died in a tragic accident. To hear his Lordship tell it, Edward had locked himself in his bedroom for weeks, and shredded everything in sight, including the costly paintings and tapestries that hung upon the walls. When he seemed to come out of this derelict state, he supposedly fell in love with Rebecca, who spurned him from the first time she met him.

After Edward had persuaded her father, Jeremiah Webster, to allow him to court Rebecca, Jeremiah became suspicious of Edward's motives. Then, Edward paid a man to accuse her father of thievery, and planted evidence against him. Jeremiah's property was seized, and Jeremiah was cast into prison where his once robust body wasted away quickly from starvation and infectious diseases contracted in that awful dungeon.

In an effort to appease Edward's punishment of her father, Rebecca had agreed to his marriage proposal. She went to live at Blackwell Tower shortly after her father's imprisonment. Edward promised to arrange for her father's release after she married him and their wedding date was set. Rebecca soon discovered that Edward wanted her in ways that were improper outside the marriage covenant. Because she refused him on several occasions, he had whipped her brutally, and promised the beatings would only get worse if she did not hasten their wedding date. She finally agreed to a quick ceremony, to take place in March of 1635. A few days before the wedding, Rebecca's father died from prison fever.

With her father dead, Rebecca had no reason to continue the engagement. In a desperate attempt to escape Edward Blackwell, she stowed away aboard the bark, *Warwick*, where she met and married John Dunton.

Now, she was expected to forgive the man who lashed her so severely her back would always carry the scars. But worse than the beatings (which she knew in her heart could be forgiven), Jeremiah Webster, her beloved father and confidante, was dead, and Edward was responsible. How could she forgive Edward for that?

Only after her father's death was his good name cleared through the efforts of the Earl of Portland, and his dear wife, Penelope. Thanks to them, her father's property was restored to her, and she was now able to receive a tidy rental income from it.

As she walked amongst the orchard trees, their barren branches looking much like arthritic fingers reaching out for comfort, Rebecca pondered these memories and questions in her heart. John had volunteered to watch Jane for her while she left *John's Cottage* for a brief respite. He seemed to know how difficult it was to be responsible for a toddler all the time. Whenever he was at home, John was most attentive to Rebecca's needs.

She loved John for all that he did for her, but mostly for the fervor with which he loved her back. Theirs was a solid marriage. However shaky their marriage began, it was now built on a strong foundation that stood the test of many hurdles and challenges.

Now, Rebecca would face this new obstacle, and she did not know what to do. To forgive the man who, in her opinion, had murdered her father, was more than any husband should ask of his wife. If Edward had not conspired to send her father to prison, her father would be playing with his granddaughter this very moment.

Yet, that wasn't entirely true. Jeremiah wouldn't have a granddaughter to enjoy if Edward had not set in motion the events that had shaped Rebecca's life. She may never have met John Dunton. She very likely would not be married to John, nor be the mother of his daughter.

Memories flooded over Rebecca as crisp and as fresh as if they'd just happened. Within four days of her marriage to John, they had all been captured by pirates. Rebecca had been ransomed back to Lord Blackwell, while John, Thomas and all the crew had been taken to Salé, Morocco, to be sold on the auction block. During the ransom attempt, Rebecca's captors failed to outwit his Lordship's men, and the pirate, Aligolant, had to flee from England without Rebecca or his gold. He had taken out his revenge on John Dunton upon his arrival in Salé, Morocco.

If Edward hadn't betrayed her and her father, John might not have been sold to Aligolant. If he hadn't been sold to him, he might not have had the opportunity to mutiny the ship and bring the pirates to justice. All sixteen crewmen, including Thomas' grandfather, could have been killed.

Every event that happened between Rebecca and John in the past two years was set into motion by Edward Blackwell III.

How was Rebecca to know what to do regarding Edward? She might despise what he did, and blame him for her father's death, but his conduct had also been the determining factor that saved John's life and the lives of his sixteen crewmen. Edward's actions had definitely sent Rebecca into John's world, into John's arms; her little daughter could not have been fathered by John, otherwise. In some regards, Rebecca should be thankful towards Edward.

If only he had not sent her father to prison.

Chapter Three

The Truce

"For if ye forgive men their trespasses, your
heavenly Father will also forgive you."
~Matt. 6:14

Having just taken baby Jane next door to stay with her grandaunts, Rebecca returned to the cottage and soon heard a knock at the front door. Her stomach began to do flip-flops as her chest tightened and constricted her breathing. Rebecca had not seen Edward Blackwell III since the night she ran away from him, when he and his guards searched the docks at Chatham for her.

The knocking sounded again, startling Rebecca, whose mind was anywhere but in *John's Cottage.*

Slipping past her, John went to the door and opened it. "Edward, you're looking well," said John, shaking Edward's hand. "Come in, sit with us. My home may not be as grand as Blackwell Tower, but it's—"

"No need to apologize," Edward said quickly, cutting him off. "I find your cottage charming. If I've learned nothing else over the past two years, John, I have learned to appreciate the quiet comforts of home and family."

John directed him to a cozy chair, then stepped into the kitchen and took Rebecca by the hand. "I shall stay by your side for as long as you want me," he whispered as he led her into the parlor. His words and his presence comforted her, and she swallowed the lump in her throat, sucked in a great breath of air, and followed him. In the parlor, she sat next to John on the settee, resting her hand in his.

Rebecca suppressed a whisper of surprise, for she was truly shocked by the gaunt look of the man who had once robustly whipped her. Edward's slate blue eyes were pale and sunken into his face, making his straight nose more prominent than usual. His cheeks were hollow, his skin sallow. His hair, once dark and thick, was now wispy-thin and streaked with silver.

"Rebecca," said Edward kindly. "You're looking lovely, as always."

Even his voice had changed . . . from one filled with rage and hatred to one tendered with timidity and frailty. Once demandingly husky, he now sounded like a man broken down by life, desperately helpless.

She lowered her eyes to her lap as she bit her lower lip. With all the changes that Edward had undergone in the past two years, why did he still make her feel such a craven disposition? This man had brutalized her and her father. She must stand up to him now or forever cower in his presence. With these thoughts in her mind, she lifted her head staring at him with distaste.

If Edward had changed little since she last saw him, it would have been easy, but he was cowed in demeanor, thin and pale. His eyes were accentuated by dark circles, as though he hadn't slept well in months, and had a haunting quality that they'd not had before. His hair was longer now, and he wore it tied at the nape of his neck with a piece of leather.

"Thank you," she said, gathering courage from his tortured demeanor. "But we are not here to speak of pleasantries, Edward. What is it you have to say for yourself?"

He gulped, started to speak, stopped, then started again. "I cannot ask that you forgive me, Rebecca, for what I have done to you or to your father. There is no forgiveness for a man who betrays the sanctity of a father's trust, and treats that father's daughter as though she was nothing more than chattel."

"Then, we've nothing to speak about," said Rebecca, standing to dismiss him.

Edward held his hand out, beseeching her with desperate eyes, "Forgiveness is earned, I respect that, and I have done nothing worthy of your forgiveness."

"No, you have not." She sank down onto the chair again, the weight of John's hand pulling her there.

"I deserve all that has befallen me since you fled from Blackwell Tower," confessed Edward. "Ninety-seven men died the day the *Neptune* was captured. And of the twenty four who were enslaved by the pirates, only two were rescued by the Salé Fleet, myself and William Moore. Counting your father in the tally, I am responsible for the deaths of one-hundred-twenty men. Yet because of Thomas' compassion toward me, I lived to remember it all in vivid detail." Edward stood and stepped to the fireplace, his back to John and Rebecca.

"One-hundred-twenty men, all of whom had wives, sweethearts, parents, daughters or sons. The families I destroyed can never be reimbursed for their losses. You are only one of the hundreds I have tread upon with no thought as to the consequences."

He remained with his back to her, but Rebecca could see the trembling in his shoulders, and heard the great, wracking sobs he tried to suppress.

"My captivity and torture was insignificant in terms of the retribution I must pay for the rest of my life . . . and beyond. There is no heaven for someone wretched as I."

"Then why have you come?" asked Rebecca, softening under his self-incriminating manner, regardless of her attempts not to do so.

Edward turned and stared at her, his eyes suddenly ablaze with determination. "I am alive only because Thomas had compassion upon me and William Moore while we were in Algeria. He found us upon the roadside, nearly dead from starvation and thirst, and he hid us in a haystack and brought us food and water several times, and provided warmth for us by giving us the cloak from his own shoulders. When we were well enough to make our escape, we begged him to come with us, but he refused. He said it would be easier for the pirates to track down three fugitives than one little boy, and that he would make his escape when he felt it was the right time for him."

"These are matters of record," Rebecca said evenly, not trusting herself to believe that Edward had changed so drastically. "But you

have not told me why you came to see me."

Going down on one knee in front of her, Edward took her free hand and held it in his trembling one. "I cannot ask your forgiveness, Rebecca, but I can ask that you allow me to help Captain Dunton search for Thomas. Without your permission, he will not take me with him."

John had not mentioned this to her before, and she looked at him curiously. He gave her a timid smile, and she felt relief in knowing that her wishes were uppermost in his heart. Her husband knew how badly this would hurt her, and he would not add to her torment of his own free will.

She looked down at Edward, still kneeling and clutching her hand. "What will you do to help my husband if I grant my permission?"

"I pledge my life to John and to your son. I will do everything in my power to return them both to you. Rescuing Thomas will never replace the life of your father, nor will it remove any scars from your back. But Thomas' presence in your home will mend the hole left there when the pirates took him from you. Admittedly, my motives are somewhat selfish. Thomas left a rather large hole in my heart, as well, and the only way I will ever be able to mend that hole is if I find him and bring him home to his family."

"I am disinclined to trust you," said Rebecca harshly. "The only reason why I am even considering your request is because you may know more about Algiers than John does. That is the only advantage that you have, and the only reason that will have any sway with me. I cannot forgive you, at least not today. But if you are helpful to my husband in his quest to rescue our sweet Thomas, I will revisit the issue of your forgiveness once again, when you return."

"I can ask for no more than that," Edward said, kissing the back of her hand tenderly. "I promise you this much: if our search brings us into the jaws of death, and it will, I shall offer my own life as a sacrifice before I will witness any harm come to those you love most . . . including Thomas, your husband and Simon Harris, as well."

"If you are able to keep such a promise," Rebecca acquiesced slightly, "It will help soften my anger toward you."

"Rebecca, I am truly sorry for all the harm I have brought upon you. Anger and grief such as I have caused cannot be easily swept away. We will speak of this matter again, when the *Warwick II* returns safely to Chatham with your family. But do not fear to tell me, even then, that you cannot forgive me. I expect no forgiveness from you . . . or from God. Not in this life, nor in the life to come."

Pulling her hand gently from his, Rebecca turned to her husband. "John," she said, "you have my permission to take Edward with you in your search for our son. Forgiveness can only come if he proves himself worthy of my trust. However, you must watch him closely. I cannot help but distrust him at this time."

John stood, as did Edward, and shook hands. "Very well, Rebecca," said John. "I will take Edward with me, but not as master of my ship. He will serve as a deck hand until he proves himself worthy to move up the ranks."

Rebecca smiled as John continued speaking, this time to Edward. "The *Warwick II* does not belong to King Charles, or the Royal Navy. She is my ship, and mine alone, to command. My word on her shall be law. If you cannot abide my word, you must speak of it now, and remain behind."

Saluting him, Edward replied, "Yes, Captain. I shall not fail you, sir."

"See that you do not," said John. "For the day you fail me, I shall feed you to the sharks that follow us, awaiting any scrap of food."

Edward paled momentarily, then recovered enough to respond. "If I fail you, sir, I shall deserve whatever punishment you choose for me."

🌴 🌴 🌴 🌴 🌴

"WOULD YOU REALLY?" Rebecca asked John later that evening as she watched him rocking their daughter to sleep. It was a time of day that Rebecca particularly liked. Dinner was over, the dishes were nearly finished, and John was rocking Jane. It was his special time with her, and when she fell asleep, he often stayed in the rocking chair for an hour or more, conversing with Rebecca while their daughter slept on his shoulder.

"Really what?"

"Really feed Edward to the sharks?"

John smiled. "No, I suppose not. But it sounded good, don't you think?"

"If Edward didn't see right through it," she suggested.

"I'm caught in a quandary where Edward is concerned," John explained. "You and Jane became two of the greatest blessings in my life because Edward mistreated you. On one hand, I owe such happiness as I have to him. On the other hand, he deserves at least six months in prison for what he did to you and your father."

"He deserves more time in prison than that," she argued.

"No," he disagreed. "Most men do not last longer than six months in prison, and after the two weeks I spent there when I ran the *Warwick* aground, I've realized that six months in prison is enough to cure any criminal of his crimes, or kill him, whichever comes first."

"Do you suppose he'll ever stand trial for what he's done?"

John shook his head. "Power and wealth tend to control England more than justice does. I do not expect he'll ever be held accountable by the royal courts."

"It's wrong," she insisted.

"It's also wrong to punish a man who lived through a pirate's enslavement for sixteen months. That was far worse than prison."

"I know, I just—I cannot help thinking about my father. What would he be doing right now?"

"Well, he wouldn't be coming to visit his granddaughter, Jane Dunton, that's certain. And, you probably would have been promised to someone else by now, and married to him. Would you love him?"

"I love you," she reminded.

"Then it would serve you well to remember that without Edward Blackwell, the third, you wouldn't be married to me."

"I shall never forget that," she whispered, drying her hands upon a towel. "Let me take Jane up to bed."

John tenderly gave his sleeping daughter to Rebecca.

As soon as Rebecca returned from putting Jane to bed, she found John stoking the fire in the parlor. In a romantic mood, she came up behind him and wrapped her arms about his waist, impeding his work with the fireplace. Soon, he gave up and turned himself around, pulling her into his arms. Rebecca sighed deeply, and rubbed her cheek against his doublet. "Mmm. You smell nice."

John laughed. "You always say that. Though I use nothing more than the soap you make and fresh water."

Snuggling closer, Rebecca said, "You have your own scent. That's what I like so much."

Scooping her up into his arms, John cradled her tightly. "Come on, Goodwife Dunton. Let's go to bed early tonight." He carried her up the stairs.

"Why, John," she teased. "I thought you'd never ask."

LATER THAT NIGHT, John considered all that had happened. He was not surprised that Rebecca could not forgive Edward. If she distrusted him as much as she did, the last thing he wanted was to make her feel threatened by Edward's serving under him as master. Certain that Edward had seen through the ruse, he doubted he would need to explain himself later on.

Offering a silent prayer to God that they would be successful in rescuing his son from Algeria, John knew his chances were slim, at best. Subterfuge might be the best battle plan, and he had been tossing ideas back and forth between Simon, Edward and Lord Blackwell for the better part of the week. Between the four of them, they would come up with several plans that might work, none of which could possibly be approved by King Charles.

"Are you asleep?" asked his wife, whom he thought was fast asleep beside him on the bed.

"No. Too many concerns in my mind for sleep."

"Me, too." She rolled over and snuggled into his shoulder.

Pulling her tight, John said, "When I return with Thomas, we'll have to make some decisions."

"Oh?"

"I haven't given up my plan to settle in America. Jamestown is growing like wildfire, as is the Massachusetts Bay Colony. With my own ship, I could begin trading between the colonies. Would you consider moving there with me?"

She giggled. "John Dunton, I will go anywhere you want me to go. I thought you already knew that."

"It will not be easy, giving up all that you have here to move to a strange country."

John hoped that by voicing his concerns, he would learn the mind of his wife on the matter of a move so far away and foreign to her. He was pleased when she answered, "Without you and our children, I have nothing here."

"You've grown close to Naomi and Ruth, as well as Simon."

"They'll go with us, of course."

"I couldn't ask them to move from Stepney Parish. Simon has practiced here all of his adult life. His father built the house he lives in, and his sisters have never lived anywhere else."

"Have you talked to them about this?"

"No. I haven't had the courage."

"Well, chatty women that we are, the twins and I have discussed it at great detail," she confided.

"You have?" he asked, coming up on one elbow.

"Of course."

"What do they say about it?"

"They're excited to start anew."

"They are?"

"Of course, John. You're their family. Just because you do not share the same blood lines, that does not mean they love you any less than they loved Mary."

"I know they care deeply about Thomas."

"And you, and me, and Jane," she added.

"But Thomas is their blood relative, their true grandnephew."

"In their eyes, the day you married Thomas' mother, you became their nephew. When Mary died, it made no difference in their feelings toward you," Rebecca insisted.

"They told you that?" This information surprised him.

Rebecca nodded. "And, they love Jane and me as if we were related to them by blood. Love is in the heart, John. It isn't automatic just because one happens to have the same ancestors."

"Well," he confessed. "I must admit that Simon has been as much or more a father to me than my own. I was wondering how I would ever tell Simon about my hope to move to America."

"Why America, John?"

"Why not?" he countered, thinking of the possibilities. "The land there is almost free for the taking. The forests in Massachusetts go on forever. There is plenty of fish and wildlife, an abundance of wild berries, and with the skills we have in gardening and raising our own livestock, we should do well."

"Why Massachusetts? Why not Jamestown in Virginia?"

"It is warmer in Jamestown, but that also means hurricanes reach into it. Inclement weather, no matter how warm, can still devastate the region. Besides, miasma is still rampant in that climate. I do not want to expose my children to that."

"Miasma is—?"

"Swamp fever. Chills, sweating, delirium, often death."

"I wouldn't like that either. What about small pox and cholera?"

"You're going to find those wherever you go. But there's no reason to expose the children to more than is necessary."

"What of the Indians?"

"They seem a little less civilized the further south you go, which is another reason why it might be better in Massachusetts. Besides, my cousin's family settled in a little town northwest of Salem. He told me a few years ago that the country offers a great way of life if you want freedom from religious oppression."

Rebecca laughed. "And that's important to you?"

"Not particularly, but it might be important to you," he said, thinking of her vision of her father a few days ago. If news of that got out, she'd be the laughing stock, perhaps even sanctioned by the Church for even speaking of such things.

"I follow the teachings of the Church of England, John."

"Except where visits from your father are concerned," he cautioned. "I do not believe that would be acceptable behavior in our current community."

"I would never tell anyone else what happened , John."

He smiled, relieved to hear of her trust and confidence. To hammer his point well, he said, "I know, my dearest. But in England, the very walls have ears. We claim we have liberties, but do we really? Why do you think I prefer the mariner's life to dwelling in the city?"

"Because, you love the sea?"

"No, because I love the freedom. I could never attain the status of merchant in England because the King would never agree to my post as a Captain."

"Why not?" she questioned. "You've already proven yourself to the King."

John shook his head. "I disagree that men should be made to walk the plank or languish in prison until they die of starvation, scurvy or prison fever. It was the one thing General Rainsborough and I tangled about when I was serving under him as master of the *Admiral.* The men of his Majesty's Royal Navy are taught a certain standard on how to govern their ships and crews. I, for one, will not lash a man for having a mind of his own. I may put him in chains and bring him back to stand trial for his crimes, but it is not my place to punish him more than that."

"So you have no desire to be a supreme ruler, a king?" Rebecca questioned, a lilt of teasing in her voice.

"Only master of my own destiny, my own ship, my own home," John admitted. "Anything more than that would be wasted on me."

"I see no harm in a Captain having compassion, John," said Rebecca, pulling his head down so that their lips were merely an inch apart. "After all, your kindness and empathy is what drew me from Blackwell Tower."

With a lingering kiss, John agreed.

Chapter Four

The Search Begins

"Judge not, that ye be not judged."
~Matt. 7:1

*I*t wasn't until May, 1637, that the *Warwick II* was finally ready to sail. In the interim, John was requested at an audience with King Charles, who had given John his blessing for the trip to Algiers, even if he could not give him much other support. In addition, King Charles provided papers for each member of John's crew, stating that they were on the King's errand, and that should a man be found with one of the papers in his possession, he was to be taken immediately to the King for clemency. In return, John agreed to provide his Majesty with a complete list of the crewmen he hired before setting sail.

Edward, true to his word, became a relentless force in implementing John's instructions, going beyond that which was required of him in every instance. John was pleased, if not proud, of the progress Edward had made in restoring John's confidence in him.

Aboard the *Warwick II*, the hemp had been replaced with fresh cannabis chords in all the seams, and tarred sufficiently to withstand years of hard ocean crossings. All the lines had been replaced with new from the twelve-hundred-foot ropery at Chatham.

The sails had been cut and sewn from new sail cloth, in quadruplicate; they were all triangular, a sail plan John had learned from the pirates themselves. This would be no square-rigged ship. Not only was there a set of creamy-white sails, but three additional sets of sails were dyed. One set looked like sandstone and granite. If the ship were set at anchor near any cliff along the Strait of Gibraltar, it would become almost undetectable from a distance. At night, the sail sheets would be replaced with others that had been died a deep, midnight blue, the color of the night sky. Other times they could use sails dyed a thick, rolling gray, to look like a storm on the horizon. Drapes were made to cover the gunwales, thus making camouflage an important part of the devious subterfuge John planned for this voyage.

Loaded aboard ship were a multitude of flags, and several costumes, as well. What the crew wore would depend solely upon whom they encountered; they could appear as fishermen, Moorish pirates, French Warriors, Spanish Conquistadores or King Charles' Royal Navy. Lord Blackwell had spared no expense in providing John and his crew with every possible disguise.

Every conceivable tool for stratagem, stealth and concealment had been designed into the *Warwick II*. There were false barrels for hiding within, false floors for smuggling humans, undetectable wardrobe backs that slid open for storing costumes, hidden panels for hiding extra weapons. Sewn into the captain's quarters' tapestries were hidden pockets with duplicates of the men's papers, showing them to be loyal subjects of King Charles, should the need ever arise to prove themselves.

Edward had insisted that the ship be double-hulled at the stern, with a space between the stern's exterior and the hull's interior for twelve men to stand, shoulder to shoulder, flat like sardines, for hours on end, if need be, hidden behind the inner hull, with breathing corks accessible only from the inside. As an avenue of escape, or if the ship needed to be scuttled, the crew could hide between the two stern hulls, remove a panel of timbers that would drop the false stern into the water, forming a rescue raft for them. They could then pull out the hemp from the inner hull and sink the ship. While saving themselves, they would allow their captors to drown. To counter balance the weight of this false stern, an artificial pocket was built into the bow of the ship, and loaded with cannon balls and keg powder. If the ship were searched, even by an able pirate, Edward's designs were nearly undetectable.

Supplies had been shipped in from all over England, many in the form of anonymous donations from grieving families whose loved ones had not been returned to them from Salé, Morocco.

When the *Warwick II* was finally slipped from dry dock to the sea, she floated like a gentle warhorse, awaiting battle.

Now, all John needed was a capable crew. Not many would be willing to risk their necks for such a fearsome venture. With Edward and Lord Blackwell's assistance, they worded the crew request and hung it on every shop door within a ten-mile radius. The parchment that John posted around the docks would bring a colorful lot to them, but his needs were more specific. The notice read:

WANTED: Able seamen willing to risk their lives in pursuit of English captives, particularly my son, now enslaved at Algiers. Compensation will be paid at double the King's rate (half upon departure, half upon return) for a period of not less than twelve months. Apply in front of the Chatham ropery, ready to sail on the fifteenth day of May 1637.

Signed:
Captain John Dunton of the Warwick II, *now lying at anchor in Chatham Bay.*

On the fifteenth of May, John and Edward sat at a wooden table, outside the ropery, waiting for able seamen to come along. Though it shouldn't have surprised him that very few men came, John was bitterly disappointed. Three older men who'd likely never sailed a day in their lives came forward early on. Their sons had been captured several years previous and were not among the rescued by the Salé Fleet. Now, they wanted vengeance, or to locate their sons' remains, whichever came first. John was forced to take their names down because he had no other prospects. Two women came, wanting to sail with them in search of their husbands, but they were turned away.

As the day wore on, discouragement settled in. John was just beginning to think that the voyage would be cancelled due to lack of crew when a crowd of men came across the quay toward them. Perhaps two dozen men in all, they were led by fifteen seamen John knew well from the first bark *Warwick*. They, too, had been taken captive the same time as John, yet lived to tell the tale.

Michael Downe, a Welshman in his mid-twenties known as Big

Mike had wild hair and glaring green eyes. He smiled down at John as he approached. "We brought men whose kin were taken or killed by the pirates, Captain Dunton." Big Mike introduced the men, saying, "Some are old, some young, but they're all willing."

Elias Fox, gaunt and weathered, had deep creases in his face much like a walnut, and nearly as dark from a lifetime spent at sea in the sun. Leaning upon the table, he said, "But we'll teach 'em everything they need to know, Captain." He nodded, winked, then shook John's hand vigorously.

"I do not understand," said John, standing to shake hands with the others. "Why would you risk your lives for a suicide mission such as this?"

Peter Bayland spoke up next. He had been John's first mate on the bark *Warwick*, and was a short, stocky fellow with a penchant for rum and brawling. "We wouldn't be alive if it weren't for you, John. We're all proud to serve under you, sir."

"Hear! Hear!" said the crew in unison.

"Of course," Peter added, "We'll want the double pay you offered if we survive the voyage. Otherwise, we'll want it sent to our next of kin."

Edward spoke up. "I am authorized to send half to your next of kin when you sign on."

The new arrivals glared at Edward, many with animosity inflaming their faces. Robert Boyer, a swarthy, peaceable man with bald head and long mustache, diverted the men's attention back to John. "Elias has been teaching me to swim and cook, Captain Dunton."

"Great!" said John, shaking Robert's hand. "We shall make you assistant cook, under Elias' tutorial. I'm pleased to know you can swim as well."

"My wife is pleased, too. Thank the good Lord that our children are still safe with her. But like me, she knows that we have a man's job to do, looking for young Thomas. It's a shame he wasn't at Salé when you went there last year with the armada."

"Thank you, Robert."

"Is *he* going with us, Captain?" asked a squeaky-voiced man about forty years old, with bright red hair, green slits for eyes and a round, bulbous nose.

John turned to the side and saw Red Taylor pointing an accusatory finger at Edward Blackwell. Red had lost some of the use of his vocal chords when he'd fallen from a yard spar several years ago, and was caught around the neck by a ratline, nearly hanging himself. Ever since then, Red's unmistakable voice ranged somewhere between a squawk and a squeal.

The other men seemed to wait with bated breath for John's response.

"Yes, he is," John answered, allowing his voice to ring with authority and finality.

"What's he got to gain in this venture?" squeaked Red.

Edward stood before John could answer. "Sanity," he responded, his voice low and almost trembling. "Young Thomas saved my life in Algiers. I want to return the favor."

A hush went over the crowd. John turned to the group and held his hands up. "Edward will be our map into Algiers. Much the same as I memorized the prominent features about Salé, Edward knows many details about Algiers that will benefit us. He was forced into slavery there in May of 1635, and did not escape Algiers until April, the following year."

"But can he be trusted?" This from Elias.

"As much as any of us," smiled John. "He's been through the refiner's fire, men, and deserves a chance to prove himself."

"He slips up once," warned Peter, "and you know what I'll do to him."

"He's not coming on as Master, is he?" demanded Red.

"No. There will be no master aboard the *Warwick II*," said John. "I will resume full responsibility for both positions, until such time as one of the crew proves himself to my satisfaction. Peter Bayland, you've been a good first mate, and if you agree, I shall keep you in that position. Big Mike will be midshipman, Red will act as gunnery deck captain."

"Hear! Hear!" echoed the men in approval.

When all the assignments were handed out, the crew of the *Warwick II* added up to twenty-nine men, including John and Edward. Simon, the ship's doctor, who would be arriving at the docks first thing in the morning, would bring their total to thirty. It was a sparse crew, but it would do well enough.

Simon, Thomas' grandfather, would soon be bringing Rebecca, Jane, Naomi and Ruth. John looked forward to their arrival in the morning, knowing the women would not let the ship sail until they had said their farewells.

Later that afternoon, while standing at the stern, atop the aftercastle, John's thoughts turned homeward. He pictured Rebecca in his mind, and could almost inhale the sweet fragrance of her long, blonde tendrils, see the turquoise in her oval eyes. He remembered her long eyelashes curled as she held Jane close to her bosom, mother and child napping.

Anxious to hold his beloved Rebecca, whom he hadn't seen in a week, John prayed it would not be their last embrace. As his thoughts turned to Rebecca, John thanked God for bringing her into his life, and asked for her health and safety until he could hold her in his arms again. His prayers turned to his children, Thomas and Jane, who had never even met. How he loved each one! Then, to the search for Thomas, John beseeched the Lord in earnest, praying that He would empower him with whatever cunning, stealth and courage he might need to effect the safe rescue of his son. John dared not ask the Lord to show him the future, however, for fear it would not be pleasant.

His attention was diverted from his private thoughts and communications with God by a call down below, one that had been relayed from the Chatham Dock.

Several wagon loads of supplies were delivered to the dock, donated from King Charles' private stores, along with a parchment praising the men for their devotion and willingness to embark on such a hazardous voyage. There were cases of wine, wheels of cheese, barrels of flour, boxes of fresh eggs, bricks of chocolate (apparently from Spain), a dozen baskets of wintered apples and squashes, two-hundred rashers of smoked pork, seven barrels of dried peas and twelve kegs of rum. There were also a dozen wooden boxes filled with fresh cabbages, carrots and onions. In fact, so many items had been delivered that John ordered the crew of the *Warwick II* to lift anchor, land-line the ship to port, and bring her up snug against the wharf.

Storing the last of the supplies late into the night, John worked harder than any of the crew to finish before dawn. It was difficult finding room for all the items King Charles had sent. Even the Captain's quarters were stacked with goods. The men on this voyage would certainly not want for food.

At the break of day, John was awakened when a carriage arrived with an odd little man from London. Coming out on deck, John hailed the man from the gunwale. "May I help you?"

"I'm looking for Captain John Dunton," said the aging man who was peculiarly dressed in striped breeches and a silk waistcoat and held a lop-sided, green wool cap in his tiny hands. He wore wire-rimmed spectacles and had a patch of white-speckled, sandy hair standing almost straight off the top of his head. John guessed his age near sixty.

"You've found him," said John. "What do you want with me?"

"King Charles ordered me to sail with you and your men, sir. I trust I'm not too late."

John laughed aloud. "Not yet, my good man. Come aboard. What shall I call you?"

"Barnabus Martin, at your service, Captain." Martin stepped up the gang-plank, carrying a heavy trunk with him.

"And your area of expertise?"

"Languages, sir. I happen to be well-versed in several dialects, Arabic, Spanish, French, Portugese, Latin and English."

"That would be useful, Martin." To Red Taylor, John said, "Fetch Barnabus Martin's other trunks, Red. Let's put him in the forecastle cabin with Edward Blackwell, shall we?"

"Straight away," squeaked Red, who hurried down to the trunks and began loading them aboard.

As Martin passed by John, he dropped the trunk he was carrying and it opened, spilling an entire library of books upon the weather deck. John stooped to help him pick them up, while listening to Martin's numerous apologies more times than he cared to, until he noticed several of the books were filled with nothing but blank pages.

"These prove useful to you, do they?" he asked pointedly.

"It's the rage in France this season," explained Martin. People are using them for their daily records, instead of parchments. I thought perhaps you would want me to scribe for you while I'm aboard."

"Yes," John agreed heartily. "I do not have a master aboard ship for the voyage, so a scribe would come in handy. Perhaps, you'll be a useful addition to the crew."

"There is one small oversight. Captain, I refrained from mentioning it sooner, but you'll soon learn the truth about me, and I'd rather you heard it from me than spread about the ship as gossip." Martin seemed to squirm a little more prominently.

"And that is?" questioned John.

"I've never been aboard a ship before, having spent most of my days teaching languages at the University."

Another landlubber! thought John in disgust. Since the King had sent Martin to translate, and apparently scribe, for the *Warwick II*, John could not turn him away. "Very well, then, Martin. As soon as you've grown your sea legs, I will expect you to take copious notes of the voyage, as well as a running inventory of all the ship's stores, a list of the crew and another of the rescued Englishmen, should we find favorable conditions in Algeria."

Martin gulped and paled considerably. "Did you say Algeria, sir?"

"Yes, Martin. I certainly did."

Trembling with fear, Martin stammered, "B-but the King did not say you were sailing to Algeria. This will not do at all!" he protested in a blubbering fashion.

"Where did the King say we were sailing?" John wondered aloud.

Martin seemed to think about the question for a moment before he answered. "To be truthful, sir, he did not say. I suppose I must have assumed it would be to the Americas." He shrugged weakly. "But Algeria?"

"I'm not likely to repeat myself," offered John. "If you choose not to go, you should report straight back to King Charles with your decision."

"Oh."

From the poor man's beleaguered expression, John could tell he would be staying with them for the duration of the voyage. John laughed aloud. "At least the King knows how to humor us." To Peter Bayland, John said, "I'm going back to my quarters. Wake me when my wife arrives."

"Yes, sir," said Peter from the helm.

It was nearly ten of the morning before the carriage arrived from Stepney Parish, carrying John's wife and daughter to bid him farewell, in addition to Simon Harris and his twin sisters, Naomi and Ruth.

John stepped down the gang-plank, with Edward following close behind him. When he reached the dock, he stepped forward, took Rebecca into his arms and kissed her, not caring who might see them. After all, she was his wife, and he had earned the right to such familiarity as this.

Afterward, he picked Jane up into his arms, hugged Naomi and Ruth, and gave a welcoming handshake to Simon. For a while, the five spoke in hushed tones, John sharing the week's events with his wife and family hurriedly. As he did so, baby Jane stroked his face with her tiny hand and whispered, "Papa, Papa." Nothing except finding Thomas could have pleased him more.

Lord Blackwell's carriage soon arrived, and Edward joined his father for one last farewell. When John noticed the two of them headed toward him, he turned to Rebecca. "You shall be in my every thought this voyage. For I will not return to you until I have Thomas in my possession, one way or another."

"I trust you completely, John."

It was the words he needed to hear. His wife had pledged her heart and her loyalty, but trust was earned, and these words encouraged him more than any others could have. "Thank you, Rebecca," he said. "I shall do everything in my power to honor that trust."

He hugged Rebecca once again, then released his wife and daughter, and hurried over to greet his Lordship.

🌴 🌴 🌴 🌴 🌴

REBECCA GAVE SIMON a hug, then watched him board the ship. Naomi and Ruth went to the carriage to wait for her.

Staring in wonder at the *Warwick II* tied up at the wharf, Rebecca still could not believe her eyes. Although slightly larger, the ship was almost the same as the original bark that John had deliberately run aground near Hurst Castle twenty months ago, with exception of the triangular sails that had been rigged completely different from the square sails the old bark had carried.

Feeling reassured by John's earlier comments, Rebecca was relieved to know that, included in the three-score crewmen, were sixteen loyal souls with John this voyage, men whose lives had been spared at John's insistence and ingenuity. He had pleaded that their lives be spared, putting himself in harm's way for them, had fed them shellfish to keep them alive, and returned them home to England, twenty months ago. They apparently felt they owed him that much. It was a motley crew, thought Rebecca, but a fierce one.

The *Warwick II* would be the only ship, accompanied by one small shallop it would tow behind. Their appearance did not have the grandeur of the Salé Fleet, but what they lacked in presence, they certainly compensated for in determination and raw courage.

Knowing John so well, and what he had learned of pirating, Rebecca accepted that he had made his plans and battle stratagem with cunning and care. The crew, who had sailed with him before, called him Captain, now. John seemed willing, finally, to accept that designation.

She watched as Lord Blackwell shook John's hand once again.

"The *Warwick II* is yours, John, now and when you return.

John nodded. "Thank you, Sir. There is no guarantee we will succeed. But we shall put up a good fight . . . to the death, if necessary."

"To the death, Father," agreed Edward, embracing his Lordship as though it might be the last time they would be together.

Two more unlikely comrades than John Dunton and Edward Blackwell could not be found. John had compassion on his side, and hated force and brutality. Edward had delighted in control and abuse, but had shown outward signs of commiseration. They had committed their allegiance to each other and to their desperate search for a missing, ten-year-old boy.

Who better to go with John than Edward? thought Rebecca, her anger easing more with each passing day. Although she had not forgiven Edward, his willingness to search for the boy who'd saved his life had softened Rebecca's heart towards him. Perhaps Edward's eagerness to serve under John's command, at the peril of his own life, had ultimately been the turning point for her. She did not know. She still did not trust him, not entirely. But John did, and he was a good judge of character. That would have to be enough.

When the men were finished with their farewells, John came toward Rebecca. She lowered Jane to the wharf and thrilled as the child lifted her arms up and toddled steadily toward her father. "Papa!" Jane said, in a sing-song way that delighted Rebecca. "Papa!" Her golden curls bounced around her head as she went toward him.

John scooped Jane up into his arms and twirled her around. After giving her a kiss, he handed her to Ruth, who was sitting beside Naomi in the carriage.

Taking Rebecca into his arms, John said, "I cannot promise success, Rebecca. But I can promise we will do our best."

"You will be in my heart and my prayers day and night, until you return to me." She kissed him tenderly, then let him go.

Because the wind was favorable and the men were waiting for John to come aboard, he said "Goodbye," and stepped up the plank to the deck. The moment he did, Rebecca heard him issue sailing orders. The plank was hauled aboard and the docking lines were loosed. Triangular sails unfurled and caught the wind eagerly, and the *Warwick II* inched away from the timbered dock, pulling the shallop behind it.

Into the noon sun and toward Algiers, her dear husband, Captain John Dunton, sailed away. Pride, fear and hope filled Rebecca's bosom and gave her pause. Stepping to the carriage, she snuggled Jane while the toddler waved goodbye to her father.

Rebecca knew that John may not find Thomas in Algiers . . . or even alive, for that matter. Many experienced officers of his Majesty's Royal Navy had told them the rescue of Thomas Dunton could not be done. They said it would require an armada with several hundred warships to take on Algiers. Some even wagered how long the *Warwick II* and its odd assortment of crew would last, one ship alone against all the Algerian pirates. But none of their urgent protestations held sway with her husband. These more experienced officers did not realize John had no plans to take young Thomas by force . . . but by stealth, subterfuge and prayer.

John was a determined man possessed with a father's courage, a father's love. And, nothing but death would stop him. Knowing this, Rebecca was both fearful and comforted. How she had learned to love and trust John Dunton!

A scripture filled her heart, though she couldn't recall its reference: *Greater love hath no man than this, that he would lay his life down for another.* That was John Dunton.

Now it was up to John and God and, perhaps, Edward Blackwell III. The first two she trusted completely.

But . . . Edward?

Rebecca was quite certain that Edward was the man her father was referring to when he told her she must learn to trust those whom she did not. Could she really trust Edward? For this question, Rebecca had no answers.

Chapter Five

Stormy Hearts

> *"Articles of Peace, Accorded and Agreed upon, between the*
> *High and Mighty Prince, CHARLES by the grace of God,*
> *King of Great Britain, France and Ireland . . . ."*
> ~John Dunton

As John read, and reread, the articles of peace between his Majesty, King Charles, and the Right Excellent Lord Siddie Hannet Laishi of Safi, Morocco, he realized that the armada's conquest of Salé had afforded him an edge in slipping into Algiers with little interference. Fortunately, he had asked the King for a certified copy of the document, which gave him Lord Laishi's seal. With a little assistance from their new scribe, Barnabus Martin, they could draw up a false agreement which would allow the *Warwick II* free trade with Algeria, as an aligned pirate of Salé. To make the ship seem even less British, John had a false name installed over the *Warwick II*, which read *Warhorse*. In Moorish tradition, the warhorse was a noble animal. As a ship, a warhorse was known to have been through many battles, usually emerging victorious.

Working on the parchment day and night, to word it the way Lord Laishi hopefully would have, John and Martin finally came up with:

> *Articles of Peace, Accorded and Agreed upon,*
> *between the Right Excellent Lord Siddie Hannet*
> *Laishi, King of Morocco and all the regions round*
> *about, and Captain Barbarossa of the ship War-*
> horse, *being a descendant of the great pirate,*
> *Arnaj Barbarossa, cousin to that greatest of*
> *pirates, Kayr-ad-Din Barbarossa.*
>
> 1. *That inasmuch as free trade has been estab-*
>   *lished between us, Captain Barbarossa is free*
>   *to conduct business between Morocco and*
>   *such other pirate nations as he deems fit.*
>
> 2. *That as long as Captain Barbarossa conducts*
>   *his affairs between us in a peaceful manner,*
>   *he shall have access to any ports within our*
>   *borders.*
>
> 3. *That Captain Barbarossa has my recommen-*
>   *dation to any country choosing to trade wares*
>   *or slaves with him, particularly to my friend,*
>   *Pasha Aligosa, Governor of the Port at*
>   *Algiers.*
>
> *Signed aboard Captain Barbarossa's ship, the*
> Warhorse, *at Safi, Morocco, this fifteenth day*
> *of June, 1637.*

John had heard that Arnaj Barbarossa, a distant cousin to the infamous *Kayr-ad-Din Barbarossa*, who waged a thirteen-year war with Algeria until he'd overtaken the country and organized it as a pirate's haven back in the early 1500's, had later established a pirate's colony in the Caribbean, and never returned from that region. Barnabus Martin's knowledge and teaching ability became an important factor in the crew's understanding of pirates. To John's surprise, Martin had made a study of Arnaj Barbarossa through interviews with seamen who had been to Arnaj's island paradise. They spoke a form of Spanish, interspersed with some Turkish dialect, and he'd been instrumental in writing an entire volume on this odd language.

It took the crew the full month's voyage practicing their guttural sounds and sentences as Martin taught them to learn the basics of the Arnaj Island Spanish and Turkish, as well as counting their money in doubloons and ducats. They also learned many familiar expressions, such as "Yes." "No." "Out of my way." "Give that to me." "How much?" "Too much."

The crew needed no entertainment, for watching one another stumble over longer sentences amused them entirely. If that were not enough, John and his sixteen crewmen were busy reciting to the others their own observations of how pirates interact with one another.

While they were at sea each day, and long into every night, John and Martin worked on the seamen's learning Turkish in many more sentence variations. John and the sixteen crewmen who'd been captured with him two years ago had already learned some of the language from their captor, Aligolant. This was something John had insisted upon when they were held captive in Morocco for six months.

Now, they learned more practical usage, and how to respond without raising suspicion.

Martin spontaneously challenged the men with many Turkish questions, and even if they did not understand them completely, they all seemed able to respond well enough. Of course, there was still a moment of laughter when Red, supposedly asking the price of sorghum, squeaked in Turkish, "How much for your cow of a sister?" and Big Mike answered, "Less than the donkey you call your wife!"

Tireless in his efforts to educate the seaman to a pirate's ways, Barnabus Martin worked alongside John with equal enthusiasm. If the mission failed, the blame would not fall upon Martin's attention to details. For the entire month, the crew labored under a schooling environment, and during the last week of the voyage, they were required to speak Spanish or Turkish. John was pleased that King Charles had sent such a fine tutor to accompany the *Warwick II* on its voyage.

Because they had once been Aligolant's slaves, John and his seamen knew other peculiarities of the pirate's life. Dyeing false tattoos, similar to those worn by all pirates, upon the inside of their wrists was painful, but Simon assured them that these tattoos were temporary, and would wear off completely in about a month. Some of the men set to coloring their skin darker and their hair coal-black. Fortunately, Simon had a great skill with plant dyes and herbal medicines. By the time they were done, the crew were a fierce looking bunch of pirate misfits as one would ever want to encounter. Some of the men, those with light-colored eyes, would pretend to be John's slaves, whom they now exclusively called Captain Barbarossa.

By the time the ship reached the Strait of Gibralter, the men were keyed up and anxious. Fortunately, when they stayed as close to the cliffs on the Spanish coastline as they could, they were not intercepted. Flying the pirate's flag seemed to assist them in their deception. The Spanish would not send a fleet to stop them, provided they passed by Spain's borders without stopping, and the other ships passing recognized them as pirates and gave them a wide berth.

"It's too easy," whispered Edward to John as they passed the Strait and headed toward Algiers' Harbor.

"No, Rebecca has been keeping us in her prayers," John responded. "God will not allow us to fail this time. We have divine intervention in our behalf."

Arriving without incident on the twelfth day of June, 1637, they anchored at the Port of Algiers and waited for the port authorities to arrive. Tensions were high, but the ship was in good stead and the authorities had little to complain about. John welcomed them aboard with a great grin of glistening white teeth against the dark background of his skin, and gave them liberally of their stores. After all, the *Warhorse* had brought cases of wine, and John passed bottles out freely to the new arrivals, who glanced only momentarily at the articles of peace from the King of Morocco to Captain Barbarossa.

After a few minutes of pleasantries, John escorted them from his ship after ascertaining where the auction block could be located. Before they left, he asked, "Could you tell me where *El Djazair* might be found?"

The three men looked at him strangely, but answered. "The ship, *El Djazair,* is at the far end of the bay. Or did you mean to inquire about Abu Benjamin El Djazair, who owns it?"

"The ship, of course," intercepted Martin. "For Abu is as stubborn as always, is he not?"

The men laughed, said something unintelligible to John, and left the *Warhorse* without another word.

"A ship?" asked John.

Martin nodded. "Either that, or its owner."

John nodded toward Edward, who was coming toward him from the forecastle. "El Djazair could be the name of a man, or his ship. Do you recall how Thomas may have used the name?"

Edward seemed puzzled. "'I must get back to El Djazair,' those were his exact words."

"But he didn't say, Master El Djazair, or the ship, *El Djazair*?"

"I wish he had," said Edward. "The city of Algiers is also called El Djazair, did you know that?"

Feeling his heart sink inside his chest, John shook his head. "No, you never mentioned it before now."

"I thought you knew," said Edward, remorsefully.

"I had no idea. Weren't you in Algiers, or El Djazair, when Thomas said this to you?"

"I was, John. But Thomas could have meant El Djazair anything, local markets, inns, brothels, the El Djazair Ropery for all I know."

"Tomorrow, we will go into the slave auction and buy as many English subjects as we can without raising suspicions," said John. "You will look around, see if anything looks familiar to you."

"I fear that I will be almost useless within the city," admitted

Edward. "For that is not where we were when Thomas found us. We were trying to escape from Algiers, inland."

"Yes, I know. But Thomas isn't likely to be on that same road every day, is he?" asked John.

"Very likely not," agreed Edward. "When he said he must get back to *El Djazair*, he always headed toward the city."

"And this happened three times?" John questioned, just to be certain there was no mistake in their communication.

"Yes. On three occasions, he brought us food and water."

"Then, we stick to the plan. We begin our search of the city from this point and spread outwards. While we are at the auction block, the rest of you who are acting like pirates will mingle, walk amongst the buildings, check out all the young boys you see, inconspicuously, of course. If Thomas is alive, someone will have seen him."

"And if we're caught?" squeaked Red.

"You aren't going anyway," said John, "what's your worry?"

"We'll still be aboard. People will be watching what we do aboard the ship."

"You'll act like a slave, with the pirates oppressing you as they always do."

"Pardon me," said Barnabus Martin. "Who are we selling at the auction block?"

"No one," said John.

"But they'll be expecting us to sell some of our slaves, won't they?" persisted Martin, his hair pointing out in all directions.

"Not if we're buying slaves," said John. "We can sell some of our stores, in limited quantities, if it worries you."

"I was thinking," said Martin, "that it would be far more likely that we've come to sell slaves, rather than buy them."

"Now, that is something I do have knowledge about," said Edward, raising his voice slightly. "When I was sold here, there were many who were strictly buyers. The pirate trade isn't based on the barter system. They do not usually trade in their worn out slaves, they dispose of them. If you men seem vicious enough to them, they'll know your slaves are dead or nearly so. Trust me on this, Martin, they will not ask for credentials, just gold."

"We cannot purchase all the slaves that go through the market place each day without making ourselves look suspicious," warned John. "This will be the hardest part of our time at the auction. If we are to remain in the good graces of Algeria, we must be able to justify how many slaves we buy."

"We can also try to help as many escape as possible, can't we?" suggested Miles Weatherby, one of the elderly men whose oldest son, Daniel, had been taken captive and never found at Salé.

"Without meaning to sound callous, Miles," warned John. "No, we dare not. This voyage has been undertaken with one goal in mind, finding my son, Thomas. If we are fortunate to find your son, as well, we shall consider him a gift from God. But I will not risk the mission for every slave held captive here."

"Who will decide, then, which slaves will be bought into freedom, and which will not?" asked Miles, his eyes filling with tears.

John reached out and placed a hand upon Miles' shoulder. "I will purchase every slave I see come over the block, but I will limit myself to two or three batches each day. I will not be there any longer than that, for my own sanity. And I suggest you avoid the auction block entirely. Your son has likely been sold to someone else, long ago. The only reason I shall go there each day is to keep up the performance required of me as Captain, and to free as many slaves as is possible. But we cannot fool ourselves into thinking we can take all of them, and we cannot deceive these pirates all the time. The moment our subterfuge is discovered, we are all dead men."

Miles' mouth fell open as he realized, apparently for the first time, that this rescue mission was not for his own son. John shared his anguish. "I will promise you this much, Miles. If we locate your son, regardless the costs, I will bring him with us, even at the peril of my own life."

"We all will," said Peter quickly. "We came on this voyage knowing we were staring death in the face. We came for Captain John Dunton. We'll all die before he will. We owe him our lives."

All the men nodded, shook hands, pounded one another on the backs. But John noticed there wasn't a dry eye among the seamen, and he whispered, when they were finished with their affirmations, "I've never been more proud of the men serving with me than right now."

Later that day, John climbed the ratlines and scurried up to the crow's nest, where Red Taylor was keeping a cautious vigil. Removing his spyglass from his doublet, John held it up to his eye and studied the terrain carefully.

The city of Algiers was far different than John had expected. Even with Edward's keen memory, he hadn't been able to explain the massive size of the place. The buildings were huge, many were like palaces, several stories tall, with lofty turrets and pinnacles. The city seemed to stretch on forever, and John could see no end of the buildings or the square, squat houses that trailed off in every direction. There seemed to be no rhyme or reason to the layout. Algiers seemed to be thrown together around the river, with side roads branching out haphazardly in all directions. He knew the population was nearly a hundred-thousand, but even London had its order, and assimilated into the countryside in a predictable manner. In Algiers, all logic had been thrown to the wind, and streets were laid out chaotically, according to the dictates of the confused.

Finding Thomas among the thousands of buildings and houses that he saw would not be an easy assignment. To the west of the city, the houses thinned out and farm fields replaced a good share of the buildings. Somewhere in this expansive and enormous city, or the surrounding area, they would find his son. Somewhere.

EARLY THE NEXT morning, John left the *Warhorse* with six of the crew, who rowed the shallop over to the quay. Edward came as the Captain's personal slave, carrying a large palm frond with which to fan his master, which he did continually.

Just as John stepped out of the shallop, he noticed a large sailing vessel coming into the harbor, that sailed right past them so they could read her name, *Larache*.

"Smooth as fine silk," said Peter. "She slips through the water in a grand, comely manner. A beautiful ship, this one."

John turned to Peter and smiled. "Someday I'm going to own a ship just like the *Larache*."

"Why? Do you not like the *Warhorse*, Captain?" asked Edward.

"I love the *Warhorse*," John said quickly. "But if I am to have a fleet of merchant ships someday, the *Larache* would make a healthy addition, don't you think?"

Peter smiled. "Must be eighty feet long," he said dreamily.

"A hundred seventy, maybe eighty, tons burthen," added Edward. "Did you know my father is building a ship over one hundred twenty feet long, forty feet at the widest beam?"

"Blimey," said Peter. "That's a warship, that is. What's he building it for?"

"He's been commissioned as a privateer," explained Edward. "He has permission from the King to take on any pirate or enemy ship he chooses, without provocation, take all their plunder and only split half of it with the crown."

John was dismayed to hear this news, knowing it would only lead to more bloodshed with the pirates than they had already seen. "I pray he will exercise such a powerful position wisely," said John. "We have enough trouble with pirates as it is."

"Legalized piracy," interjected Peter, "is what it is, Captain. That's how Rainsborough got so famous, you know."

"Yes," agreed John. "And a finer captain is hard to find."

Big Mike sighed, almost wearily, it seemed to John, "No, sir. We're signed on with the only one that matters. You think Rainsborough woulda' stuck his neck out for us back in Salé?"

"It's hard to say what a man would do unless put to that kind of test," said John. "I did nothing heroic in Salé, I merely did my job. If I had done more, my son would be with me now, and we would not be searching for him."

This seemed to silence the chatter, and the men quickly dispersed to begin their search of the city, as they had previously planned. John and Edward walked through the streets of Algiers toward the auction block, which Edward seemed to recall with startling clarity. As he waved his palm frond, cooling John's pathway, he muttered, quietly "Yes, I've seen this. Oh! Yes, this way. Quickly. It's right over here."

Before they reached the entrance to the market place, Edward whispered to John, "I've heard the men tell of your heroics, John. You mustn't downplay it so much in front of them. It will dishearten them."

"I appreciate their loyalty, and yours, Edward. But I did none of it for praise. I did it for survival, theirs and mine."

"I've never done anything one would consider heroic," said Edward. "I was a bloody coward that day on the *Neptune*."

"Young William Moore said otherwise," John whispered back to him. Then, loudly, he said, "Clear the way! Slave! Shall I slit your throat now or wait until I can enjoy it? Do you think I want to fight my way in line like swine to the fodder?"

"No, Master! Clear the way! I tell you clear it now!" Edward yelled, appearing truly horror stricken. "This way, Master," he guided John as others pressed themselves along the corridor, out of their way.

"Aw, it is Captain Barbarossa, is it not?" asked a swarthy pirate at the gate. When he spoke, it was not to John, rather to Edward, his *slave*. "Come in, we have heard of your arrival. Will your master be interested in slaves today? Women? Men? Or children?"

"My master will make his own choices," said Edward irritably. "He will only be seated for fifteen minutes time. He shall see what prizes you are capable of, but if he is not pleased, he will not buy. And if he does not buy, he will not return."

"We have a wide assortment today. Come, sit down here near the front, where you are better able to see them," said the man. Then, turning to another, he said, "Bring in the next group."

Across the front of the large tent came a line of twelve men not unlike the motley crew he and his own men made up more than two years before. Tall, short, old, young, yet they all shared the same conditions: filthy, starved, unshaven, weak, trembling. Their appearance inflamed John, and it was all he could do to keep his anger under control.

Glancing furtively at the people around him, John noticed their glee at the depravity with which these slaves had already been treated. They seemed almost joyful, pointing and belittling them in front of everyone. Some remarked how bad their teeth, how swollen their ankles, how useless their muscles, how terrible their stench, bringing their bargaining price to the bottom of the scale. It hadn't seemed so bad when he'd been on the other side, but this! This was intolerable!

The auctioneer started the bidding, but the moment that he did, John stood, interrupting him. "How much?" he asked, his voice hot with outrage.

Backing down, the auctioneer squeaked, "We never get less than twenty ducats apiece, Captain Barbarossa."

John whirled around quickly. "Any challenges to that price?" he demanded.

Everyone shook their heads, apparently afraid of him, frightened by the danger they saw in his livid eyes.

"Pay the man, slave!" John barked. Then, he threw a small bag of gold at Edward's feet, and left the tent in haste.

What would they think of him now? Would he ever be allowed in the auction block again? Had he endangered lives by his reaction to what he had seen there? How humans could trade in other humans' lives, he could not comprehend. He had not expected to respond the way that he had, and now he feared that he had put the mission in danger. More precisely, he had jeopardized Thomas' rescue.

John swallowed a lump in his throat, found his heart pounding inside his chest, and hastened down a narrow alley to the quay. Numerous displays of jewelry, blankets, fruits, vegetables and wine bottles were lined up for display in the open market, and John casually looked at some of these, while waiting for Edward to join him with the slaves.

A man who looked vaguely familiar was disembarking from a shallop that had, apparently, come from the *Larache*, for the shallop's oarsmen headed back toward the *Larache*, the moment the man stepped ashore.

To his horror, John recognized him as a man who had often attended the auctions at Salé, Morocco. Indeed, John had often seen him when he'd gone into town to get supplies for Aligolant, and his old master knew the man well, for they dined together on several

occasions aboard the bark *Warwick* while John was there.

Quickly, John turned aside to examine reams of brightly colored cloth next to him, waiting for the man to leave. Relief flooded over him when the man finally passed by him without giving him a second glance. John was immediately grateful that he had used Simon's dying potions upon his skin and hair, for John now looked as though he was a true Moroccan.

Within another few minutes, Edward was escorting twelve shackled Englishmen out of the small alley and onto the quay. Seeing John, he nodded, "Shall I take them straight to the *Warhorse*, Master?"

"Yes," said John, trying to keep his voice steady. "And put them in the hold. We do not want any of them escaping now, do we?"

"I will take them straight away, Master," said Edward.

"I shall go with you," John insisted, "for I am in a foul temper and will have sport with them shortly." He said it loud and with fervor, and noticed that several vendors had stared at him in horror, and backed away, apparently frightened by him. Without smiling, John felt some satisfaction, although he regretted having to make such an outlandish statement when he saw the looks on his new slaves' faces.

CLIMBING ABOARD THE *Warhorse*, John waited until Edward had the men secured in the hold before he went below to speak with them. He brought Barnabus Martin with him.

To his dismay, he found them cowering in one corner, fearing the worst from him. In a soft voice, John said, "You've nothing to fear from me, men. I will not harm you."

They continued to shrink from him, as John swept his hair back off his face in frustration. Then an idea occurred to him. Quickly, he slid off his right boot and removed the stocking from his foot, then said, "My real name is Captain John Dunton. Look at the true color of my skin. I'm white as you. The color on my hands and face is a dye. I'm an Englishman, same as you. I, too, was captured by pirates two years ago, along with my son, Thomas. My men and I have come in disguise to Algiers to rescue my son, and those few whom we can, without disclosing ourselves. You have my deepest apologies for frightening you."

Some of the anxious men seemed to let down their guard. "Blimey," said one, "his feet are white as snow." This seemed to convince them that John would not harm them.

"Thank you, Captain Dunton. I've heard of you, sir," said another. "I served aboard the *Row Bucke* at the siege of Salé a year ago. I was real sorry we never found your son, sir."

"Thank you," said John, shaking the younger man's hand, noting the gaunt appearance behind the shocking blue eyes. "Your name, please. Martin, write these down in turn, record their origin and capture information, as well."

Martin pulled out a notebook and quill, sat down on a barrel and held a bottle of ink between his knees as he began writing.

"Samuel Streeter, sir. From Somerset. I have a wife and child at home, sir. I cannot tell you what my release will mean to them."

"When were you captured?" John asked.

"Three months ago. We had set out for the Americas on the merchant ship, *Lockley*, sir, from Hurst Castle. Of seventy-two men aboard, we twelve survived to the auction."

Another man came forward, this one not much younger than John. As he took John's hand, he collapsed in a dead faint. "No more," said John, catching him. "Get Simon, quickly," he told Martin, who stopped his ink bottle and raced up the ladder for assistance.

Edward helped John lay the man down on the floor. "When you're refreshed, men," said John. "Then we'll talk."

Simon arrived momentarily, and began his task of doctoring the emaciated men. "Sorry I wasn't here sooner, John. I've been in the crow's nest with Red Taylor. The *Larache* has us both a little worried."

John nodded. He knew their concern was well-founded.

"Edward, remove the chains from the rescued, feed them and see to it they are bathed and looked after by the doctor."

"Straight away, Captain," Edward agreed, and John heard the singsong happiness in his voice. He, too, was delighted to release the few captives they'd bought freedom for that day.

"When you've both finished, come to my cabin. Simon, bring Red with you." Turning to the newly rescued captives, John said, "In order to keep the pirates from knowing you've received your freedom, I must ask you to remain below decks at all times. It will not do to let them know Captain Barbarossa feeds and clothes his slaves."

Leaving Simon, Edward and Martin to assist the rescued Englishmen, John hastened to his cabin, stretched out upon his bed, and then realized his entire body was trembling. His performance in Algiers had shaken him more than he had imagined. Seeing the familiar face of the pirate who frequented the slave auctions at Salé, Morocco, studying John at the quay in El Djazair today, brought to John's mind the grave peril they would encounter now that they had begun the most dangerous part of their mission.

Chapter Six

A Father's Son

"... *a wise son maketh a glad father.*"
~Proverbs 10:1

oward evening, the emaciated men had been refreshed, cleaned and were now sleeping peacefully below decks, knowing for the first time in three months that there was some hope they would be returned to England.

For John, that hope seemed fleeting, at best, as he discussed the affairs of *Larache* in the Captain's quarters with Simon, Red, Edward, Big Mike, Elias and Peter, as they sat around the rectangular wooden table, voicing opinions.

"It's a different ship than he sailed before," admitted Elias. "I remember because I was serving the pirate, Aba Masmuth, one night when he came to dine with Aligolant, back when we were slaves. He had a ship called *Dismalta* at the time, I heard him mention it."

John opened up the journal he'd kept aboard the *Admiral* during the siege at Salé a year ago. The name *Dismalta* jumped out at him from one of the pages as he perused it. "Yes, it was the *Dismalta*. We sank her last summer at Salé, though several of her crew dove into the water and escaped."

"What we don't need is a hot-headed pirate discovering your true identity, John," said Peter. "He'll have every pirate in this vermin-infested place after us!"

Sighing wearily, John said, "We cannot risk my going to the auctions anymore. Peter, you'll have to go in my place. Tell them I was outraged that they had such paltry offerings and let it go at that."

"We must not risk bringing anymore slaves here," said Simon. "Thomas' life is at stake, and we dare not risk it."

"I cannot ask Peter to go to auction and not bring any slaves back. It's inhuman to even think about," said John. "And, it would not be prudent to avoid the auction block because that is why all pirates come here . . . to buy slaves, or sell them."

"You both have points of value," admitted Edward, speaking for the first time. "I am the only one whom this Aba Masmuth has not seen. Perhaps if I go to the auction, and bring back those I can. It will appease the pirates enough that our presence will still be valid."

"If someone recognizes you from when you were here before, Edward, what good will that do?"

"I will tell them that Captain Barbarossa is my master now. Believe me, John, your actions at the auction today spoke volumes about your temper. No one would dare question which pirate 'bought' me a year ago, not with you as my master. You scared all those who were there. Even me."

"Sorry," said John. "It was all I could do to keep a civil tongue

while they were humiliating those men."

"And they saw it as a fit of bad temper. They will be relieved if you do not attend with me."

"We could have some screaming on board," said Elias. "Some shrieking out in pain. Especially at night. That'll make them think you torture your slaves, and that's why you buy so many of them. It'll scare them out of their skins."

"Yes," said Simon. "It might work. Men fear what they cannot see, sometimes far more than what they do see."

"We can gather large stones by day. They have a small quarry just west of here," said Big Mike. "And throw them over the gunwales late at night. It'll sound like we're throwing bodies overboard. Then those who go into town can pretend to be terrified of Captain Barba-rossa. They can spread stories, how he tortures his slaves for sport, how they have to tie up their bodies with stones and sink them in the harbor. Make them fish bait. We can paint you pretty terrible, Captain. That is, with your permission."

"The rest of you," said John. "What do you think of this plan?"

"It could work," squeaked Red. "We could say that Captain Barbarossa especially likes young boys as slaves. Will pay handsomely for them. That might bring out Thomas' master."

"It could," agreed Peter. "Or it could backfire. Perhaps Captain Barbarossa is so terrible, the pirates would rather kill him than let him stay here."

Edward laughed. "You think they do not torture for sport?" he asked incredulously. "I've witnessed their barbarism. Why do you think the Barbarossa pirates gave credence to the term barbaric?

England never had such a word in their language until that murderous group of pirates took power here. It was to our great relief that they finally settled in the Caribe Islands. Cannibals, they were!"

"Then it's agreed," said John. "The only question remaining is what to do about Aba Masmuth, who now has possession of the *Larache*."

"And several of his crew," inserted Red. "They could recognize any of us."

"As slaves?" questioned Edward. "I think we're all overreacting. Those going ashore don't even look like slaves now. Dark skin and hair. Pirates' clothing. The only one who may have a problem would be you, Captain."

John nodded. "Should my real name be had amongst these people, you'll all be slaughtered."

A shudder went through the room.

"We knew the risks when we came aboard," said Elias. "What odds did the Royal Navy give Captain Dunton?"

Peter's mouth dropped open, Red rocked back on his heels, but Big Mike said, "Ninety-nine to one. It's still realistic."

"So, even before you came, you figured we'd never return alive?" John asked.

"We knew it was a fool's mission," admitted Peter. "We reckon we gotta die sometime. Might just as well die heroes, as running from pirates the rest of our lives."

"I did not come to die a hero," said Edward, standing. "I came to find Thomas. I'm not going to let my fear of some pirate named Aba Masmuth stop me."

"Of course not," said John. "After all, we're about to spread that kind of fear in the pirates about Captain Barbarossa, when we all know I'm the weakest link among us."

"Perhaps you should grow a mustache and beard, John," suggested Simon. "And let your hair hang over your brow. With more skin dye and the right attitude, no one will recognize you."

"You're right," said John. "We're not doomed to fail, as some of you might think. I'd lay my odds a little better than yours. Say eighty-five to one against."

The men laughed at that, and the aura of impending doom was lifted from the room. They stayed up, long into the night, some of them men screeching out in terror, as though in horrific pain. Sometimes, John's loud, booming voice could be heard across the harbor, laughing maniacally or cursing. It took a great deal of courage to keep up a steady barrage of this activity until around three in the morning, then the deathly silence that filled the night sliced through the air as a few of their precious cannon balls were thrown overboard.

Just before dawn the next morning, Robert Boyer, who'd learned to swim during the last two years, dove overboard, secured the cannon balls within cloth bags, tied them fast with a long rope, and brought the long ends up to the crew, who hauled the cannons back aboard. They may need those cannon balls later in their voyage, and could not risk running low on them.

While his men began their daily excursions into the city, John remained aboard, growing his beard and mustache, and helping Simon with the new arrivals.

It was tedious work, attending to sores and spoon feeding some Englishmen who were so weak they were practically incapable of feeding themselves.

John's frustration mounted daily. He was finally in Algiers, but unable to leave the ship because his disguise hadn't quite grown enough. He wished he would have thought of growing his facial hair while they'd been at sea, for it would be long and healthy by now. In his wildest dreams, he never imagined he might be recognized by someone from Salé while he was in Algiers. And, daily reports from the crew who went ashore were less than cheerful, for they'd heard rumors about John Dunton and his siege against Salé almost two years earlier, although the pirates were particularly secretive in the information they disclosed, and John's crew dared not press too hard for more information, lest the pirates became suspicious.

By the end of two weeks, the men had kept up their daily excursions into town, covering more and more territory, searching for any sign or clue that might point them to Thomas' whereabouts. Their nightly vigilance of seeming terror and mayhem aboard the *Warhorse* was also continued. In addition, Edward managed to buy thirty more slaves, including two young brothers, George and Scotland Bremmett, ages eleven and thirteen.

The eldest brother came to visit John within a few days of his arrival aboard ship. At the time, John was assisting Simon as he redressed a number of nasty, festered wounds upon the back of a new arrival.

The lad was tall for thirteen, and thin, with dark hair and hazel eyes, and a jittery look about him, but he was also well-mannered and went straight to the point of his visit. "Sir, I wonder if you might tell me about your seaman, Miles Weatherby?"

"Not much to tell. Scotland, is it?" asked John.

"Yes, sir. But the men call me Scotty." He swept his blonde hair off his forehead with one swoop of his thin fingers.

"Well, Scotty. What ever possessed your parents to name you Scotland?"

"I was born there, sir, while my parents were visiting Mum's grandmother. She favored the name, I suppose."

John smiled. "Something to tell your children, isn't it, Scotty? Not too many Englishmen were born in Scotland. What would you like to know about Weatherby?"

"Sir, it's just . . . there's another Weatherby slaving for a relative of the master my brother and I served. It's a common English name, sir. But I couldn't help wondering."

"Do you know where this relative lived?" John asked.

"Yes, sir. About a kilometer away from where my master lives, sir."

"First, Scotty. You are your own master now. It does not matter how long you've served someone else, your days of servitude are over," John said, tousling the lad's hair. "And second, tomorrow you and I will venture into the city together. You will pretend, only for the day, that I am your master, although I am not and will never be. We will take Edward with us, for he is known in the city as my slave, and his presence may make for fewer questions. You will show me where this Weatherby is serving. If it is at all possible, we will bring Weatherby back with us. But you must not mention our plans to Miles, lad. It is best not to get his hopes up."

Scotty's smile brightened. "Yes, sir. I won't say a word to anyone. It's always safer that way."

"Thank you, Scotty. Tell me, how is it your former master came to sell you and your brother at the auction?"

"My brother, George, has been ill, sir. I thought he would die soon, and I told my master I would not serve him again, unless my master provided medical attention for George. He was very angry, said he would sell us to someone who would beat us into submission."

"Meaning he couldn't?" asked John.

"No, sir. I still refused to serve him, even after he—" Scotty hesitated, then said stubbornly. "He dared not beat my brother, sir, for I swore in my wrath I would kill him . . . and, I also think he did not want George's death on his hands."

"Are you healed enough now to accompany me tomorrow?" Having heard the Bremmett brothers' story, John was now concerned about the physical toll that going into Algiers would place upon young Scotland.

"Yes, sir. I think the Lord preserves my strength, so that I can take care of George. He's always been the weaker of us."

John smiled and rubbed Scotland's shoulder affectionately. "We'll have quite an adventure tomorrow, then."

"Yes, sir."

"Now, Scotty. Are there any other lads in servitude in Algiers, about your brother, George's, size or age, that you recall?"

"Several, sir. But most of them passed away. None of them were named Thomas, sir, except for one boy about six years old who came to my master's—" he corrected himself, "to the pirate's house where I was enslaved, but he died of fever the same winter."

"Very well, Scotty. If anyone should happen to remember a Thomas, you will alert me straight away?"

"Yes, sir. I'm very sorry about your son, sir. Slavery is not an easy life."

"I'm quite aware of it, Scotty. I wish we had found you a few years earlier. Your adjustment would not be so painful now."

"Both our parents died when our ship was taken," confessed Scotty. "I was seven years old then, and it fell to me to take care of my brother. Fearing that we would be separated, that has been the worst for me, sir."

"Well, when we return to England, we will seek for a relative to care for you and George."

"I doubt my grandmother survived losing my mother to pirates. She was her only daughter, and I'm sure the loss was terrible for her, sir."

"Do not worry, Scotty, we shall find someone to take you in."

"And if we do not," said Edward behind them, "my father will adopt you both and you can become my brothers."

Scotty smiled. "That's very kind, Sir Edward. I'd best get back to the galley," said Scotty. "Elias told me not to be gone long."

"We'll talk more later on," said John as the lad hurried off. He turned to Edward. "I didn't hear you come down the ladder."

"You were involved in young Scotland's story," said Edward, "as was I. Do you think this Weatherby might be Miles' son?"

"We will know soon enough," said John. "Will you join me tomorrow?"

"Nothing would please me more, Captain."

"You'd best be careful, John," said Simon. "Rumors are that Aba Masmuth was asking about you at the auction block the other day, when Edward purchased the Bremmett brothers."

John raised an eyebrow to Edward. "You never told me this."

"I did not feel it was anything to worry about," said Edward. "I heard from another servant that Masmuth had stated, in a rather boisterous voice, that he'll be glad when Captain Barbarossa makes an appearance, for he would like to tell you that he grows weary of the nightly moaning coming from the *Warhorse*."

"You do not suppose we're overdoing it?" asked John with a wink.

Edward laughed. "Why do you think I added my voice to the screaming last night? Let the cries of terror fill their pirate dreams. They deserve to lie awake nights, recalling their own secret horrors."

Later that evening, when the rest of the seamen reported in from their excursion into town, they gathered on the gunnery deck to discuss the day's accomplishments. John was disappointed to learn they had searched nearly the entire city without any clue as to young Thomas' whereabouts. Tomorrow, they would begin searching the outer regions that were less populated.

If that wasn't bad enough news, Edward had yet to find any particular area that seemed more familiar than another. He just couldn't seem to locate the hayfield in which he'd lain that early spring day, fifteen months ago, when Thomas had rescued him and William Moore.

Worse still, the correct place with the name, *El Djazair*, that kept coming back to Edward, could not be found. Although the men had found *El Djazair* nearly everywhere, as the official name of bakeries, markets, wineries, loom shops, brothels, inns, and government offices. But at each and everyone of these, they had found no Thomas.

And, there were no ships in the harbor bearing the name *El Djazair*.

EARLY NEXT MORNING, John, Edward and Scotty joined the men in the shallop for the daily excursion into town. The other crewmen separated from them upon arrival at the quay, leaving the three to find the location of Weatherby's master's house.

Scotty knew the city well, and it did not take long to find the house where the slave named Weatherby worked. It was in a less influential area of the city, and John was surprised to learn that even the poorer class Algerians had English, French and Spanish slaves. Made of rough sandstone, the house was so small, it couldn't possibly hold anymore than two rooms.

While John remained behind him, Edward went to the front door and knocked. A man perhaps twenty-five years old answered, his light eyes and skin telling them he was an Englishman even before he spoke. "May I help you?"

"My master is looking for a slave named Weatherby," said Edward, his hand flowing out to proceed a deep bow toward John.

"I am Weatherby," said the man. "Daniel Weatherby."

"Then, I must speak with your master," said Edward. "For Captain Barbarossa would buy you from him."

"My master is not at home," said Daniel. "And I don't believe he would sell me. I serve him well." A look of fear settled in his eyes the moment he heard Captain Barbarossa's name.

"Is there anyone in your Master's family at home?" asked Edward slyly.

Daniel cleverly answered, "I will check." Then, he closed the door abruptly.

"Edward, you stay here," whispered John. "Scotty, you go left, I shall go right around to the back. Apparently, my reputation has preceded me."

Scotty nodded and was off to the left before John could turn toward the right side of the house. Within moments, John was at the back door, where Scotty joined him.

John whispered, "Any windows he could escape through?"

"Only one, sir. I'll guard it."

"We can only hope that he will not try to get through the one on the other side," said John, but his words were lost in midair for Scotty had already headed back.

Quickly, John opened the back door and peered inside. Daniel Weatherby cowered in a corner of the small kitchen, holding a fire poker in his hands. "I'll not go with you, Captain Barbarossa. I am a good servant. My master is pleased with me."

"Hello, the house!" yelled John. When he received no response, he noted that the house was empty with exception of himself and Daniel Weatherby.

"I am not here to debate the issue," John said quickly, in perfect English, so the young man would let down his weapon. "I am here to offer you freedom from slavery, and a chance to return to your father, Miles Weatherby."

Daniel dropped the poker. "You know my father?" he gasped, incredulously.

"I do. He crews aboard my ship."

"That's a lie," Daniel said, reaching for the poker at his feet while keeping his eyes upon John. "My father is a carpenter."

"Who went to sea to find his oldest son," said John. "I assure you, Daniel, we are not the enemy you have perceived."

"But I've heard the rumors," insisted Daniel. "You torture people upon your ship at night. Everyone is talking about how the terrible—"

"It is a ruse," John explained. "There was no other way for us to safely search the city."

"Search it for what?" Daniel asked, fear raising in his eyes.

"For my son, Thomas Dunton," said John.

"Your son is in Algiers?"

"Taken captive when our ship was taken by pirates in March of 1635."

"Then you're . . . you're John Dunton!" Daniel exclaimed, his eyes wide with surprise.

"How do you know that?" John asked.

"When Salé fell, it was your son for whom his Majesty's Royal Navy searched. Your story is still alive, all over the country. The great John Dunton, how he persuaded the King of England to help him rescue the English in order to find his son, Thomas Dunton."

"This is common knowledge in Algiers?" John was amazed, and concerned, that such a story had reached this far east of Salé.

"It is all the pirates talked about for months afterward, those who escaped the armada. There is a price on your head, too."

"Ten thousand ducats," said a voice behind John. "I'm going to collect every bit of it. You did well, Daniel, keeping John Dunton's focus on yourself while I entered the house. You shall be rewarded for your loyalty."

John whirled around. Standing in the doorframe was a stout Algerian about fifty years old, with yellow teeth and a vicious smile. His black hair hung in greasy tendrils around his squat face. In his hand, he held a long dagger, its blade glistening in the light from the far window . . . the window where Scotty would be watching and listening.

"Pity it's only ten thousand," said John, rubbing his fingernails upon his waistcoat lapel. "I suppose you know that I have resources at my command that would net you perhaps forty thousand ducats . . . if you cooperate."

"If that were true—" said the man, but he did not finish his sentence. A rock in Scotty's hand had hit him soundly over the back of his head, and he fell to the floor with a thud.

"I motioned for Daniel to be quiet," explained Scotty, "knowing the element of surprise could work for me, too. I hope I served you well, Captain."

John nodded, then Scotty bent over the fallen man, to assess his condition.

"My father, is he really aboard the *Warhorse?*" asked Daniel.

"He is," said John. "But tell me, has your master treated you well?"

"Better than most," admitted Daniel. "He's never whipped me, and he allows me enough food."

John removed a bag of ducats from his pocket. "Write him a note. Tell him to buy a new slave, and treat him well. If he does not, he will answer to Captain Barbarossa."

"But he knows who you are. Do you think he won't tell anyone?"

"When he comes to, he'll know I did not kill him, and that I can at any time."

"No need," said Scotty. "I already did."

"Then," said John, "we must leave at once. He will soon be found and people will look for his servant."

"We can put his body in the well," offered Daniel. "Perhaps it will be days before he's found."

"It will buy us enough time to get you safely aboard the *Warhorse*," said John. He stepped through the adjoining room and opened the front door. "Come, slave!" he boomed. "I will need your help with this!"

To John's surprise, Edward was cowering near the road, as though he had been afraid of Weatherby's Algerian master. He had played his role well, and now stepped with exaggerated obeisance toward the front door.

Once inside the house, John decided to wait until dark to remove Daniel's dead master to the well. There were too many people around. The risk was too great to take.

The day wore on in agony. John knew the other men would be worried when they did not return to the shallop by sundown. Hopefully, they would keep their wits about them and go on back to the ship to wait.

Finally, the sun set in a glorious display of reds, oranges and pinks as darkness crept upon the city. Edward and John hoisted the dead man into the well behind the house, while Daniel and Scotty kept a lookout. Then, they put a hooded cloak over Daniel, to keep his face covered. They did not want him to be recognized. As the lights of the neighboring houses flickered out one by one, they crept surreptitiously through the shadows and made their way quietly to the quay.

Since neither Daniel nor Scotty could swim, Edward and John taught them the basics about breathing deeply and holding that air within their lungs to keep them afloat longer. Then, they carried them on their backs as they sank deep into the water and treaded out to the *Warhorse*. As silently and quickly as the water permitted, they soon found themselves at the ratlines and climbed aboard.

The other seamen were waiting for them, blankets outstretched to warm them after their chilly swim. But the water wasn't that cold, and John quickly discarded his. Daniel looked around for his father, and for a moment, his expression bore disappointment.

"This way," said John, taking him by the arm and striding toward the companionway.

Miles Weatherby was down in the galley talking with Elias when the dripping men entered together. John ached inside when he heard the bellowing cries of Miles Weatherby as he recognized his son, and wrapped him in his aging arms. Father and son wept upon one another's shoulders for a good long time.

It was a bittersweet reunion for John. They had rescued one man's son. But where was Thomas?

Chapter Seven

Clues and Courage

*"For the Lord your God is he that goeth with you, to
fight for you against your enemies, to save you."*
~Deuteronomy 20:4

*E*arly the following morning, the men departed at their usual
time. John had stayed below with Simon, dressing the wounds
of a savagely beaten slave, and he'd assumed that Edward had
gone into the auction block to purchase more slaves. He was surprised
to hear Edward calling him from the gunnery deck. John climbed the
stairs and went through the companionway hole where he found
Edward pacing back and forth.

"What is it?" John asked. "Why didn't you go with the others?"

"Because I've been up all night pacing in my room," Edward
admitted.

"That's true enough," said Barnabus Martin, writing upon a
notebook near a cannon where he was curled up on the thickly
planked floor.

"When we were at Daniel's master's home yesterday, while I was waiting for you to bring him out the front door. I turned around and found that I could see a good share of the country from the doorstep."

"Yes, it was sort of at the top of a little knoll, wasn't it," agreed John.

"It seemed familiar to me, though I cannot say why. The master I served lived in a much larger house than those upon that street. But the view, John. I remember that view in particular. It frightened me. I do not know why, but it did."

"That's just great," said John, his heart falling in his chest with a resounding thud that echoed in his eardrums, "because we've just put the owner of that house down a well, Edward."

"How can we possibly go back there now?"Edward asked, the fear etched in his voice.

"We may have a few days," said John. "Perhaps they will not find his body for a while. Daniel did say his master kept to himself. But when his body is found, the neighbors will remember that you were standing on his doorstep yesterday for a good fifteen minutes. If you're seen in that area after his body is discovered, you could be arrested."

"Perhaps if we travel by cover of darkness, we can search the surrounding area. If I can find the house where I was enslaved, I will be able to find the field where Thomas rescued me." Edward continued his pacing as he spoke, the drive in his eyes now gleaming, changing from fear to purpose. "It's the first time since we arrived that I've found someplace seemed familiar, John."

Nodding, John said, "Then, we formulate a new plan after the men return. Word of the murdered master will reach the city soon.

If we wait until the men report in, we'll know whether or not it is safe enough to venture out tonight."

Edward agreed, though his pacing did not ease.

"Go to bed, Edward," John encouraged. "If we are able to venture into the city tonight, you will need your rest."

"I will try," he answered, and headed for the companionway that led to the forecastle.

"You should try, too," said Barnabus Martin behind him. "You look terrible, Captain, if you'll forgive me for saying so."

"I haven't slept much in the two weeks we have been here," John admitted. "And last night was particularly difficult."

"Last night, you saved another man's son instead of your own," observed Martin. "That had to be difficult to swallow."

"And Scotty killed Daniel's master, so now we've got that to worry about, not to mention the fact that I'm a wanted man in these parts. Here I am, in the city where my son was last seen, and I can hardly go out to search for him. Ten thousand ducats for my head, did you hear?"

"Yes, the men were discussing it long into the night. Which is why you're here and not in town looking for Thomas."

"If someone recognizes me," nodded John. "If this disguise isn't foolproof, they'll slaughter my men to get to me. You'd be surprised what a man would do for that much money."

"What is that?" Martin asked, "About ten times the value you're paying your own men to help you find Thomas?"

"None of them would betray me," John insisted. "Not one."

"Perhaps not," admitted Martin, "but no one knows what's behind the minds of these men you rescued from enslavement."

"Their freedom is worth more to them than—"

"Ah . . . but you don't really know that, do you, Captain? Perhaps one of them would be happy to turn you in, take the gold and set themselves up in piracy. Perhaps, one of them faces a worse fate in England, now that they're going back."

"That's ridiculous," said John, but even as he said it and stormed away, he realized that Martin's words were true. He recalled a conversation he'd had with Robert Woodruff at Salé two years ago. Woodruff had been taken as a slave, become friendly with the pirates and, eventually, bought his way out of enslavement. When he tried to return to England, he found that the constable had a warrant for his arrest. He had become a fugitive because of his participation in piracy. King Charles did not look kindly on men who were captured and then helped their masters plunder upon English ships.

As Scotland had pointed out in their discussion late last night, not everyone knew the rumors about the infamous John Dunton. Scotland certainly had not heard of the reward offered for his capture. Still, John was only infamous to pirates. And, Daniel's master had maintained close ties to pirates. There was no reason to believe that all of Algeria knew about the high reward offered for John's head.

John firmly believed that he could trust everyone aboard the *Warhorse*, but to be safe, he ordered that none of the rescued men would be permitted above the hold of the ship until such time as they sailed away and considered themselves safe from capture, even Scotland, though the lad was sorely disappointed.

When evening came, the seamen returned with news of another fruitless day. However, there was no reason to believe that Daniel's master had been found, for there was no word about him within the city, and rumors usually traveled fast.

With this encouraging news, Edward and John went over the gunwales and silently slipped into the water, where they swam quietly to the quay in the dark of night. They did not bring the shallop for this might raise someone's suspicions as to what Captain Barbarossa was up to now.

Staying in the shadows of the buildings they passed, the two men crept deeper into the city until they reached the knoll and began a search of buildings and houses around the poorer section first. It wasn't until nearly dawn that they found a street that looked familiar to Edward, and when they'd located a row of two-story houses built of sandstone, a stronger memory returned to Edward.

Stealthily, they climbed up onto the balcony of one of the homes and waited for the sky to lighten briefly, so that Edward could be certain of his bearings. Before the sun could pop over the horizon, they were well away from the area and on their way back to the ship.

When they reached the quay, they heard a sharp voice that stopped them cold. "Captain! Captain Barbarossa!" John recognized the voice immediately. It came from the pirate, Aba Masmuth.

John froze, but Edward turned quickly and lashed out at him, "Why do you disturb my master when his only desire is to reach his ship?"

"Your master does not know how to speak for himself?" questioned Aba Masmuth.

Turning, forcing a look of hatred and anger upon his face, John glared at him, his brow crinkling together in a deep frown. "Who dares question me?!" he roared.

"Captain Masmuth, of the *Larache*."

"Hmmpf!" snorted John, trying to fit into the mold of Captain Barbarossa. "What is it that you want from me, Masmuth?"

Masmuth approached cautiously. "Have we met, Barbarossa?"

John glared even more ferociously. "Praise be to Allah that we have not!"

"Your behavior is bizarre, Captain, to say the least. Surely you can find a more convenient time to torture your slaves than the wee hours of morning? You keep the others awake in the harbor, including myself." His voice had a hint of warning in it.

John refused to back down. "What is that to me? Do I presume to tell you how to run your ship, Captain?"

"Are you certain we've never met?" asked Masmuth. "I know that I've heard your voice before, seen your face somewhere."

"It is the Barbarossa blood you see, Masmuth. You've obviously been to the Caribe Isles." John began to get nervous. He could feel his palms sweating, and a cold chill ran up his spine.

"Yes, of course, but— no, that is not where. Perhaps Salé? I went there often before the war."

"Perhaps," said John noncommitally. "Now, bother me no longer, Masmuth. I must return to the *Warhorse*."

"You would be wise to consider my suggestion," said Masmuth

dangerously. "Better pirates than you have crossed me. They never lived long enough to regret it."

"You dare to insult me, Masmuth!" John roared. "We shall soon see if the consequences were worth the price."

"Idle threats do not concern me," said Masmuth quietly. "You have no idea who you're dealing with."

"Indeed!" barked John. "Do you see me cowering in my boots, Captain?" He gave what he hoped was an evil, menacing smile.

"Captain!" came another voice from down the quay behind him. "We're here with the shallop, Captain Barbarossa, sir." It belonged to Peter Bayland.

John turned quickly, noticed both Peter and Big Mike walking towards him, then turned back to Masmuth. "Peter," he said sternly. "Get this vermin off the quay."

Peter whipped out his dagger while Big Mike curled up his fists and pounded them together with a loud thunk-thunk.

Masmuth turned quickly and slipped into an alley, departing in haste.

When they were safely back aboard the *Warhorse*, they breathed a sigh of relief, then went into the Captain's cabin to discuss the situation in which they found themselves.

"It's only a matter of time before Masmuth remembers who you really are," insisted Edward. "He was moments from grasping it while we stood there."

"So we've got the body *and* Masmuth to contend with," said Peter.

"And still no sign of Thomas," moaned Simon.

"At least we're getting closer to finding the area where Thomas was last seen by Edward," inserted John. "That's a first step towards finding him."

"We know he's not in the city," said Big Mike. "We've covered every step of it. If he'd been there, we'd have found him."

"But" said Elias, "five ships came into the eastern part of the harbor last night some time. Maybe one of them is named *El Djazair*."

"Maybe," said Peter. "With Masmuth now suspicious, it'll be risky finding out their names in daylight. Everyone aboard the *Larache* will be watching us, wherever we go."

"Then, we wait until nearly dark," said John. "Peter, you and Edward will come with me. The rest of you will wait aboard."

"Of course!" said Edward, without any provocation at all. "We will need to bring Martin with us, John. We'll need an interpreter."

"Why?" John questioned. "We're able to speak the language almost as well as he can."

"No, we cannot. Don't you recall Masmuth saying your voice seemed familiar to him? He was that close to putting the face with the voice, John." He held up his hand, his thumb and forefinger spread a half inch apart. "You've got to stop talking. If anyone else recognizes your voice and puts it together with your face, the game's over."

"What if you run into Masmuth again?" asked Simon, the worry over losing another family member apparent on his aging face.

Edward had an answer for that, too. "We'll say you've lost your voice, so your slave, Martin, is interpreting for you."

"Why Martin?" John asked. "He is our weakest member, Edward."

"I resent that," said Martin obstinately, "but since we all know that Edward's vocabulary in Barbarossa's Turkish/Spanish blend is hilarious, at best, I shall overlook it. However, the King did not tell me I was to offer myself as the sacrificial lamb."

Sighing, John said, "Then it's settled. Tonight we go ashore, Edward, Peter and Martin. Peter will watch our backs, Martin our language. We will locate the spot where Thomas hid you, and work our way in the direction he always left you from there."

Edward nodded, but John noticed for the first time that great beads of sweat were dripping off his forehead and his face was pale and drawn.

"Are you not feeling well?" John questioned.

"Fear," said Edward, swallowing hard. "Much as I hate to admit it, the moment I heard Masmuth's voice, I felt my stomach knot up, and I wanted only to hide myself in a corner, like a coward. I had no idea I would react like that, and I am fully ashamed."

"No one is immune to fear," consoled John. "When your moment comes, you will act your part well. I have confidence in you."

"And yesterday," Edward confessed, "when we were after Daniel Weatherby. I cowered in the open street, and I thought the whole time, I wish I had a place to hide."

"But you didn't hide, did you?" said John. "And today, you've shown real courage in the face of overwhelming odds, Edward."

"I must help you find Thomas, I must," whispered Edward, his voice now nothing more than a soft moan.

Realizing Edward had probably overextended himself through their journey last night, and had not rested the night before either, John comforted him. "You shall help us find him, Edward," said John. "We have all prayed diligently for Thomas' rescue. We are all working toward that goal every single day. God watched over us before, and He shall do so again. He led Scotland to us, and He led us to Daniel Weatherby. Surely, that should give you hope that He'll lead us, through you, to Thomas, as well."

"Do you trust God?" questioned Edward quietly.

All the men looked at John with this question. He could see the longing in their eyes for his answer. "I didn't for a long time," John whispered. "But when we retook the *Warwick* nearly two years ago, I felt His power work for our good. Since then, I've learned to trust Him more eagerly."

Edward paled further and seemed to sink toward the deck. John grabbed his arm and kept him on his feet. "Will you be able to go with me tonight?"

"I will force myself," said Edward. "Until then, I think I'd better lie down for a while."

John and Martin helped him to the forecastle. "You'd best take a nap until midnight," John suggested. "Both of you. Sleep is something that you may not be afforded for a while."

Edward sat limply upon the bed as John lifted his feet and helped him lie down, covering him with a blanket. "If you cannot sleep, I suggest you devote the next few hours to prayer, Edward, for we will surely need all the help we can get."

"Prayer," scoffed Martin. "We would be better off arming Peter with a dozen knives."

"You're entitled to your opinion," John warned. "But you will keep those opinions to yourself under my command."

Martin swallowed hard. "I hadn't expected a crusty sea captain such as yourself to lean toward spiritual matters, Captain."

"Because you do not know me well. The past month you have taught my men and me languages, but you have learned nothing in return. You are here at the King's command. We are here out of duty, loyalty and love. Your books and learning have hardened your heart toward the more important matters, Martin, and you would be well-served to spend some of your life reading the Bible and letting God become your teacher."

Martin nodded, but did not respond.

John turned and went out of the room. Martin was a good man, diligent in his loyalty to the King, but would he be loyal to those around him, knowing they depend upon Deity for their strength? Martin had expressed concern about a traitor amongst them. Perhaps it was a warning. Perhaps Martin would betray them. John brushed the thought from his mind, for he recognized it as pure foolishness.

Peter, who had just turned over his watch to the midshipman, approached John from the aftercastle deck. "I'll be turning in, Captain," he told John.

"Yes, all four of us should. It may be a long night, and we'll all need our strength." John nodded, then retired to the Captain's quarters to wait until nightfall.

Stretching out on his bed, John knew he would not sleep. He

tossed for a short time, then got out of bed and headed for the weather deck, where he spent the next hour at prayer in the crow's nest. It was a quiet place, and the closest to God he could get on a ship. It used to seem silly, when he was a young seaman, that he would spend part of his time in the crow's nest talking to God. He hadn't done so in many years, but when he was finished, he felt comforted. He left the nest and returned to the captain's quarters, where he finally slept a few hours.

By the time night had fallen upon them, John had nightmares about his young son, lost in a city where his father was always just around the corner, but could never find him. When he awoke, his chest felt constricted and painful. Worrying and waiting for his son's rescue had become almost unbearable. And, tomorrow was Thomas' eleventh birthday.

Around midnight, the four men slipped silently into the water and swam toward shore as surreptitiously as possible. John had to give Peter a crash course in swimming, but Martin and Edward took well to the water. They did not dare take the shallop, for fear they would be stopped. When they reached the wharf, they pulled themselves up onto it and pressed the water from their clothes as best they could.

Edward remained true to his promise. He led John, Peter and Martin through the outskirts of town in an eastward direction, toward the familiar place he had seen from one of the larger homes atop the knoll they had tracked out the previous night. After about six or seven miles, the houses thinned out and large farms took their places. Several miles later, Edward stopped in front of a huge wheatfield. In his excitement, Edward started dancing around, "This is it, John! This is where William and I were dying when Thomas found us!"

John looked around at the rows and rows of wheat, as though he almost expected Thomas to pop up and say, "Hello, Father."

"I know it's wheat now," Edward said, "but in this field over a year ago, there was a hay field, and stacks of hay interspersed throughout. I remember it clearly because of the roof on the farmer's house. See, it has two chimneys, and one of those is missing some bricks from its northwest corner."

"Very well," said John. "We've arrived where Thomas hid you. We must find out which way he went after leaving you, and try to retrace his footsteps."

"He always went west for about two fields, then turned right," remembered Edward.

"Let's go then," said John. "Lead the way."

With Edward leading them, they retraced their footsteps for about a mile, then turned right at the only road they found in all that distance. This they followed for several miles, until daylight began to lighten the darkness and settle the dawn upon them. By now, their clothes were dry and their boots dusty. All they could see around them were fields of wheat and beans. They stopped long enough to purchase food from the only farmhouse within several miles, and to drink water from the farmer's well.

While they were refreshing themselves, Martin struck up a conversation with the farmer. "We're looking for a lad about eleven years of age, with dark brown hair and eyes, who answers to the name of Thomas."

"Thomas Dunton," the man said quickly.

John's heart skipped several beats, but he forced himself to be calm as he listened to the man explain.

"Yes, he travels between his master's ship and the wheat fields once each week when they are in port. I've tried to sell him wheat from my fields, but his master is specific, and will only buy from his wife's cousin, who grows wheat ten kilometers beyond my fields."

"And you know this because?" Martin asked.

"I told him once that his master would never know, and he could save half the money for himself. Does Thomas listen? No. Instead, the lad obeys his master, and will not do anything other than what his master tells him."

John tried to reveal no interest, and noticed that Edward and Peter did the same. If they understood what Martin and the farmer spoke about, they did not show it.

"Has he been by lately?" questioned Martin.

"No. *El Djazair* was due back in port sometime soon, but I have not seen him yet. Is there some reason why you're seeking young Thomas?"

"We were told he might have been in the area when one of my master's slaves went missing. Perhaps he saw something."

"Your master sends four of you out to search for a missing slave?"

"The slave stole a family heirloom."

"And your master is?" questioned the farmer.

John nodded slightly to Martin as he stood up, indicating the conversation was over. "From the descent of Barbarossa, of course," said Martin, leaning his head toward John. "Surely you see the family resemblance." He gestured toward John.

The farmer studied John cautiously. Then a moment of recognition, very likely feigned, passed between them. A big smile cracked the farmer's face, a forced smile, as though he was gritting his teeth in horror behind his lips. "An honor it is, Captain," he said with an elaborate bow.

John glared at him. "It took you long enough. We must be going!"

"Yes," agreed Martin. "Thank you kindly for your generosity."

The man merely grunted as though he had been insulted. Then, he turned away, ignoring them as though they had never shaded his doorstep.

When they were out of hearing range, Edward said, "You offended him."

"How?" asked Martin.

"You never thank a Turk for his generosity. It is an insult to them."

"How would you know that?"

"Believe me," said John. "You do not tell them that they are generous."

"Why not?" Martin persisted.

"Because," snarled Edward, "they do not understand the concept. You should have said, 'Good day,' and been done with it. To speak anything good about their character is always an insult."

"Oh, I should have said, 'You're ugly and your stench is exceedingly ripe,' that would have been a compliment?"

"Better than to say he was generous. It's a term they do not want people to use to describe them. They want to be remembered as someone ferocious, less respectable than any one else." Edward turned toward the sea.

"But he fed us," Martin complained, apparently unable to grasp the situation.

"We bought his food," Peter reminded. "It wasn't an act of generosity, it was an act of piracy, for we paid five times what the food was worth."

"Forget it," warned John. "Just be more careful in the future."

When they could finally see the harbor from their position on the road, a distance of about a mile or two, John eagerly quickened his pace. When they were atop the last knoll before reaching the harbor, John brought forth his spyglass, and watching over the rooftops of the houses below them, he studied the ships lying at anchor. Two additional ships had come into this end of the harbor while John was away. John realized that they would have to travel through the city again to reach the harbor, though this easterly portion was less populated than the western end.

There were seven ships at anchor in this end of the harbor, and it was impossible to tell which one, if any, was the *El Djazair*. When John and his men reached the wharf, they still could not decide which ship was the right one, so John sent Peter and Martin back to the western end of the harbor, to the *Warhorse*, to report their progress, while he and Edward waited for nightfall.

While remaining in that general area, John and Edward were approached by several vendors, offering wares and foods. They purchased a large, flat round of bread and a sweet, ripe melon, which they ate eagerly, then waited in the shadows until night fell upon the city.

The good thing about Algiers was that there were so many people. A pirate and his slave blended in easily and did not seem to raise suspicious eyes anywhere. What was one more pirate and a slave in a city filled with them?

When the city seemed to quiet down around midnight or later, John and Edward went into the water, this time swimming as soundlessly as possible out to each boat. John swam towards the four boats farthest from shore, Edward towards the three closest. Fortunately, there was a little moon shining between wafting clouds, so John was able to determine that the four ships to which he had assigned himself were not the *El Djazair*. John was just heading toward one of Edward's three ships when he saw Edward's arm wave him back. A voice yelled, "Who goes there?"

Dunking his head under water, John swam down as deep as he could, yet still heading toward Edward. When he surfaced, John realized he had nearly reached the boat's ratlines. Suddenly, Edward was yanked upward out of the water and hauled aboard the ship nearest him. John swam into the ship's shadow and watched in horror as Edward was captured by pirates.

"Got us a live one here!" barked one of them.

Chapter Eight

The Act of Restraint

"... *for my onely sonne is now slave in Argeire . . . and
like to be lost for ever, without Gods great mercy* . . ."
~John Dunton

"And another live one down here," John yelled loudly,
waving for the pirates aboard the *El Djazair* to notice
him. "I thank you for capturing my slave for me." With
those words he swung himself up onto the ratlines and climbed
aboard. "Permission to come aboard," he bowed. "Captain Arnaj
Barbarossa, of the *Warhorse*, at your service."

A chinking sound was heard from the captain's quarters and a
barrel of a man with dark, swarthy skin and high-set forehead came
forcefully forward. "Captain Barbarossa," he challenged. "We have
heard of you from others within the city. Your reputation is deplor-
able." He gave a menacing snarl, and John perceived that this was
a compliment, rather than the reverse.

Edward pulled himself free from the two pirates who flanked him, and flung himself at John's feet. "Master, forgive me. It will not happen again," he begged in Spanish. "Mercy, Master, I beseech you."

John removed the belt from Edward's waist and slipped it around Edward's neck, pulling it snug enough to look painful, but not so snug it would actually harm Edward. "I will show you mercy when I get you back aboard the *Warhorse!*" he yelled with as much ferocity as a vicious wolf. "You lazy dog! You'll need a few more lashings to go with these!" John ripped Edward's shirt off his back, revealing the healed scars of many vicious whippings.

Cowering fearfully, Edward began to tremble. "No, master. I beg you!"

"Silence, dog!" John growled.

Edward fell silent immediately, though he was still shaking like a frightened pup.

John gave Captain El Djazair a hand sign that Aligolant had often used when greeting an equal, which the captain returned, as he shook John's hand vigorously. "Thank you for capturing my slave," said John with a little bow. "He dove overboard nearly an hour ago and I have been swimming after him ever since."

"How is it that the feared Captain Arnaj Barbarossa goes after his own escaped slaves?"

Smiling sheepishly, John replied, "I am the only one who knows how to swim."

Just then a motion caught John's eyes, and he saw a young boy, perhaps eleven years of age, approaching cautiously. Recognizing his son immediately, it was all that John could do to restrain himself from running over and gathering him in his arms. Thomas looked much better than John had expected, with his dark hair, sprinkling of freckles and eyes exactly like John's. How could he warn him not to say anything? He gave his son a firm, menacing look, which he hoped Thomas would read as "Keep your mouth shut and your ears open." It did no good, Thomas Dunton came quickly toward him. Then, Thomas went straight to Edward, apparently not recognizing John in his pirate's outfit, dark skin and pitch black hair. "Edward?" he asked. "Is that you?"

Edward's eyes widened and tears filled them. "Thomas?" he asked, then he cowered again. "Forgive the child, Captain Barbarossa. He gave me his supper once, when we were waiting at the auction block. Lay not my escape to his charge."

"You know this man?" questioned Captain El Djazair.

Thomas nodded. "Yes, Master. He— " Stopping in mid-sentence, Thomas looked up at John, and the recognition between them John realized immediately. He gave Thomas another silent glare, hoping the lad would be able to pick up on the clues Edward had given him.

"It's you!" Thomas accused, looking almost angry at John. "Captain Barbarossa!"

John smiled with what he hoped seemed like an evil smile, though he knew Thomas had assessed the situation and was now "acting" his part well.

"You're the one who nearly starved Edward to death?" Thomas asked.

Shrugging, John nodded. "And you're the young man they call Thomas, the kind one, the one who serves his master without complaint, and without thought of escape."

"That he does," said El Djazair. "And I'm not selling him, if that is where this conversation is going."

"I did not offer to buy him," said John. "He may serve you well, El Djazair, but I've heard that he takes pity on other slaves at the sacrifice of his own well-being."

"I have heard the rumors," admitted El Djazair. "But you are not here to talk about a young slave. You are here to collect your own."

"If you will allow me, Captain El Djazair" John nodded. "My slave shall be punished the moment we arrive at the *Warhorse*."

"You may take him," said El Djazair. "But you must call me Ben, as do my friends. I am Abu Benjamin El Djazair, the father of Benjamin, who was lost at sea when he was about young Thomas' age."

"Thank you. And call me Arnaj," insisted John.

"I have heard of your ancestors," said Abu El Djazair. "They settled in the Caribe Isles, did they not?"

"On their own island, which they named *Arnaj*," said John. "However, my mother was English, having been captured and sold to my father, who loved her and took her as one of his wives. I am the only son my father has, and he prizes my life dearly." With these words, John nodded toward Thomas, who gave him the briefest of smiles.

Apparently, Abu Benjamin had not noticed the exchange, and said to John, "We will send you back to the *Warhorse* in one of my shallops. You there," he said, pointing to two seamen. "Deliver Captain Barbarossa and his slave to their ship."

"I must thank you for capturing my slave for me, Ben," said John, bowing elaborately. "Will you do me the honor of dining with me aboard the *Warhorse* tomorrow night? I have a load of fine foods from an English merchant's ship, and would be honored to share it with you, before it goes to the auction block."

Abu Benjamin nodded. "It would be my pleasure."

"Bring the lad," suggested John. "For I have yet to see a slave serve his master as eagerly as I have heard regarding yours. Perhaps, if some of my men see his example, they will emulate him."

"He is a rare breed," confessed Abu. "My other slaves are jealous. They are always pestering him to change his ways."

"I shall warn my slaves that they would do well to follow his example. After all, my whip master has not had much sport lately."

"From what I hear, your whip master is deprived of his sport because you like to torture your slaves yourself," said Abu.

John laughed vigorously. "We all have our little secrets. Tomorrow night then?"

"Very well," said Abu, considering. "And I shall bring a woman or two for your pleasure, as well."

"No," said John quickly. "They make my men restless, and my heart belongs to my wife, I'm afraid."

"Hmmpf!" snorted Abu. "You're either a man deceived by love, or a man enslaved to a woman, Arnaj, something which I had never anticipated."

"Rebecca is one of my only weaknesses," John confessed, watching the joy spread on young Thomas' face as he said it. "Until tomorrow, then."

Quickly, John tugged Edward along, handing him down to Abu's crewmen who rowed them in a captured English shallop back to the *Warhorse*. To contain his excitement, John forced himself to curse and shout at Edward the entire way. It kept his mind off other, more important matters, and would, hopefully, not give their ruse away. "Filthy dog! You will be punished severely for your cowardice you mangy son of a cow!"

Noticing Edward weeping the entire time, John wished that he could do so, as well. As Edward cried, he blubbered, "Yes, Master. Whatever you wish, Master."

While John knew that Abu's able seamen would think Edward was weeping for fear, John knew he was really weeping for joy.

REBECCA AWAKENED WITH a start. The dream she'd had was so strange, yet somehow she knew it was also true. She had seen Edward and John in a shallop, being rowed to the *Warwick* by a couple of pirates she did not recognize. John was yelling and cursing at Edward, while Edward was cowering in the bottom of the boat, whimpering like a lost little child.

What could it mean? Had Edward failed to help John? Was John cursing him because he had cost Thomas' life? Why else would John act like a man possessed of such an evil disposition?

The nightmare disturbed her so that Rebecca went downstairs and pulled the Bible down from its resting place on the mantle. She lit Thomas' candle upon the mantle, which she lit every evening in remembrance of Thomas, and brought it with her to the kitchen table, where she placed it beside the Bible. Then, she knelt in prayer, pleading with the Lord to help her understand the dream she'd had about her husband and Edward. When she had finished, she sat in a chair and turned the pages of the Bible until she found the verse she felt the Lord wanted her to read:

> *"And being warned of God in a dream that they should not return to Herod, they departed toward their own country another way."*
> ~*St. Matthew 2:12*

Reading it over and over, Rebecca pondered why John would be cursing Edward, why Edward would be crying, and why they would be in a boat with two pirates. Perhaps it was nothing more than a foolish dream. What did the words of St. Matthew have to do with John and Edward? Unable to fathom the mysteries of God, she wrote the scripture on a piece of parchment, folded it neatly and tucked it beneath her chemise, near her heart, knowing that in His own due time, the Lord would eventually show her why this inspirational passage was so important.

THOMAS COULD SCARCELY sleep all night. After the disturbance upon the weather deck had awakened him, he'd gone up to see what the problem was, and to his great astonishment and joy, he'd found his father dressed as a wet, though ferocious-looking, pirate, and Edward, whom Thomas had fed and comforted more than a year ago on a country road in Algiers.

Praying that he hadn't given anything away, for it was obviously a charade that Edward was Captain Barbarossa's slave, Thomas had striven diligently to prevent himself from throwing his arms about his father's waist and hugging him with all his strength. He couldn't do that, not yet. His father had come to rescue him, of this he was certain. Whatever else Thomas did, he must be ready, instantaneously, whenever the moment arrived, to secure his rescue.

For the first time in two years, Thomas allowed tears to surface in his eyes and slip unashamedly down the sides of his face. The longing and the prayers in his heart were finally to be answered. He felt so joyful he could scarcely contain his happiness.

Something else seemed just as important to Thomas as his pending rescue. Many times, the other slaves had tormented him, saying that his father had forgotten all about him. Now, Thomas knew his hope and belief had not been in vain. A true Father never forgets his own son!

During that brief encounter on deck, John had given Thomas two veiled messages. The first, when John said , "I am the only son my father has, and he prizes my life dearly," was meant for Thomas' heart alone. Thomas was his father's only son, and his father prized Thomas' life dearly. That his father was here, upon this very ship, dressed in a pirate's costume and claiming to be Captain Barbarossa, was evidence enough of his love for Thomas, but John had apparently said those words so Thomas would know, without question, where his father's heart was centered.

The second message was more subtle, yet its impact was no less miraculous. John had said, "Rebecca is one of my only weaknesses." This could only mean that John and Rebecca were together somehow.

Since his father had said it in Edward's presence, and Edward, too, had nodded toward him, Thomas could only conclude that Edward had given Rebecca up, that the two men were now acting out splendid roles in their effort to rescue him. Thomas' father and mother were together again. Would she be on the ship, *Warhorse*? Of course not. Father would never allow that, not again. Not after their capture in March of 1635.

It had been twenty-seven months since the bark *Warwick* had been captured by pirates. Twenty-seven months of deprivation, starvation, hard labor, loneliness, heartache and constant worry—were his parents still alive or not? Twenty-seven months of sheer torture, physical and emotional, with the only fringe benefits received . . . stale bread and an occasional bruised mango.

Now, young Thomas had the answers to his questions, and many of his trials would soon come to an end. His mother was alive! His father, too! Alive! And his father had finally come to rescue him!

I will be ready! he vowed. *Whatever my father plans, I will be ready!*

Then, Thomas remembered one more blessing. His silent tears turned to the biggest smile he had ever known. Surely, God had allowed John to find him today because this day had eternal significance.

Thomas' heart fairly sang with the memory: *Today is my birthday!*

JOHN AND EDWARD both waited silently until the shallop was completely out of earshot before they gathered the men below decks to lay out the next strategy of their plan and to tell them all that had transpired. Peter and Martin had made it to the ship safely, and seemed just as anxious as the others to hear what had happened.

Unable to hold back the tears any longer, John stood bravely and announced the great news, his face glistening with moisture in the candlelight. "We found Thomas alive and well aboard the *El Djazair*. He is enslaved to Captain Abu Benjamin El Djazair, who will be dining with us tomorrow night. We must all go into our roles more convincingly than we have ever done. If all goes well, we will be soon be sailing out of the harbor with Thomas.

The looks of joy upon the men's faces only added to John's tears. "Edward, I trust you will forgive me for treating you as a slave. Your performance was splendid. Absolutely inspiring."

"Of course," smiled Edward through tears of his own. "As was yours, Captain Barbarossa."

"Martin," said John, eager to give out assignments and get their plans well underway. "Go into the market first thing in the morning and purchase a young lamb for Elias to dress and prepare for our dinner tomorrow night. Send it back with a slave and a pirate. Afterward, speak with the auction master. Make arrangements for us to return in two weeks with a new load of goods for the auction block. It will be an appointment we will not keep, but it will give the auctioneers the sense that we are here to stay, to trade stores between voyages from other cities. Then, purchase whatever stores the ship is low in, and have them brought aboard in abundance. Take several of the slaves and at least two pirates with you. Play your roles well, and we may all survive this rewarding adventure."

Martin nodded as he scribbled notes in one of his books.

"Elias, prepare the lamb straight away, saving the blood for Simon.

Rub the carcass with spices and herbs, and bake it all day, until the meat falls from the bones. The Turks love it this way. Prepare fresh carrots and caramelized onions, get some assistants to make several batches of flat bread for you, so that all day the ship smells of baking breads and savory lamb. Anything you can think of to add to the meal that is not traditionally English will be useful. I'm sure Martin can make some suggestions here."

"I will get some rice from the market," said Martin at once. "It is a staple food and when cooked with a stout chicken broth is quite tasty. Also an assortment of fresh, local fruit."

John nodded. "Good. Now to the slaves' roles. Tomorrow, you must spend all day cleaning. Make the decks sparkle, the glassware glisten. Our Pirate actors should stand watch over you, without helping. We want others in the harbor to see that we are going to great lengths to greet our guests.

"Seamen, make all the sails and lines ready to deploy at a moment's notice, but do it in such a way as to make it appear that you are merely inspecting gear and rigging. We must not seem to be preparing to sail, for that would look suspicious.

"Above all else, keep your prayers said," John reminded. "The good Lord will see us through the next thirty hours only if we are diligent in calling upon Him. He's willing to help us, but He still wants us to ask for His help."

"Simon, it's time to prepare the wine. Take Peter and Edward with you, and make two full cases ready. These will be taken to *El Djazair*, with the Captain Barbarossa's blessing. Then prepare Edward's back so that it appears as though he has been lashed severely. Make the sores look terrible, for we will tie Edward to the foremast before dinner. To Captain Abu, it will seem as though Edward has already been punished. Be sure to leave a bloodied whip nearby, so there will be further evidence of our brutality."

"I can use narrow strips from the lamb to accomplish this," said Simon. "It will look very effective, John."

"You cannot call me John," he warned. "I am Captain to our pirates and seamen, Master to our slaves. You are a slave, Simon. Please, be very careful."

"Forgive me, Master," bowed Simon ceremoniously. "I wasn't thinking."

"If I yell at you while Captain Abu is aboard, you must understand that it is a ruse. I fear I may have frightened poor Edward to death on the way over from the *El Djazair*."

"Nearly," Edward confessed.

"We heard you cursing him," squeaked Red Taylor. "It sounded like music to our ears."

The men laughed a moment at Edward's expense.

John held up his hands to stop them. "I will tell you this," he encouraged. "If it were not for Edward's quick thinking tonight, we both would have been strung up on the spot, gutted and fed to the sharks. You may laugh, if you wish, but if we had been found out, their next move would have been to seize the *Warhorse*. Without Edward's ingenuity, your fate would have been terrible."

"And yours," whispered Edward, humbled. "A finer Captain I've never served."

"Hear! Hear!" echoed the men.

"Get some sleep, then," said John. "For tomorrow the Lord God will deliver Thomas into our hands."

"What of the other slaves?" asked Martin. "Surely, there are some we can rescue, as well."

"We will take all those aboard *El Djazair* that wish to go with us," agreed John. "But we cannot take all the slaves from Algiers. We haven't enough ships for that, nor enough food. And, we'll still have Abu's men to contend with when they awaken and realize we've gone."

"Will they chase after us?" asked Martin, a hint of edginess in his voice.

"Of course they will," laughed Peter. "But they won't catch us."

"How can you be so sure?" Martin wondered.

"Because we will sabotage their ship. Once they're out at sea, they'll begin to sink."

"I wondered why you brought that tin of cannabis weevils aboard," Red squeaked, winking at Simon.

"And why he never let them out of his possession," added John with a smile. "They are not aboard to scuttle our own ship, Red."

When their plans were finalized, Elias, Martin and seven other men went ashore before dawn, so that Elias could bring the lamb back early enough to slaughter it and cook it for the evening feast. Meanwhile, Martin and the others continued their own assignments.

For John's part, he did not sleep at all. How could he, with his son less than a mile away, enslaved on a ship lying at anchor in the same harbor? He paced back and forth in the captain's cabin, jotting down notes on parchment so that he wouldn't forget any details. Over and over in his mind, he memorized every element regarding how Thomas' rescue should happen. Cunning, stealth and grand performances would be the only way they could rescue Thomas. But when they did, John doubted he would ever let the boy out of his sight again.

When the men returned with the lamb, they brought grim news. A murdered Turk had been found stuffed down his own well, and the city was searching for Daniel Weatherby as the most likely suspect. If that wasn't bad enough, Captain Masmuth, from the *Larache*, had been looking for Captain Barbarossa, swearing in his wrath that when they next met, he would kill him slowly.

Chapter Nine

A Stratagem Is Set

". . . and I will not be too tedious to set downe every point
of our subterfuge, . . . because I will make it
as short as I can."
~John Dunton

When Captain Abu Benjamin El Djazair came aboard the *Warhorse*, he took one look at Edward, who was tied to the foremast, and said to John, "I can see that you truly are related to your Barbarossa ancestors, Captain."

John looked over at Edward and felt immediate relief to know that all the blood came from the lamb Elias had slain. The strips looked like raw flesh opened on Edward's back, but they were really narrow strips of lamb's flesh. The whip curled up nearby was still dripping, an effective display of the whip master's talent.

Growling ferociously, John yelled at the whip master. "Swine! Get that slave down and clean up this mess! Do you not know we are entertaining guests tonight?"

"Ye-yes, Captain," stammered the whip master, Big Mike. "Straight away, sir. You two! I thought I told you to take this slave down an hour ago. Throw him into the hold."

"But he's half dead already," complained a seaman.

"If he dies by morning, throw him overboard," ordered the whip master.

The two complied as John led Abu Benjamin and young Thomas to his cabin. Thomas' eyes were wider and more fearful than John imagined they would be. Either his son was horrified at what he had seen, or he was a fine actor. He hoped the latter would be the case, for he did not want his son to think him a monster.

"I've asked the cook to prepare our finest meal for you, Ben. I trust you will enjoy it. While we are dining, I have asked some of my men to take a gift of wine, fine cheeses and breads to your men. Perhaps Thomas can assist them."

"My men don't deserve to be coddled," Abu barked.

"But Master," argued young Thomas. "You have always told me that my kindness toward the men would be rewarded. Would not yours, as well?"

Abu nodded briefly. "Tell them you have smuggled the goods aboard, lad. They ought not learn that their captain has a soft spot."

Thomas grinned. "I shall indeed, Master." Then he quickly followed Big Mike down the companionway to the gunnery deck, where the galley was also housed.

While they were gone, John and Peter entertained Captain Abu in the captain's quarters dining area, while Elias and Robert Boyer waited on them with skill and finesse John hadn't thought possible. Small talk led to pirate boasting, and John told as many tall tales as he dared, as did Peter.

Before the evening was over, they drank several bottles of wine, and all the time, John kept praying that the other plans were going equally as well.

WHEN THOMAS WENT below decks, Big Mike clamped his hand over the lad's mouth, but Thomas bit his finger. "You think me a fool, that I can't keep my own mouth shut?" he demanded in a tight whisper.

"Sorry," said Big Mike. "I thought seeing your grandfather, you might—"

"Grandfather?" Thomas whispered. Footsteps sounded somewhere behind him as Big Mike ushered Thomas deep into the hold's stern.

When Thomas turned around, he was grabbed so tightly by Simon he could scarcely catch his breath. "Grandfather," he whispered. "I've missed you so."

"And I, you, lad. Now, we haven't time for fussing yet. That will come. Right now, you must accompany Big Mike, Red and a few of the others back to *El Djazair*. When you arrive, you will present the pirates with food and wine. Make certain none of the slaves drink the wine, Thomas, for it is filled with a powerful sleeping herb."

"Yes, sir," said Thomas, pushing his feelings down for the moment. It would soon be over, but he had duties to perform first, and he would be faithful to the last moment.

"Big Mike and the others will pretend to row back, but will await your signal to return. When the captain's men are asleep, tell the slaves they may all come back with us, only if they will pledge their allegiance to King Charles and swear off piracy forever," Simon explained.

"I can manage that," said Thomas.

"I'm giving you this tin of cannabis weevils, Thomas. You know what to do with them."

"Yes, sir. You can depend on me." His heart was beating so hard and fast in his chest Thomas wondered why it did not just explode all together.

He knew exactly where to place the cannabis weevils because he had the assignment of checking the hemp on a weekly basis to make sure there were no weevils aboard. These busy little beetle-like insects loved to eat hemp, a chord-like material made from the cannabis plant, which was used to stuff seams and cracks in a ship's outer planking, making them water-tight. In the warmer climates, the cannabis beetle had become the scourge of the Mediterranean sailor. Many a ship had been sunk by them, and seamen were overly cautious not to let them infest the ship. The weevils did not like tar, which coated the outsides of the ship's seams. But the inside was normally not coated with tar, which gave the hemp room for expansion and kept the strong tar odor out of the hold. Thomas put the tin into his pants pocket.

After Thomas helped the men load the shallop with two cases of wine, two rolls of hard cheese, and several loaves of fresh flat bread, he went with them, directing them back to *El Djazair*, his heart singing with happiness.

When they approached the ship, Thomas called out, "Ahoy, Master Tovie."

"Ahoy, Thomas. Didn't get to dine on the *Warhorse* after all?" asked an older Englishman with a fierce scowl. "Knew it was too good to last."

"No, but we were able to smuggle these goods back to you. Thought you could do with a spot of refreshment."

"Does Captain Barbarossa know?" asked Tovie, apparently fearful of Thomas' father.

Tovie, though technically a slave, had pleased Master Abu much the same way and for many more years than Thomas. He was the slave with the highest position aboard ship, which is why all the slaves called him Master Tovie.

"Why should we tell him?" asked Thomas. "He's got plenty where this came from. He'll never even miss it," offered Thomas.

"That's a good lad!" exclaimed Tovie. "Come aboard, then. You men care to stay and sip with us?"

"They heard about the dancers at the Pirate's Den tonight. I promised them you'd give them a good alibi, should the captain wonder where they've been."

"Right, then. What's your names?"

"Squeaky Red and Big Mike," said Michael Downe. "Just say the lad brought us aboard to show us your ship, and you can have all the goods we brought."

"It's a deal, then," said Tovie, handing the wine and food up to the others on deck. "Off you go. Have a nice peep at the dollies for me, will you, lads?"

Big Mike nodded as he shoved off and they rowed away and slid behind a boat nearer the wharf to await Thomas' signal.

Thomas tore off a hunk of cheese and half a flatbread for himself. Tovie and the pirates did not seem to mind. Soon the pirates were all on deck, feasting on cheese, flatbread and wine, laughing and roaring rowdily. It took the sleeping herb a while to take effect, but soon the pirates, and Tovie, were all snoring loudly.

Quickly, Thomas went below and awakened the slaves. When he'd roused them all, he said, "The pirates are all asleep. If you want to escape your captivity, and will pledge your allegiance to King Charles of England, come with me. If you choose not to go, stay here and remain slaves."

One of the more shrewd slaves, James Merrit, said, "Why should we trust you, Thomas? What have you ever done for us?"

"I've not turned you in when you've disobeyed Master Abu, nor when you've tormented me," said Thomas. "I find no pleasure in securing your freedom, but you are Englishmen, same as me."

Duly chastened, James said, "Where will you take us? To the city where we will be found and hung until we are dead? For that is one of the punishments for slaves that run away, you know."

"We shall be aboard Captain Barbarossa's ship, sailing away just as soon as we arrive there." Thomas held his ground and did not back down. "You will only be given this opportunity once. If you do not care to go, James Merrit, that is your choice. Those of you who will choose freedom, come with me." He turned to lead them, but James

placed his hand on Thomas' shoulder, stopping him.

"Why would Captain Barbarossa allow us to escape Master Abu? Surely he will enslave us, and we will be no better off than we are now."

"Captain Barbarossa will not enslave any of you," vowed Thomas. "I will stake my life on that."

"What makes you so certain?" said James.

"Because he's my father, come to rescue me," said Thomas, his heart soaring as he said it. "All of you said he would never come, but he's here. I'm going with him. Whether or not you will go with me is entirely up to you."

He shrugged James hand away, turned and left them in the hold. Sixteen of the twenty slaves followed him. Two of them picked up sleeping Tovie on the way by. Thomas grabbed a lantern and swung it high from the aftercastle deck at the stern rail. Then, he instructed the slaves, "Tie the pirates up and gag their mouths. Put them in the hold. They will sleep for a good, long time."

By the time James and his two companions joined them, the deck was awash with activity. Pirates, bound and gagged, were being lowered into the hold by the slaves, and several crewmen from the *Warhorse*.

When all the slaves were safely boarded on shallops and pinnaces, they were rowed to the *Warhorse*. While waiting for one of the shallops to come back for him, Thomas took the tin of cannabis weevils down to the hold, at the stern, which rested lower in the water than any other spot on the ship. He used a knife to dig little holes in the hemp, insert a weevil inside, then plug the hole back up with the hemp he'd removed. Thomas did this in several places down low in the hold, below the waterline. When the ship started to sink, the weevils would tunnel upward, above the waterline, thus making deep hemp channels that would eventually sink the ship, but be less likely detected.

When he was finished, Thomas started hauling the barrels of food stuffs and supplies up to the weather deck, and while the crew from the *Warhorse* loaded it into the shallops and pinnaces, he went one step further. He took the cannon balls, one by one from their cradles, and dropped them overboard. Then, he rolled the barrels of gun powder out on deck to the crew and loaded it aboard a shallop.

Satisfied that he had done everything he could to disable *El Djazair*, he took one quick look around, then descended the ratlines and stepped aboard the waiting shallop. This time, Simon was there waiting for him, and held him tight against him all the way back to the *Warhorse*.

"Grandfather, tell me everything," Thomas whispered, feeling safe and snug at last. "How did Father find me? Is Mother well? He didn't really whip Edward, did he?"

Simon smiled. "All these tales shall be told, in time, Thomas, by your father. As for Edward, I'm afraid I was the culprit. You'd be surprised what you can do with a little lamb's blood and a few strips of lamb flesh. I hope you weren't too horrified."

"I wouldn't blame Father, for Edward was cruel to Mother. But I thought, now that he'd seen the other end of the whip, he wouldn't need further punishment."

"Ah, Thomas, you and your father are of the same mind. No, John is just as gentle as he ever was, though fierce when it comes to finding you. He's been searching for you ever since the day we saw you at the auction block in Salé."

By this time, Thomas could contain himself no longer. He picked up one of the oars and started oaring toward the *Warhorse* with all his strength. It was time for his father to hold him, and he was most anxious to return the favor.

Soon the big ship loomed into view. "Grandfather, where is the bark *Warwick*? Mother told me I was to look for it if ever I escaped."

"The *Warwick* is before you, Thomas. The *Warwick II.*"

"What?"

"The old *Warwick* was run aground at Hurst Castle when your father and his men mutinied against the pirates and took it back. Your father had no choice. The pirates were alive in the hold, and were pulling out the hemp. It was the only way your father could stop them from sinking the ship."

"He'll have so much to tell me. I suppose it will take weeks and weeks."

"Indeed, it will. Well, here we are. He's waiting for you."

"What about Master Abu?" Thomas asked as he started to climb the ratlines up to the gunwale.

A hand reached out and took hold of his, pulling him easily up to the deck.

"He's sleeping off a very large portion of sleeping herbs, son."

The instant Thomas heard his father's voice, he fell limp against him, weeping and laughing all at the same time. "Father! Father! I knew you'd find me. I never doubted it, not once! Thank you, Father."

Then, his father was kneeling and they were hugging and holding each other as they had never done before. John was even crying, something Thomas had never witnessed.

And, for that moment, it did not matter where they were, whether they were safe or still in harm's way, they were together, at last.

🌴 🌴 🌴 🌴 🌴

"FORGIVE ME IF I stare at you all the time," Thomas said, as he took his turn at the helm with John. It had been a dark night, and only the stars to steer the vessel by, but the wind was selfish and it seemed they had to wring each puff from the air that they could. The ship had weighed anchor silently around three of the morning, and they were now sailing northwest, toward the Strait of Gibralter, a destination at least five days ahead. Because of the lack of wind, the men and rescued Englishmen strong enough, had set themselves to the task of oaring.

"I do the same," said John, his heart warming at Thomas' apology. "I hope you'll be patient with me."

"I've learned patience," said Thomas in a philosophical tone. "I've had to, Father."

"So have I, son. It has been a hard way for you to learn such a skill, but we are together now, and I will not allow us to be separated again."

"Do you suppose we'll get away from the pirates for good this time?"

"We'll do our best, though with this wind we'll have to do some mighty oaring, as well."

"The wind comes up best a few hours after sunrise. It's nearly always calm at night in this part of the world," Thomas explained. He leaned back against his father, as though making certain that John was still standing firmly behind him.

"If we can get into the tidal current going out, that will help us. By the time the pirates awaken and learn of our deception, the tide will be against them." John wanted his son to feel safe, but they were far from safety at this point. His heart wanted to soar, as Thomas' seemed to, but John was too cautious for that just yet. They had thousands of treacherous miles of ocean still to go, and the pirates would not give up without a fight.

Looking back on their fierce experiences in Algiers, John realized that finding Thomas had been the easy part of his son's rescue. Keeping Thomas would be far more dangerous! But John and his crew had committed themselves to this voyage for just that purpose. None of the men would consider giving up now, regardless what obstacles the pirates threw at them. Not unless they were all dead.

The main concern in John's heart was the unfavorable winds they would find when they reached the western coast of Portugal and Spain. Blowing down their noses, the prevailing wind would force them to tack back and forth without making much headway. It's one thing to sail south with the prevailing winds at your tail, while looking for your son. It's quite another to have found him, and try to sail against those winds, which would take three times as long, if they weren't driven south all together. Tacking back and forth would leave them vulnerable. That is where they could be overcome. However, if they headed west, across the Atlantic, they would have the prevailing winds in their favor. It would be a longer trip that way, for they would end up circling the Atlantic Ocean, which many referred to as the Great Pond, but they would find safety in American waters, where most pirates still feared to sail.

Pirates preferred their targets within a few hundred nautical miles of a coastline, and crossing the Atlantic was not high on their list of navigable seas. The problem the pirates faced was that their charts were hopelessly outdated. Some of them did not even have charts, but spent their time near land so they wouldn't get lost. While it was true that some pirates were quite good at navigation, most were not.

"Thomas, who was the navigator aboard *El Djazair?*" John asked.

"Master Abu and—"

"Son, he is not your master anymore. You are now master of your own destiny."

"Thank you, Father. I'd quite forgotten." Thomas released the wheel and turned around where he hugged his father fiercely.

John laughed and hugged him back. "I missed you, too, son."

Turning back to the helm, Thomas explained, "Captain Abu and his first mate always did the navigating. They treated it like it was some great mystery, and we never sailed beyond the Bahia de Cadiz in Spain, where Abu traded his slaves for wine, linen and other marketable goods. I don't think they navigate as well as I do. And they never use an astrolabe."

"This is good," responded John. "I was thinking of going home on the circle route."

"Won't Mother be worried?"

"Yes, but she will understand. She's living at our little cottage now, next to your aunts, Naomi and Ruth."

"Is she happy?" Thomas wondered aloud.

"As much as she can be with her son missing," John agreed.

"Does she remember me, then?" asked Thomas.

John felt the lad's shoulders quiver, as though his son was still restraining his tears. "Rebecca loves you with all her heart, Thomas. She lights a candle on our mantle every night in your memory. When I had given up all hope that you might still be alive, she refused to believe that you were gone. She even scolded me when I tried to reason with her. After all, we had not found you in Salé when I was there, and I did not know you had been taken to Algiers before then, so I could only assume that you had died in that city."

"We heard about the siege at Salé," Thomas confessed. "The pirates have almost restored the city back to the way it was before you arrived. Some boast that the English will never be the downfall of the pirates' world."

"They are an evil lot," John agreed. "But we were able to rescue three hundred and thirty-nine of our countrymen. It does not matter that the pirates have restored Salé back to its former glory, because there are people in England who praise the day we arrived there to rescue them, as do their families to whom they returned. My greatest sadness was leaving that place without you."

"We'll head toward the Caribbean, then?" said Thomas, bringing the conversation back to the matter at hand.

Nodding, John realized how much he loved Thomas for wanting

to take John's mind off weightier matters. It showed him just how much his young son had grown into manhood while they were separated. Thomas had learned to live apart from his family, and had behaved himself well enough to be treated fairly by his master. The boy was not a child anymore, and John would have to treat him like a man now, for that is what the lad had become. His eleven-year-old son had lived the life a man should never have to live, and survived it well.

"To the Caribbean," John agreed. "Then, we'll head up the coast to Plymouth, and across the Atlantic again, back toward England. Perhaps we will find a group of ships to sail with us on our voyage across the northern hemisphere, for there is safety in large numbers."

"It will seem a prayer answered to me," said Thomas, "wherever we go, for I have prayed night and day that you would find me, Father, and you have."

"I have," agreed John. "But there are other things you need to know, Thomas, and I hardly know where to begin. Since you're a man now, I suppose the best thing is to tell it straight out, like I would to any other man aboard."

"I'd like that," said Thomas. "What would you like to tell me, Father?"

John worried how Thomas would react to this news, but he had to be told, and the sooner the better. "Your mother and I, while we were aboard the *Warwick* and the *Little David*, conceived a child together. You have a seventeen month old sister waiting at home for you, named Jane."

"A sister?" Thomas asked, his voice a mixture of awe and surprise.

"Yes. A cute little thing, with curly blonde hair, eyes as turquoise as her mother's, and my dimples."

"Does she walk? Can she talk?"

"She toddles around, though I suppose when we get back we'll see her walking much more steadily. She can say *Papa, Mama, Auntie Ruth* and *Naomi, Grandpa,* and *Thomas.*"

"Thomas? She can say my name?" his son asked incredulously.

"Well, it sounds more like *Toe-mahs*, but yes, she says *Thomas.*"

"I can't wait to meet her. Are you sure we'll have to go across the Great Pond, Father? It will take so long to get to England that way." Thomas gave him a look of total frustration.

"Patience, son. I thought you said you'd learned patience."

"That was before I knew that I had a sister."

"So, the news of your sister, Jane, pleases you?" John questioned, still uncertain how Thomas was really feeling.

"Pleases me?" Thomas asked. "I think it's better news than being rescued. Well, almost."

"I'm relieved that you feel this way," John remarked. "It rather troubled me, wondering how you would react."

"Will you work on conceiving another child as soon as we get home?" Thomas asked. "I'll need a brother, too, you know."

John laughed aloud at Thomas' boldness. "Yes, son. Shortly after we get home, we'll do our part in providing you a brother."

Chapter Ten

The Chase Begins

> " . . . in the morning we saw two shippes that did give us
> chace all day, but they were so farre off at
> Sea . . . and then wee lost them."
> ~John Dunton

By the time the wind picked up and they were headed westerly on the Alborán Sea, Captain Abu Benjamin had awakened from his deep sleep, so that he knew the remainder of his crew were likely awake, back in Algiers.

Abu was furious, if his coarse stream of expletives from the hold were any indication. He had been placed in shackles, eye-bolting the wrist manacles to a post in the middle of the hold, so that his hands could touch nothing. Everything near or around the reach of his feet was also moved well away from him, so he could not harm the ship or stores, and no one but himself. They hadn't gagged him, however, and several times through the day, John wished they had.

If the prevailing summer winds held, which often went east to west, they could be at the Strait of Gibralter in five days' time.

However, a contrary wind could drive them easterly, and that was something they did not want. Rather than go that direction, they would anchor alongside some cliff near the coast of Spain, set up their cliff sails and gunwale covers, and wait it out. John knew that Spain would not welcome pirates along their coast, but they had Spanish flags as well as English flags, and they were not afraid to use whatever means necessary to escape these treacherous pirate seas.

As they passed several ships headed east that did not interfere with them, they were still flying the pirate's flag, and were prepared to carry on as though they were pirates should anyone approach them, at least until they cleared the coast of Portugal. By late afternoon, they noticed a ship far off in the distance, behind them, that seemed very much like *El Djazair* giving chase. Dark clouds hugged the western horizon, so they quickly put up all the gray sails, covered the gunwales with gray tarpaulins, and refused to use any lights on board that night, whatsoever. By the time the night darkened, they had become more noticeable, so they switched the sails to midnight blue, and were certain that they could not be seen by their pursuers. It was difficult work, changing the sails twice each day, but it seemed to give them an edge of relief. After all, if *El Djazair* could not see them against the gray of the daylight sky, or the dark of the night, they might survive intact.

Tightening up the sails made their progress a little faster, and they continued this way for several days, with the pirate's ship still in pursuit. One more night and *El Djazair* would likely catch up with them.

These hopes kept John agile and alert at his station, which he rarely left, only to catch brief snatches of sleep. When he awakened, he often found Thomas snugged up against him, sleeping as well.

The skies were still gray in the daytime, and black at night, but soon after they passed through the Strait of Gibralter, John noticed the western sky pinking up ever so slightly at sunset. This meant that tomorrow it could be clear. He had only one course of action left to him, but he first wanted to see how his crew would react.

When he had gathered the crew together, he voiced his thoughts clearly. "We can head for Spain's coast and hope to find a place to duck away for a few days where *El Djazair* will not find us, or we can head north toward the Spanish coast, put up all our dark sails and hope *El Djazair* will pass by us in the night without seeing us, or we can continue to try to outrun her. But she's been gaining on us steadily, and I expect her to reach us sometime around midnight."

"Has she even seen us?" Peter asked. "Because when we were in the city of Algiers, Martin and I swore our gray sails made the *Warwick* seem almost invisible against the gray sky. It's only been this evening that the sun has lightened the clouds at all, and then it's just been a few late shadows."

"We do not know," said John. "The fact is, she's been on our tail for five days, with no sign of giving up, and she's likely to reach our position near midnight. We've got about four hours before that, so we must decide."

"What do you want to do, Father?" asked Thomas.

"I'd blow them out of the water, if I thought I could get away with it," said John. "But in order to fire on them, we must have the element of surprise."

"I say, let's turn the *Warwick* about, put up the black sails, and as soon as she passes us, and we feel it's safe, let's chase her out into the Atlantic and sink her." Thomas grinned.

"And if she sees us before we pass, son? What do you say about that?"

"She won't," said Peter. "I doubt she's seen us at all. If we sail to her north a few more nautical miles, it's likely she still won't see us, even as she passes."

"It's risky," said John, "but bold. She will not expect that from us, will she?"

"Hear! Hear!" said the men in unison.

"But you'll need to shut that squawker up," squeaked Red Taylor.

"Has he eaten anything, yet?" asked John.

Simon shook his head. "He just kicks his food back at us, John."

"Very well. Simon, prepare a bottle of your special wine," said John. "I shall deal with him, myself." To Peter, John said, "Head us northerly." To Red and Big Mike, "Go to the crow's nest. Keep an eye on her. If she shows any sign of following us north, let me know of it straight away, but quietly. We'll soon know whether it's the *Warwick* she's chasing, or a ghost called the *Warhorse*."

The men went to their duties immediately.

"Father, why did you ask the men for their counsel?" Thomas questioned the moment they were alone.

"These men came for one purpose only, son. They came to rescue you. If I treat them with disrespect, without their input into each dangerous situation, it would be a gross injustice. They're all good men, and they need a share in what we are doing."

"Captain Abu just orders the men about like they have no feelings of their own, and whips them if they don't perform exactly as he says. I used to think your way was wrong, Father, but now I see that you've always had the best interests of the men at heart."

It was the kindest compliment Thomas had ever paid him, and John felt duly humbled. There was a time when the lad would have scolded him for his empathy toward the other seamen. "Thank you, son. It's been my belief that there are better ways to discipline men, and using the whip isn't one of them."

Thomas snuggled next to his father, wrapping his arms around his waist. Great tears formed in his eyes and dripped down his cheeks. Stammering, Thomas said, "I – I'm proud you're my father. I – I love you. I never got around to saying that before, but I want you to know."

John forced his emotions down. They had a job to do, and his blubbering around the ship would not be too encouraging to the men. In response to Thomas' confession, he said. "I love you, Thomas, more than you'll ever know until you have a son of your own. And, I'm proud of the way you've governed yourself in my absence. Every father should have a son like you."

When Thomas' had wiped his eyes, John stood back and encouraged him. "Now, no more tears for a while, son. We mustn't let the men see us struggle like this."

"Of course not, Father. It's just . . . I haven't cried for a long time now. Master Abu hates that." Thomas shuddered, as though from some secret pain that he would never share with anyone. "I gave it up, swearing I would never cry again until I was safely with you."

"You may be *with* me, son, but you're not safe. Until the day that

I tell you we're safe, I will expect you not to cry anymore either."

"Very well, Father. If you don't mind my saying it, I feel so much better being able to say Father, instead of master."

"So do I," John agreed. "Now, back to work with you. I'm going to deliver a bottle of sleeping wine to a very disagreeable man."

When Thomas had joined Red and Big Mike at the crow's nest, John went down with Simon to the galley, where Simon poured a number of herbs into a fresh bottle of wine. "The lad has changed," Simon sighed wistfully. "He's not a child anymore."

"He's a man," John agreed. "And we shall treat him as one with us. It's the only way. My son has had to grow up these past two years, something I had not hoped would happen for at least four or five more years."

"He'll be a better person for his struggling," encouraged Simon. "You must not blame yourself, John."

John chuckled at that. "I have no one else who'll take the blame, Simon. It is all on my shoulders."

"Then blame Aligolant, if you must, and remember what became of him. You did not plan for a pirate to force your son into manhood before his time." Simon swirled the herbs lazily in the liquid. "Give them about an hour, John. Abu will sleep if you can get him to drink it."

"How much can I drink without falling asleep?" he asked.

"It would be better to force yourself to throw it up after you drink it," said Simon. "And then drink lots of water afterward."

"How much?" asked John again.

"One big swallow or two," came the answer.

John nodded, then took the bottle down into the hold where it was dark and dreary. After closing the hatch, he lit a lantern, knowing the light would not penetrate into the world beyond the hold, and hung it from a hook in the ceiling.

"You're a filthy beast!" roared Abu. "Your mother should have drowned you the day you were born."

"Trading unpleasantries will not solve anything," said John patiently. "Besides, I didn't come to call names. Rather, I came to thank you for taking good care of my son in my absence."

"Your son?" questioned Abu. "Who is your son?"

"Thomas, of course," answered John. "He is in good health, has only a few minor scars on his backside, and has learned things that I could never have taught him in the two years since he was captured by Aligolant."

"You're John Dunton?!" Abu asked, though it was more statement than question.

"At your service," John bowed and opened the bottle of wine. "I've come to toast you, my good man. Because of you, my son is alive, and well." Putting the bottle opening up to his mouth, John stuck his tongue inside it, knowing the bottle was too dark to see through, then pretended to swallow several large gulps. "Although," John added, wiping his mouth with the sleeve of his shirt, and staggering a little, as though he was already intoxicated. "I fear there are scars that will last far longer than those upon Thomas' back. You see, as he grows taller, those scars will become smaller. It's the scars upon his heart that I worry about. And I wonder what you might have done different if you'd known he was my son."

"I treated him well enough," snorted Abu. "But that won't matter for long. My crew will chase you down and kill every last one of you."

"You do not suppose we thought of that when we sent that wine over to the ship for your men to drink?" John questioned, swaying a little more.

"Yes, but they're awake by now, and likely well on their way to capturing you."

"That is," John smiled, "if the wine we gave them was merely for sleeping. You see, Abu, there are potions for when one only wants to make the drinker sleep for several hours." He took another pretend swig from the bottle of wine. "And there are potions for other purposes as well. It will be days before the bodies start smelling so badly that they draw any attention. By then, no one will even want to go in the hold to see what makes it reek with such a horrible stench. More likely, they'll think the black plague is aboard, and will promptly tow *El Djazair* out of the harbor, light it afire, and let it burn until it finally sinks to the bottom of the Alborán Sea."

Abu cursed viciously. "You swine! Father of a mad dog!"

"Ahh," warned John ominously. "You may curse me all that you want to, Abu. But curse my son? That you must not do." This time John took a huge amount of wine into his mouth, then spit it in Abu's face. "You would not allow anyone to speak ill of Benjamin, nor will I allow anyone to speak ill of Thomas."

Pretending to take several large swigs of wine, John corked the bottle and rolled it over to Abu. "If you decide to change your mind about that toast," he hinted. Then he left the hold, leaving the hatch ajar ever so slightly. Laying flat on his stomach, he watched Abu for several minutes.

The portly captain cursed John over and over again, but John was pleased that he no longer cursed Thomas. After a while, he seemed to tire of this, and reached out with his feet to bring the bottle to him. It was quite a struggle, trying to hold the bottle with his feet while removing the cork with his teeth. And again while trying to get the bottle up high enough to drink it down. Finally, he secured the bottle with his mouth and his teeth, and swung the bottle up with his head, where he held it as steady as he could and drank it all down, every last drop that did not spill down his chin.

When he had finished drinking, John returned and removed the lantern. No reason to asphyxiate the poor man. Then, John waited at the open hatch and listened to Abu yell and scream for perhaps another ten minutes. Finally, Abu fell asleep.

Returning to the helm, John questioned Peter about their position. It was nearing midnight and they could see *El Djazair* heading westward, her entire starboard side visible because of the square portholes of the gunnery deck, lit up from lanterns. She showed no signs of turning north, and when she was well past them, John gave the order to come about and head on out into the Atlantic Ocean after her. She would have a big surprise on her tail come morning.

John set the men to painting a wide white stripe around the gunwale of the ship. Then, they removed the *Warhorse* sign. Now, the *Warwick II* displayed its name proudly across the stern. Perhaps when *El Djazair* finally saw the *Warwick II*, it would not realize it had once been called the *Warhorse*. With the stripe and the true name, the ship was bound to look completely different to them.

When they were back on course and chasing *El Djazair* rather than being chased by her, John went below to get some sleep. His watch would come at six of the morning, and he would need to rest.

Thomas woke his father just on time, and John slipped into his doublet and a ruffled silk shirt that hung loosely on him, disregarding the bulging muscles it hid, along with his breeches, leggings and high-top boots. He had washed his hair vigorously over the past few days, as well as his skin, and he could see that some of the dye was fading, leaving his own coloring more prominent.

By the time John was dressed and ready for the day, so was Thomas. The two arrived at the helm station precisely on time, relieving the midshipman from his post.

"Prepare to hoist his Majesty's colors," John told Red Taylor, who had come on duty at the same time. "And we want white sails out today, gentlemen."

The orders were relayed and John's crewmen went through the laborious changing of the sails. It was the first time they'd sailed the white canvas, and it might be their last time to change the sails, which would cut down their slack time, but when they were done, the *Warwick* looked majestic upon the wild Atlantic Ocean.

Before the *Warwick II* lay thirty-five hundred nautical miles of open water, and winds that would drive them to the Caribbean Sea in forty days or less. It may seem a treacherous route to return to England, but John would not stop until they'd caught up with *El Djazair*, sunk her, and arrived at one of the outlying islands that encircled the Caribbean Sea. This route was the only one that would give them some space from the pirates. John would not risk Thomas' being taken from him again. If the pirates remained within a few hundred nautical miles of land, it seemed reasonable to John that the open sea and two Atlantic crossings were much preferable to risking a dangerous tack north to England, past the coasts of Portugal, Spain and France, through pirate-infested waters.

They'd had little difficulty sailing down those coastlines when they were on their way to Algiers. The winds had been brisk on their stern the entire way, and they'd flown the pirate's flag. Should they meet pirates taking the trade winds south along that route, while they were making slow progress tacking north into a head wind the entire time, they would be vulnerable to pirate invasion, no matter what flag they flew. John would not put his son in that position again.

Along with a crew of thirty one men, John still had to worry about the fifty-nine slaves that had joined them at Algiers. Many of these Englishmen were sickly, suffering from starvation and sores that oozed from their bodies. These, Simon attended with help from some of the crew, giving them teas to drink, cleansing their sores and putting herbal salves upon them. He also increased their diets, little by little, until they started to show signs of improvement.

When the sails were unfurled and the *Warwick II* began to pick up speed, it did not take more than twenty days to catch up to *El Djazair*. It had apparently seen them coming, and set all their sails out, as well as their oarsmen to task. By the time they did overtake *El Djazair*, that ship was in trouble. She was listing to port heavily, and the oarsmen to starboard were having a devil of a time trying to keep their oars in the water.

Another day upon their tail and John heard a call from Thomas at the crow's nest. "They're waving a white flag, Captain."

John nodded, then pulled out his spyglass to see. They were, indeed, flying a white garment hung from a yard spar, waving it back and forth.

"Pull us alongside them, Peter," said John. "It seems they do not want to fight us, after all."

Thomas climbed down the ratlines as agile as ever, and at the last rung he did a flip in the air and landed right side up at John's feet. "It was the cannabis weevils, wasn't it, Father?" he asked, not missing a beat.

"It seems so," John smiled, tousling Thomas' hair. "Good job, son. No need to ask where you learned that trick."

"I can do all sorts now," Thomas told him. "Only, I still don't know how to swim. Tovie offered to teach me, but I refused. I've been waiting for you to teach me, Father."

"Just as soon as the sea is becalmed," John promised.

As the *Warwick* pulled alongside the *El Djazair*, John mused aloud, "Strange that they never fired a single shot at the *Warwick*."

Thomas gave him a conspiratorial grin when Big Mike explained, "Your son threw all their cannon balls overboard, and confiscated their gun powder."

Taking all fifteen pirates captive was a simple matter. John arranged for some moving around in the hold until all could be shackled in the same manner their captain had been. Three slaves, James Merrit and two who seemed quite loyal to James, were found with the pirates.

To his surprise, Thomas insisted that these three slaves be put into shackles also. "They cannot be trusted," he told John earnestly.

John was not about to argue with his son. Thomas would know their true nature better than he would.

El Djazair was boarded and stripped of anything that could possibly be salvaged from her, then she was fired upon at point-blank range, and sunk. It was a sad moment for John. He knew how difficult it was to lose a ship, whether to sinking or grounding made no difference. A man's ship was a part of him, and losing it to any catastrophe took a heavy toll. John heard Abu weeping in the hold for days, then began to worry that beneath the heavy crying, the pirates would make use of the opportunity to communicate a plan of escape. Immediately, he ordered the crew to stand guard in turns down in the hold, to prevent the pirates from communicating. Anyone who spoke would be gagged for twelve hours.

There was a minor scuffle when one of the pirates was being taken to the hold. Fortunately, Peter was the one escorting the pirate, and he merely pushed the pirate overboard. Unfortunately, John did not hear about it for several hours, but the other pirates in the hold heard about it immediately, since Peter returned empty handed and then taunted them with the pleasure it had given him.

It was a distressing situation, and John knew that he must release the pirates at the next opportunity. Even if it meant they would be forever left on a deserted island, they would stand a better chance of survival there than inside the hold. There were not enough able men to watch every one of them all the time and, of necessity, long periods in the hold became their way of life. John insisted that they be allowed to move around on deck for an hour each morning and evening, under careful guard. At no other time were they given an opportunity to stretch their limbs except when being taken to the head.

The life of a captive pirate under John's care was much more generous than an Englishman under a pirate's care. John was certain these differences had not gone unnoticed, for the captives seemed to complain less and sleep better. They were always hungry and thirsty, and John did not spare much for their meals.

Food would not be a problem. They hadn't sold any of their vast stores in Algiers and had only used up three cases of wine on Captain Abu and his men. However, if they should run low, they could always stop at one of the islands in the Caribbean Sea and replenish their water and a few other supplies. If they got a calm day, some of the men could do some fish diving, as well.

In the meantime, they stayed their course, unaware that there was still trouble brewing behind them.

Chapter Eleven

Into the Eye of the Storm

*"And there arose a great storm of wind, and
the waves beat into the ship. . ."*
~Mark 4:37

The clouds on the eastern horizon looked terrible to John when daylight arrived one morning well into their sail eastward. He had never seen the billowing towers of gray so high before. They were almost so tall he couldn't see the tops of them. It looked as though God had opened his mouth wide to swallow the *Warwick II*. Whole. And John couldn't understand why.

"Father," said Thomas, who was apparently watching the clouds himself. "Why do those clouds have yellow streaks in them, like they're swirling in one direction?"

"I think we have a hurricane headed toward us, Son." This was not the time to treat Thomas as though he was still a child.

"But it's not hurricane season until September."

"It looks like this one arrived a little early."

"What shall we do?" Thomas asked.

"We will do everything in our power to survive the storm," John answered. "Shorten the sails, strap the helmsman to the helm. And then we will pray without stopping, like the God-fearing men that we are. If it is His will, we will get through this safely."

"Whose turn is it at the helm?" Thomas questioned.

"Mine," said John.

"But you've just finished your shift," the young man protested.

"I am the Captain," John reminded. "Call all the men to the weather deck, immediately."

When the men were gathered together, John gave them the news. "The storm approaching us from behind has all the distinguishing features of a hurricane. I do not know how many of you have had any experience with one."

Two of the men held their hands up, Elias and Red.

John continued, "I will expect you two to prepare the others for what's ahead of us. We'll break up into two teams. Six hours on, six hours off. Edward, stand forward and choose your men. I shall take whomever remains."

"But John, you—" began Edward.

"You've more than proved your ability, Edward. And you know that they must be divided equally by their strengths. I have no ship's Master aboard, and at this time, we are in dire need of one."

"Aye, sir." Edward agreed. He started separating the seamen and rescued Englishmen, according to their abilities, into two lines. More than twenty of the former English slaves were too emaciated to expect their assistance, but when Edward was finished, he said, "That gives us twenty-three apiece, Captain."

Very well," said John. "The storm will be upon us within a couple hours, men. I will remain at the helm, lashed to it. Edward, set your group to tying everything down in the hold that they possibly can. The gunnery deck portholes are to be latched and locked, the cannons double-wedged and strapped down to the eye-bolts, and all moveable armament to be securely fastened. There will be no sleep for the first rotation. My group will step forward and take their positions."

Edward nodded and led his men below deck.

John separated his men into groups, depending upon which sails they would be working, and gave instructions to all of them. "The sails are to be shortened now, while there is time to do it, with lashings at the ready. Extra lashings, too. Prepare yourself a harness that will allow you to work, but will hold you securely should a wave try to wash you overboard. Then, nail down everything on deck. Strap it, lash it, nail it. This is not the time to worry about leaving holes. If it cannot be secured on the weather deck, remove it to the gunnery deck and secure it there. Make certain the drains are open and clear. Secure the ratlines to both sides and to the stern. If someone falls overboard, we must afford him access, so he will have a way to climb back aboard. And, trail some lines five hundred feet in the water, with knots in them for grabbing onto. If we plan ahead, we will be as secure as we can make ourselves."

"And then what?" squeaked Red Taylor.

"Why, we shall do what all faithful Englishmen have always done in this situation, Red. We shall pray, and put our lives in God's hand."

"God giveth and He taketh away," said Thomas. "We shall pray that this time God giveth."

While the men were busy, John took one final reading with the astrolabe. It wouldn't be completely accurate, for the sun was partially obscured, but it was as close as he could get it. "Take your reading, too," he encouraged Thomas. "You may need to know this someday."

While Thomas used the astrolabe, John set their course on a chart in the Captain's quarters. The winds were out of the northeast, which would drive them into the West Indies. If they survived it, they could leave the pirates with one of the Spanish colonies. Or, if the storm abated long enough for them to anchor, and if they could find adequate protection from the following storm, should there be one, they might weather what lay ahead of them.

With his pen, John drew a clockwise circle around the area into which they were sailing, then he drew arrows that pointed the clockwise way the wind would blow inside the hurricane. It was always best to know which direction the wind would blow.

Suddenly, John realized that if they turned a little farther south, they might miss the brunt of the storm, perhaps they could even survive it. Looking again at his chart, he hoped they could sail far enough south to pass the Antilles, then come back north in the lee of the islands, where it would be considerably safer.

Having made his decision, he hastened to the helm and said to Red Taylor, "Have the men set the sails full out, we are heading south."

By the time the sails were unfurled, John had the *Warwick II* on a southerly course. The wind was picking up, also on a somewhat southerly course.

Brisk and punishing, the wind filled the sails with ferocity and pushed them forward. The ship picked up speed as it sailed. Within four hours, the seas went from twelve foot swells to forty-foot monsters. When they were in the bottom of the swells, they had little steerage, for the wind was blowing off the tops of the waves and couldn't reach them.

When they were on the tops of the waves, it felt as though the wind would rip them from one wave-top to the next. Soon, many of the men were on deck, vomiting and praying, in between shortening sails and tightening lashings. Huge waves pounded the decks, and would have swept most of the crew overboard if they had not been lashed to masts and gunwales..

Their speed worried John most, so he ordered that two open barrels be strapped onto lines and thrown overboard off the stern, in an effort to slow down the ship's acceleration. The men had been unable to track their speed beyond twenty knots, but it did seem that the barrels were helping by creating a drag in the water behind them. The shallop they towed also concerned him, and he had the men play out a great deal of line to it, which would keep the shallop from crashing into the stern of the *Warwick II* while slipping the downside of monstrous ocean swells.

Edward, Peter, Red, and Big Mike had all requested to relieve John at the helm, but John would not allow it. He stayed at his post and carried the brunt of the storm upon his own shoulders. If the ship went down, it would be at his hand, not at another's.

All through the day and night, they sailed a terrific storm. At four in the morning, the *Warwick II* got knocked down by a giant incoming wave, which caught the ship broadside, busted the mizzen mast in half, cracked the foremast, and sent the men swimming aboard the weather deck until the ship righted itself.

Thomas, who had lashed himself to the mainmast long before the rogue wave hit, now sought safety by his father's side. John lashed him to the other side of the helm, then tied a line from his own waist to Thomas' waist, just in case.

John ordered the mainmast sail unfurled slightly, then had the sails removed from the foremast completely. The mizzen mast was cut loose and cast overboard. Now, they would have to depend solely on the center sail, which the men had made short and flat and tight, so the wind would bounce off it and not fill it up.

By dawn, it seemed the wind had weakened, the seas were less steep, yet there was still the terrible confusion of the waves to contend with, and John was constantly on his toes, changing the degree of reach across each wave so that they wouldn't be caught broadside again.

By noon, the mainsail was unfurled completely, the seas served gentle, twelve-foot swells, and the wind blew a brisk twenty knots. They had passed through the worst of the storm, and not lost a man among them.

Wearily, John turned the helm over to Edward, and went to the Captain's quarters with Thomas, where they both collapsed on the bed and slept until the next morning.

John awakened to a call from the crow's nest. "Land-ho!" He

scrambled out of bed, threw on his clothes, left Thomas still sleeping, and hurried up to the forecastle.

"That's impossible," he told Red, who was at the helm.

"It looks like one of them islands east of the Spanish Colonies to me," winked Red.

"It took us twenty five days to travel the first three thousand nautical miles, and one day to travel the last five hundred?" John questioned. "We must have been doing twenty-five knots, easy."

While it was true that John had never sailed so fast in his life, it was equally true he'd never been so scared. It was by the grace of God that the *Warwick II* had survived, as well as the men aboard it.

"What of our pirates?" John asked, ready to assume command once again.

"They all survived save one," squeaked Red.

"What happened?"

"One of the wine barrels came loose when we got knocked down. Killed one of them pirates and wounded three others. Simon patched them up well enough, then we sent them back down the hatch.

To Edward, John said. "Get Peter and a few men. Bring all the pirates with you. It's time we made arrangements for their release."

Edward nodded and went below.

"Gonna put them off here?" asked Red.

"Better than in the hold," said John. "We'll check the island out, of course, make sure there's plenty of water and food. We can leave them some wheat, rice and dried peas. If nothing else, they'll be able to grow food if they're careful."

Thomas joined them as John was speaking. "If they build a big enough fire when they see a ship pass, they'll be rescued. It is preferable to the hanging they would get in America or England."

"Still squeamish about that, are you?" Red questioned.

"Not in the least," said John. "I've seen my share of hangings. But these men did keep my son alive. I owe them, at the very least, their lives."

"Glad to hear you say that," said Captain Abu Benjamin behind him.

John whirled about. The pirates, ragged though they were, stood before him in a small group. "Well, then. If this island proves adequate, you men shall be given your freedom. That's more than you'll receive if we take you back to England with us."

"This is a long way to go to get to England," Abu said, stretching his arms and legs, and whisking his fingers through his unkempt hair.

"It gets my son away from pirates," said John. "I will not let him be captured by your lot again."

"So you'd sail an extra seven thousand nautical miles just to keep the lad safe, eh?" accused Abu with a vicious snarl.

"I do not have to justify my actions to you," John snapped. "I merely thought your men might like to get a little fresh air. Since their captain has no manners, they'll all be denied the opportunity. They'll have you to thank for that, Abu. Take them back to the hold, Peter. The Captain is apparently not the least bit grateful that we spared his life."

Peter smiled and led the pirates back below deck.

John shuddered. "Terrible men, these pirates. You give them their lives and they want to insult you for it."

"You took the safest route for young Thomas," said Red. "We all agreed on the voyage, we knew the course you planned to take. The seas around Spain and Portugal, England and France, are not safe anymore, Captain. We'd all be better off in the Massachusetts Bay Colony. At least that puts us out of harm's way where these pirates are concerned. Since the real Captain Barbarossa took power in Algeria, over a century ago, all of Europe has suffered. Until someone kills every last one of them pirates, there'll be no peace for the likes of decent men."

"Still," said John, "it would be better if we didn't have to do anything about the pirates, if there was no evil to contend with. I considered myself an evil man after my first wife, Mary, died. God had taken her, you see, and I refused to give Him credit for any good in my life afterwards. It wasn't until we were taken captive that I turned my heart back to God. Yet, I never realized until captivity that I wasn't an evil man at all. I still had a heart. Most of these pirates have no heart. England will not stand a chance against the pirates, I see that now. Before I went to Algiers, I thought it would be a simple matter to send another armada out. Now, I understand that the King was right, it would take the entire Royal Navy to conquer Algiers. That leaves . . . how many dozens of towns the size of Salé, still filled with pirates, to conquer next? We did the right thing. We never could have rescued Thomas if we had not gone in disguised as pirates. And, we would not be able to return him to his mother if we were captured again."

Edward stepped forward and put a hand on John's shoulder.

"Storm or not, it was better than fighting pirates. Thomas' safety is our only concern, John. If that means seven thousand extra nautical miles to keep him safe, that is what we shall do."

"If we can just reach Plymouth by the end of August," John said. "We'll be able to find someone going back to England in September. But I will not go back across the Great Pond without several ships at our sides. Thomas' life is too important to incur risk a second time."

"What if we're too late? What will we do, then?" asked Red.

"We'll wait the winter out in Virginia. It is warmer there for living aboard a ship through the cold season. Then, we shall head east with the next group of ships to take on the Atlantic." John pulled Thomas close to him.

Thomas reached out and pulled Edward and Red into the circle.

At first Red balked, but John gave him a quick frown, so Red joined them, too. The three men hugged Thomas as though their lives depended on it.

When Thomas let them go, he looked up at them eagerly, and shook their hands one by one. "Thank you," he said. "My father could not have found truer friends." By the time he was finished, the other men had come forward to hug Thomas and shake his hand, as well. Peter arrived with Simon, and joined the procession. Soon there wasn't a dry eye among them, with exception of Thomas, who said to John, "Permission to cry, sir?" John nodded, and that was when the hugging of young Thomas began in earnest, by all those who had risked everything to ensure his safety.

By evening, the *Warwick II* was anchored securely in a quiet lagoon surround by lush hills. A clear, freshwater stream flowed down from a tropical mountain, emptying in the sea at the western edge of the lagoon. There were bananas, coconuts, wild papaya, mango, and plenty of bamboo and other plants for stripping bark to make strong cord. In addition, there was a herd of wild boars that roamed the island, as well as a hoard of large, fat crabs.

At first, the seamen were worried about eating the crabs, but John assured them, "The aboriginal tribes of New Zealand and Australia have been living for centuries on crab. There's no reason why we should not do so."

Grabbing one of the crabs from the lagoon with very little effort, John asked Elias to build a fire. "Tell you what, men. I will eat the first crab. If it does not kill me in twenty-four hours, tomorrow night we shall have a crab feast you will not forget."

"Hear! Hear!" they all echoed.

That night, John and Thomas stayed ashore. It was the first time, Thomas confessed, that he had slept on solid ground in more than two years. As they gazed up at the sky, which had cleared considerably, a few stars peeked out at them. "Father, is mother as beautiful as I remember?"

"Even more than she was," John answered, longing for his wife with a fierceness that surprised him. "Having Jane has changed her in ways I hadn't hoped. Rebecca was willful and strong when we first met, and now she is twice that, yet there's a tenderness about her I doubt even you noticed while you were with her. She's closer to Deity than ever, and she senses things that you and I might let pass by unnoticed. I cannot describe the changes, really, except to say that she was nearly perfect then, but now she's so much better than she was. Does that make sense to you?"

"Well, you say that I've been made a better man by my experiences. It seems perfectly normal to know that she has become a better person, too."

His philosophical manner surprised John. "And what of me?" he asked. "Have I changed, now that you've had the chance to get reacquainted with me?"

"Very much," said Thomas. "You're still just as compassionate as you always were. Perhaps more. But you have strengths in leadership I hadn't noticed before, and the men look up to you more than I've ever seen them look up to any captain. It's almost like the bond you and I feel, Father. It's like you're their brother, and they are yours. Isn't that the way God intended men to act?"

"Yes, Thomas," John agreed. "You're right, of course. All of us, every single person, will give an accounting to God one day, regarding how we lived our lives. If He sees me as you do, I shall not worry about my standing before Him."

"Well, there is just one thing," hinted Thomas.

"What is it?" John asked.

"You still haven't taught me how to swim."

Laughing aloud, John tousled his son's hair. "In the morning, the sea is usually becalmed. I will teach you, then."

WHEN DAWN CAME, John touched Thomas' shoulder gently. "The water is flat as glass, a few turtles are coming ashore to nest, and it is the perfect time for swimming lessons.

Thomas sat bolt upright. "I'm ready." He rubbed his eyes and looked out at the lagoon. The aquamarine water shimmered, as though it was a liquid mirror, all the way out to the reef that encircled it. The color reminded John of Rebecca's turquoise eyes. The scent of frangipani hung heavily on the morning air, and several heron stood at the water's edge, stiff and straight, awaiting a tasty fish for breakfast.

John led Thomas into the lagoon barefooted, knowing the water temperature this far south was bound to be warm. He was not disappointed. "The first thing you need to learn, my son, is that water needs respect, but she can be your friend."

Thomas grinned. "Show me."

John expanded his lungs. "You know how a barrel floats if it has enough air and is sealed tightly."

A quick nod came from his son.

"Your body works the same way. Take in a big breath and you can float, indefinitely, upon your back." John sank into the water, expanded his lungs again, held his breath momentarily, and lay completely motionless, floating like a cork. "It takes some relaxation to float like this, but when you've mastered floating, we'll move onto the next step."

As he breathed out, John sank a little, but he quickly recovered the floating position when he breathed in, which he did for several minutes while Thomas watched in wide-eyed wonder.

"I never saw you do that before."

John stood up, pressed the water from his hair, and said, "I'm usually too busy catching fish. But Thomas, if you're ever thrown overboard, you can float on your back a great long time, which would give us a chance to rescue you."

Thomas leaned his head back and John put his hand below it to steady him. "That's right," he encouraged. "Just relax. Breathe deeply, inhaling a lot of air, exhaling just a little. That's right."

Although he arched slightly, Thomas was beginning to learn how to float. By the time Elias brought a pot of porridge over to them from the boat, Thomas was learning the breast-stroke.

As they filled their stomachs, Elias went over to a nearby reef and stood upon it, waiting for a turtle to swim by. He did not have to wait long. John and Thomas watched Elias dive headfirst into the water, then saw him bob back up to the surface with a large turtle. Elias turned the turtle over onto its back to disable its ability to swim. When Elias brought the turtle up onto the beach, he left it on its back in the shade of a palm tree.

"I'm going to catch a turtle someday," said Thomas. "Just as soon as I get swimming mastered, I'm going to learn diving."

While Thomas practiced the water skills taught to him all the rest of the day, John and the men made plans to repair the masts and the sails. They were glad, now, that they'd brought several sets of sails with them. During the storm, many of the white canvas sheets had been shredded, and massive repairs were needed to restore them.

The pirates were taken ashore that same day, where they remained shackled, this time to a number of palm trees. For the next several weeks, this was where the pirates spent their daylight hours, but they were hauled back to the ship's hold each night.

Every day, Thomas spent several hours swimming until he finally learned the skill well enough to survive a sinking. Then, John taught him how to dive from the gunwale of the *Warwick II*, which he practiced over and over again. John's heart filled with pride as he watched his young son show off his diving prowess.

Soon, John was able to teach him how to catch small turtles, by diving headfirst into the water and wrestling them onto their backs, keeping his hands clear of the turtle's strong beaked mouth. The lad was relentless in his desire to make the sea feed him, and for this, John was grateful. The creatures found within the water's depths could be frightening, but most of them would sustain a starving man for prolonged periods of time.

Thomas dove steadily throughout the morning, practicing the skills he'd learned continually, until he finally started bringing up clams, scallops and then lobsters. On his last dive of the day, he managed to bring up a turtle the size of a large melon. Everyone aboard cheered for him, and they ate delicious turtle soup for their supper that night.

Chapter Twelve

Marooned

"Nevertheless, the men rowed hard to bring it to land;
but they could not: for the sea wrought, and
was tempestuous against them."
~Jonah 1:13

Anchored in the lagoon of a beautiful, deserted island seemed like paradise for the first week or two. John enjoyed it, but his heart longed to return his son to Rebecca, to hold her, and to get Thomas acquainted with Jane. That could not be done until repairs were made to the *Warwick II.*

By the end of August, John and his crew had replaced the mizzen mast with a stout and sturdy coconut palm trunk, and reinforced the foremast with leather straps that tightened as they were drenched with water and allowed to dry. While the straps were curing, as well as the new mast, the ship received an extra packing of hemp because some of the seams had jarred loose in the storm.

In mid-September, they were concerned about proceeding farther north during the hurricane season. It would be wiser to remain on the island until early spring, then head north. But would they find a safer anchorage up the Chesapeake? They considered the boat strong enough to sail, but the weather worried them.

Finally, John put the issue up for a vote, and it was unanimously agreed that they would stay on the lee side of the islands all the way to the Florida crossing, then cut across and head up the coast. With God's help, they might still catch a group of ships heading to England from the American Colonies in late October, if the weather held. If the weather proved unfavorable, they would winter in Chesapeake Bay, and head east toward England with the first fleet in the Spring. When the hands were counted, all of the crewmen voted to take the risk, except one former slave, Tovie, who dissented, saying he was afraid of the Spanish Conquistadores in the islands. The majority vote ruled and the crew of the *Warwick II* began intense preparations to set sail as quickly as possible.

THE SHIP WAS stocked with bananas, coconuts, strips of bark for making rope, four wild boars, and several crates of wild papaya and mango. John and the crew refilled all their water barrels with fresh water from the stream that flowed from the island. On return trips from the ship, John had the men set upon the island four cases of rice, three barrels of dried peas, three barrels of wine, two barrels of wheat and an assortment of extra tools that might come in useful to someone marooned upon such an island. Several swords were also hidden and a map made of their location. The map was placed inside an empty wine bottle that was buried just below the surface, inside one of the barrels of wheat. He did not want to leave the pirates unarmed, in case they were attacked by an unfriendly ship.

As soon as they got a favorable wind, the *Warwick II* was well-prepared to set sail. That day came early in the afternoon on the twenty-third of September, 1637. Thomas had gone ashore early in the morning, while it was still calm, with Elias, Robert Boyer and Big Mike, intending to bring one last load of turtles aboard for their voyage. John's son wanted another chance to dive from the reef and show off his fishing prowess.

Simon Harris and Barnabus Martin were still nursing the emaciated slaves back to health, most of whom were recovering well, but were still somewhat weak.

Peter, Red and several of the other seamen had gone below to bring the pirates up, intending this to be their last day aboard the *Warwick II*, for they would be left on the island as soon as the wind gathered strength. John and Edward remained on the forecastle deck, Edward preparing to stand the first watch at the helm.

"You seem to be feeling much better, Edward," said John, noticing the glow in Edward's cheeks, the clarity of his light, blue eyes.

"I'm sleeping well, for the first time in more than two years," admitted Edward. "Since Thomas came aboard, the nightmares have gone."

"It's a good thing you've done, arranging for Thomas' rescue, participating in it. Your father will be well-pleased, as am I." John walked over to the stern rail and watched for a moment as Thomas made a spectacular dive off the reef.

"Thomas has caught another one, " said Edward, joining him.

Just then Thomas surfaced, sped forward without moving his arms, then dived below once again. "What the devil has the boy got this time?" John asked, curiosity and concern mingling in the pit of his stomach.

"One of those winged monsters you rode out of the Chesapeake seven summers ago," said Edward, standing on tiptoe and straining to watch.

Thomas and the ray then did a mighty leap into the air, the manta batting its wings to dislodge its captor. But the young man stayed with the manta ray, clinging to its shoulders with tenacity learned through his own captivity.

When the ray headed out into deep water, Thomas finally let the creature go and swam back to the reef, climbed upon it and waved to John, shouting, "Did you see that, Father?"

John waved back, calling, "Good sport, son!"

Then, Elias was patting Thomas on the back and they were laughing.

John turned back to Edward, but stopped short. Edward's eyes were wide with fear, his mouth askew slightly, and then John noticed the blood-tinged sword in the hands of Captain Abu Benjamin Djazair. Peter and Red were held tightly by pirates flanking them, knives drawn at their throats. He wondered who it was that Abu had, apparently, run through.

"It seems," sneered Abu, "that you trusted one slave too many, John Dunton. You see, some of these have been with me for years, and are quite loyal." He stroked the head of one of the English slaves that had been rescued from *El Djazair*. John was not surprised to see that it was the one called Tovie.

Unable to defend his men, John had no choice but to allow the pirates to thrust him forward and place him in shackles and fetters. Behind him, some of the other seamen men were already restrained, while still others were missing entirely. Soon, all the men, along with John, were thrown into the hold where they had only a single lantern to stave off the darkness. Simon, Martin and a few of the recaptured slaves who had been under the doctor's care, were thrown into the hold, as well.

It made for crowded quarters. Edward was leaning against the hull's interior when the Englishmen arrived. His color faded, his face went deathly white, and he stumbled forward.

John caught him quickly, helping him stand once again. When John pulled his hand away from Edward's shirt, he found it smeared with blood. "He stabbed you?" John asked, angry that his kindness toward Abu had been returned with such brutality.

"I was about to push you overboard, or at least warn you, but Abu thrust the blade in before I could get a word out. I had hoped you could get away, and stay with young Thomas." Edward's voice sounded strained. He gasped, sucking in one great breath, then fell against John, shivering uncontrollably.

Simon rushed over and tore Edward's shirt from his shoulders. "Someone rip his shirt into strips," Simon insisted. John complied immediately. Removing a small pouch from his pants pocket, Simon poured some herbs from it against Edward's wound and packed a small fold of cloth against it. Then, tying the shirt strips around Edward's waist, he held the cloth firmly in place until the bleeding eased.

Twenty minutes passed, and silence reigned among them, except for some splashing sounds they heard on the windward side of the ship, which sounded very much like someone was being thrown overboard. A shiver went through the group of men huddled in the hold.

To think that they could be captured by pirates a second time, and that John could be separated from his son once again, was unthinkable. John had no idea what the other men were thinking, but he could certainly guess that they were as angry, and felt as wretched as he did.

Soon, the hatch was opened, and Peter, Miles and Daniel Weatherby, and several more of the rescued Englishmen, were thrown into the hold as well.

Peter quickly approached John, who noticed a large bruise upon his face, and his nose was bleeding.

"Tell me what's happened," John insisted.

Peter, staring in horror as Simon applied pressure to Edward's abdomen, said to John, "I – I'm sorry, Captain. We thought their shackles were still secure when we came below to bring the pirates up. They rushed us."

"Who released their shackles?" John asked.

"One of the rescued slaves," said Peter. "The one they call Tovie."

"Was anyone hurt?"

"Two of my men were killed, Jones and Swallow. They were asleep on the gunnery deck when it happened." Peter hesitated, as though he did not want to continue.

"And?" questioned John, fearful for what he would learn.

"And the weakest of the slaves were thrown overboard, as well."

"Not George?" asked John, afraid for the young lad.

"No," said Scotland, stepping out from behind some barrels. "I hid both of us down here under your spare sails, Captain, the moment the pirates took over."

"Bless you, Scotty," said John. "That was a brave thing you did."

"It felt cowardly, sir, hiding myself as well. But I have to look after George," insisted Scotty. "I'm the only family he's got left."

"How many did we lose altogether?" asked John, turning back to his first mate.

Peter calculated quickly in his head. "Twenty-seven, sir."

"They drowned twenty-five slaves?"

"Took them straight from their beds, Captain. Stuffed their mouths with rags so they couldn't scream and tied their hands behind their backs. Tossed them over the windward side, where young Thomas wouldn't see them. That was the only kindness we saw from the butcher. I expect Captain Abu didn't want the weak rescued once again and he knows that Thomas, Elias and Big Mike all know how to swim. It was horrible," Peter said, almost shuddering.

To hear Peter admit his anguish made John realize just how much compassion Peter had for those less fortunate than himself. Peter had changed over the past two years from a crusty seaman with a penchant for brawling, to a warrior with a soft spot for the downtrodden. John was deeply touched to see that Peter was evolving into a true hero.

"They're all dead?" John questioned.

Peter nodded as the men in the hold went silent once again.

Sinking to his knees, John wondered what they should do now.

His son was still on the island. Fortunately, Thomas was still in good hands. Elias, Big Mike and Robert were outstanding swimmers, good fishermen, and they fostered a tender spot for Thomas. They had enough rations and ingenuity to last them a long time on the island. Thomas would be well-cared for, regardless the circumstances. Each one of the men would lay their lives down before they'd let any harm come to Thomas. They also knew that John would stop at nothing to get back to them.

John heard the anchor being lifted and felt the *Warwick II* give a gentle lurch forward as her sails filled with air and she headed out of the lagoon.

"What's the matter, John Dunton?" asked a voice from the darkness. "A bit of a strain to say goodbye to your son once again?" Abu stepped forward, sneering and discontent.

"You'll pay for this, Abu," warned John. "I had planned to let you live, but now I shall not rest until you're swinging from the hangman's noose."

"You dare threaten me, you fool," cautioned Abu. "I'm the Captain now, and my word is law." He nodded to four men at his sides, who stepped forward, grabbed John and Edward and dragged them up onto the aftercastle deck, where Thomas could still watch the fate of his father from shore.

Stripping John's shirt from his back, Abu smiled. "Ahh, so you're already accustomed to whipping. Good."

"Do not do this to Edward," pleaded John. "You've already wounded him. Isn't that enough?"

"Not at all, Dunton. For it was Edward's fine performance that led me to fall into your snare in the first place." With those words, John and Edward were tied to the helm and whipped mercilessly. John closed his eyes and refused to cry out, for he did not want his son to hear it. Apparently, Edward was either unconscious, or had the same strength of will as John.

From the shore of the lagoon, John heard the shouting of his young son, Elias, Big Red and Robert, yelling with all their might pleading that they release John and Edward, but soon their voices faded into the distance.

When Captain Abu was finished, he had his men dump John and Edward into the hold, then taunted, "We'll see you for another round tomorrow, slaves. You'll see that I'm the kinder of the two of us, Dunton. There'll be no need to fasten your shackles to an eye-bolt. After all, no man would sink his ship while his son was marooned and waiting for another rescue."

The lantern was removed from the hold, the hatch was closed and locked, and darkness settled upon them. Within a few minutes, candles were brought forth and lit. The door to the hold was quickly fitted with a strong lock from the underside, effectively locking the pirates out. These were some of the many defenses Edward and John had designed into the hold of the bark *Warwick II*, in the event they were captured and imprisoned there.

Once the lock was in place, they started pounding strips of thick planking over the door, making it even less likely for the pirates to make a quick entry, then stationed two men with hammers at the sealed opening, to break any fingers that might try to break their way through.

To give the captives fresh air, John went to the stern and pounded out two cylindrical plugs three inches in diameter. These air vents Edward had designed aft, near the ceiling of the hold, both port and starboard. They gave fresh air to the otherwise airless hold. If necessary, two holes forward could also be pounded out. In heavy seas, these holes would have to be corked or risk filling the hold with water. John stationed a man aft, his solitary job was to keep an eye on any encroaching water.

Captain Abu's men, apparently hearing the noise from securing the interior locks, had scrambled to try and open the trap door, to no avail. And John knew they had no tools to make their entry save the knives in the galley and their own swords. It would take them a good twelve hours to cut their way through the six inch thick boards with those weapons. Whatever plans John and the men made would have to be executed quickly.

These safety measures taken, the men gathered around Edward and Simon. "Edward will not last another round," John whispered as he looked at his friend laying unconscious on the hull's floor beside him.

Peter and Red spoke up, almost simultaneously. "You've got to deploy the stern raft, Captain."

"Agreed," said John. "But it will only hold ten men. Twelve at most. Since it may be the only means by which Thomas and our fellow seamen escape the island, that only leaves eight positions now for you men to leave. Edward will have to go. He cannot live through another beating. Who, besides myself, will stay behind?"

"You're going," Peter said.

"I will not ask any of you to bear the whip master's stripes for me," argued John.

"Why not?" squeaked Red. "How many times did you bear them for us?"

Peter looked anxiously at each of the men. "If you don't go, none of us will take Edward out of harm's way. If you stay, we all stay!"

"Hear! Hear!" the men cried in one accord.

John swallowed the lump in his throat and the pride in his heart. "Will you scuttle the ship, Captain?" he asked Peter.

"We have thirty-five hundred nautical miles to make that decision," grinned Peter in gratitude. "We know the pirates won't take the Great Circle, as we have, because it will put them in harm's way with the Spanish and American Colonies. They'll go eastbound, tacking through the trade winds. It will take them near three months to make the crossing, provided they don't run into another hurricane."

John nodded, agreeing with this assessment. "You'll have ample time to ambush them. But they haven't our compassion, Peter. They may just slaughter all of you."

"We have plenty of hiding places, Captain. But your point is well-taken." Peter seemed to think on the challenges ahead, then said, "I promise you this. If we haven't successfully mutinied by the time we reach the Strait of Gibraltar, the *Warwick II* will never cross through it again."

"Thank you," said John. "You've shown true leadership, skill and cunning. When I get back to England, I will expect to see you there."

"You'll see me next aboard the *Warwick II*, sir. When we retake the ship, we're coming back for you," Peter insisted.

Red Taylor added, "The remaining seamen and Englishmen will draw straws to see who's staying."

"No," said Peter. "Simon must go. He's Thomas' grandfather. I won't be responsible for taking another of Thomas' family from him. The brothers, Scotland and George. And Miles Weatherby, with his son, Daniel."

"You're right," agreed Red. "Children first, and Simon because both Edward and George will need his skills."

"This leaves only one vacant spot," said Peter. When the straws were drawn, Red Taylor drew the shortest one.

John was amazed at Peter's kindness toward those who were together as families. It only increased Peter's value in his eyes.

They had to wait until dark to deploy the stern raft. This would give them a narrow edge in escaping, since the pirates would be hard-pressed to see them.

In the meantime, they soon had their shackles removed and the men moving freely, silently about, packing supplies into the space for the castaways, in case they did not reach land in a timely manner: an axe and scythe, four oars, warm wool blankets, additional seeds, flour and food stuffed into flour bags, some canvas to sail with if they had wind, to funnel the rain if they needed water, and two wooden flasks the size of watermelons filled with water. John then insisted that the remaining men, including Englishmen and seamen, go to work preparing their hiding places. Since they'd hidden tools and lumber all over the inside of the hull, this was not a difficult task.

They soon had barrels with false bottoms securely set into their cradles. They could house twenty men in all the barrels and false floor space they had built into the ship at the Chatham repair yard back in the Spring. But there would still remain a dozen men vulnerable.

After much deliberation, it was decided that all the slaves and Barnabus Martin would go into hiding before the stern raft was dropped. The remaining seamen would take their chances in a mutiny, as soon as it was feasible to do so.

By nightfall, the men had their plans well under way. John was the last to climb into the narrow space between the stern of the boat and the false stern built onto it. A narrow opening was secured with a few planks, and would need shoring up before stormy weather. The way it was designed, the entire stern was actually two sterns fitted together. The outer stern was false, and would drop off into the water, hopefully right side up, and become a raft for escaping prisoners. It would make a great crashing sound in the dark, but the men had a plan for that, too. At the time the stern raft was deployed, the vulnerable twelve seamen would start pounding on the hull with hammers, and yelling with all their might. If the pirates heard a splash over their racket, perhaps they would think that it was a diving whale, or some other sea creature. John could only hope that by the time the pirates could investigate the noise, the black night would have swallowed them up.

With all the supplies that had been removed from the false barrels, including medical supplies, which Simon divided equally between the crew and the castaways, there was not much room left for another person aboard the raft.

Shortly before midnight, everyone was in position. The remaining refugees were tucked into barrels and under floor boards. Hopefully, when the pirates did break in, they would believe that most of the

Englishmen had preferred drowning, by crawling off the boat through the hole in the stern, rather than face a pirate's life.

Miles and Daniel Weatherby, Scotty and George Bremmett, Red, Simon and Edward were stuffed into the space between the stern and the raft.

John said his farewells to the remaining seaman. He gave Peter a great handshake. "We'll see you again, soon," said John. "I have every confidence in you, Captain Peter Bayland."

Peter nodded, then pulled John forward, gave him a big embrace, then released him. When he did so, John noticed they both had tears filling their eyes.

As John squeezed into the last position on the stern raft, which was entered through a small crawl space built into the top of the stern, he did his best to cling closely to the crawl space, so as not to crush anyone below him. There were five men and two young boys down there, much more snug than he was at that moment. But they would have to remain cramped a few more minutes while the men inside the hold released the remaining bolts that secured the raft to the stern. With that job done, John waited until he heard the remaining seamen pounding against the hull and screaming fitfully, to mask the noise. Then, he pulled the last retaining bolt from its topmost position, and shoved against the stern with all his might,.

The timbers creaked and groaned a moment, then began to fall, top up, thank goodness, into the sea. With a great splash, the raft plunged into the water, throwing John off on impact. Quickly, John grabbed onto the raft, but it crashed down once again, bouncing beside him, almost striking him in the head. If it were not for his keen reflexes, it would have knocked him out cold. Amazingly, no one aboard the raft made any noise, in spite of John's tumble into the Caribbean Sea.

Quickly, and silently, John pulled himself aboard the raft, and asked in a low whisper, "Is everyone all right?"

He could faintly see their nods in the dim starlight. Simon was cradling Edward, who was still unconscious against him. John thought for a moment how blissful Edward must be feeling.

The *Warwick II* sailed on, away from the raft and its eight seamen. By the time the pirates brought lanterns to the stern, to see if something had fallen overboard, the raft had slipped into the black night like a ghost.

The men on the raft settled in for a long night, praying for current and wind, in their favor. Taking turns, they began oaring vigorously on a course that would carry them back towards the island where Elias, Big Mike, Robert and Thomas had been marooned.

In September, Rebecca was busy stripping the last of the peas from their pods as she sat on the small side-porch at *John's Cottage*. Her twenty-month-old daughter, Jane, was playing in the yard. She looked up when she heard Jane laughing with delight.

An orange and black butterfly rested on Jane's fingertips. For several minutes Jane held very still, more so than she'd ever done before, except when asleep. Jane cooed and talked to the butterfly, and wrinkled her nose in a funny expression. When the insect flew away, Jane let out a squall that could be heard as far away as London.

Putting the bowl of beans down, Rebecca went over to Jane and picked her up. "It's all right, Jane. Butterflies aren't meant to live with people. She would have had a terrible time living with us, missing her mama and papa."

"Papa?" asked Jane through her tears.

"Papa will not be home today, darling. He's off searching for Thomas. Perhaps he's even found him by now. Perhaps they're on their way home right this minute."

"Papa . . . home this minute," said Jane.

Gasping, Rebecca couldn't believe her ears. "What did you say, Jane?" she asked, wondering if Jane could possibly know herself.

"Papa home now," said Jane. "Papa home this minute." The child pouted as though she completely understood what she was saying, and was equally frustrated that John was not at home with her, at that very moment.

"Papa cannot come home yet, Jane. He has to find Thomas first," Rebecca coaxed.

"Papa home now!" Jane insisted stubbornly. "Want Papa. Jane want Papa."

Big tears filled Jane's eyes and Rebecca wiped them away with the corner of her apron. "He'll come, darling. Do not cry. Papa will find Thomas, then he'll come home."

"Gwampa says no," Jane told her.

"Grandpa is with Papa, looking for Thomas."

"Gwampa not. Gwampa libs wif Jane."

Rebecca caught her breath. "Jane, are you saying Grandpa visits you?"

"Libs wif Jane!" she pouted.

"But Jane, your grandfather, Simon, is with Papa."

"Not Simon," Jane cooed.

"Gwampa wif hair." She put her fingers up to her head and twirled them around in her hair. "Like Jane's."

"You've seen Grandpa Webster?" Rebecca asked, her own eyes filling up with tears now.

Jane nodded. "Wif hair like Jane's," she agreed. "Gwampa libs wif Jane."

"But Jane, Grandpa lives in Heaven, with God."

"Wif Jane," her daughter insisted.

By now, Rebecca was completely bewildered. She sank onto the ground and held Jane close. "What did your grandfather say no about?" asked Rebecca, remembering Jane's earlier sentence.

"Papa. Thomas. No come home."

"What?" Rebecca asked.

Jane smiled up at her, the dimples deepening in her oval cheeks. "Must go get them," said Jane. "Gwampa says."

"Grandfather said that we must go get Papa and Thomas. Why?"

"Dunno." Another butterfly flitted into the garden and Jane's attention was distracted. "Look! Butty-fly!"

"Jane, why must we go get Papa and Thomas?" Rebecca persisted.

But whatever memories had stirred in her daughter were gone as Jane stood up and pursued the new butterfly. Rebecca watched her for a long time and mulled Jane's words over and over in her mind.

Papa. Thomas. Not come home. Must go get them. Surely she must have dreamed all this. Then, Rebecca remembered Jane's tiny fingers twirling around in her hair. Jeremiah Webster had a full head of hair, golden with streaks of silver, and curls that twirled around. He used to play with one particular curly lock that hung down over the right side of his forehead when he was concentrating on something difficult. Had he done that? Had Jane actually seen him. *Why not? I have.*

Rebecca had tried to bury the memory of when her father stood by the mantle, and told her to trust him. But the recollection was just as vivid today as it had been the day it happened.

Had Rebecca closed the door against her father's intrusions so strongly that he could no longer get through? Was he using her daughter to tell her what she needed to know?

For the rest of the day, Rebecca could not get Jane's words out of her mind. She prayed over them, fretted and stewed, but when night fell, they whispered through her dreams and became a part of her. It seemed as though she, too, had received Jeremiah Webster's message.

Papa. Thomas. Not come home. Must go get them.

Chapter Thirteen

Desperate Measures

"Why standest thou afar off, O Lord? Why hidest
thou thyself in times of trouble?"
~Psalm 10:1

*T*homas stood atop the island mountain, looking far out to sea. If he'd had his father's spyglass, he might be able to see the ship. Elias, Robert and Big Mike had watched with him as the *Warwick II* sailed off into the darkness last night. Today, they'd hoped to catch a glimpse of the ship from the mountain, so they'd started climbing shortly before dawn, and arrived atop it by noon. But there were no ships on the eastern horizon where Captain Abu had sailed away. He suspected that his three companions already knew that Thomas would not see his father's ship, but they had to let him try, regardless.

Bitterly disappointed, Thomas had held his sorrow inside himself. He did not have permission from his father to cry, and until he did, he would continue to swallow his sorrow. But it left an ache inside his chest that was more painful than when they'd been captured the first time.

Of course, the men had tried to convince Thomas that they could mutiny in a variety of ways because deceptive designs had been built into the ship when John bought it. John and his men would find a way, somehow, to retake the *Warwick II* and come back to get them. After they listed all the ways the crew of the *Warwick II* could stage their attack, Thomas felt more confident.

At the top of the mountain, a barren area stood out in prominence. Great rocks, having been washed clean of all smaller particles of earth by the numerous and harsh rainstorms that often rolled over it, stood like sentinels, guarding the island. Within a hundred yards of their pinnacles, however, the jungle encroached upon it, and in time, Thomas suspected that even the rocks would be covered in a lush, green blanket of vines and foliage.

It had taken all morning for the men to reach the mountain top, even though it was less than a thousand feet tall, but the thick vegetation made penetration almost impossible. Elias and Big Mike had to clear a path with machetes while Robert and Thomas laid the trimmings aside in neat stacks for further gathering, before they could pass through the dense jungle to the top.

Discouraged when they arrived and could not see the *Warwick II* any longer, Thomas sat down and pulled his knees up to his chest, then wrapped his arms about them and rested his chin there. "Why did they have to whip him?" he asked Elias. "Father has been more than generous with them."

"Because they're pirates, lad. They don't need no more excuse than that." Elias' gaunt and weathered face had deep creases much like a walnut, and his skin was nearly as dark from a lifetime spent at sea.

"Aye," agreed Big Mike. "They're savages, really. We'd probably have been better off not taking them from their sinking ship, but let the lot of them drown that day."

Thomas turned to face him. "Is that what Jesus would have done?"

Robert, a swarthy man with bald head and long mustache, answered. "No. He would have taken care of them until He could arrange for their safe refuge, just as your father did."

"Thank goodness Father provided for them so well," said Thomas, cheerily. He did not want the men to think of him as an insolent child. "Because he was generous, we will have food to spare."

"Speaking of food," said Robert. "We'd best be planting some of that grain he left, or it will never be ready for harvest. We don't know how long we'll be marooned on this island, but even if we were rescued tomorrow, someone else might appreciate our efforts."

"Right," agreed Elias. "Come along, Thomas."

As Thomas stood up, Big Mike patted his shoulder. "That's a good lad," he said. "Soon as we get down—"

"Wait a minute!" said Thomas as he looked out across the horizon to the north of the island. "What's that?"

Thomas pointed toward a black, flat object at least fifteen miles north of them that floated and bobbed on the surface like a cork.

"Blimey!" exclaimed Elias. "That could be the stern raft we told you about."

"Then they're going to be swept past the island and miss us

altogether," Thomas said. "Maybe they can't see us. Quick, build a fire."

He dashed down the mountain trail to one of the piles of thick brush they had cached en route to the top, and brought as much of the dryer timber as he could carry to the top of the mountain. The three men followed his example. Soon, they had a handsome pile. Since Elias was best at using a flint and stone, he had the fire roaring hot in only a few minutes.

"There's not enough smoke," said Thomas, realizing that all their efforts were going up into the atmosphere as nothing more than hot air.

Racing back partway down the mountain, he pulled wetter branches from the bottom of their cached piles, and cut some short palms, then brought them up to the top and laid these directly over the fire. For a moment, Thomas thought he'd doused it, but soon the spiky leaves started to curl, piling up stacks of smoke as it burned through the damp leaves.

If there was anyway they could help his father realize their position, this was it, so they stayed hard at work on the fire, creating smoke all afternoon, and tall, shooting flames all through the night.

IT HAD BEEN a colder night than John had expected, mostly because of his wet clothes. His men had been equally drenched in the raft's splashdown, and suffered as much as he did. The daytime sun made up for the coldness of the night, which was a blessing and a curse all at one time. They had warmed up from the brisk, long night, but now they were too warm, and getting too much sun, with no sails to shade them. By evening, they would all be burned because they hadn't thought to pack an extra shirt or two, or a swatch of canvas.

Even with the men oaring in shifts, they still seemed to be caught up in the northern current. Calculating the speed they were traveling by counting seconds off whenever he set a sliver of wood adrift, gave him an indication that they should, at the least, be able to see the island by now.

By the time John saw the smoke far off in the distance, he'd already been worrying the raft was drifting off course. "We're too far north," he said, sitting up straight and studying the smoky puff far away on the horizon. "And Thomas is sending us a signal."

The men did not have to be told what to do. They took their positions on the long sides of the raft and began rowing more vigorously. Shoveling water past them, heading toward the smoke. Over and over, relentlessly, without stopping they rowed, trading off oars in rotations every half hour. For hours they couldn't even see the island, but the puff of smoke kept them steadily oaring toward it.

By nightfall, the smoke became a flickering light that seemed to get taller as the night wore on. By dawn, they were so exhausted they could scarcely row another stroke.

Simon rationed out what little water they'd been able to bring in the two flasks, but they worried they would drink it too fast, so each man kept his consumption down to one swallow each. As the sky began to turn pink and rosy, they could see the outline of the island well, but they had still had miles to go, and doubted they would have the strength to continue.

Edward, who had revived earlier that morning, had lived through the night. His shivering and sweating had eased and all that remained was to let him rest and continue to heal.

Realizing they were not going to get out of the northern current without more vigorous rowing, and seeing his men so exhausted they were shaking as they rowed, John looked down into the deep, clear water, worrying how they could manage a more southerly direction. Swimming about two fathoms below them was a school of mantas with wing spans about twelve feet wide.

Suddenly, it dawned upon John. If a man could harness one of these gentle giants, the men's need for strength would be greatly reduced.

"How much line have we got aboard, Red?"

"I dunno, exactly," squeaked the answer. "Ten fathoms, at most."

Looking into the water, Edward protested, "John! You're not thinking what I think you're thinking!"

"It will be a whale of a ride," said John. When Edward gave him a scowl, John added. "I will choose a small one, if it makes you feel any better."

Giving a bewildered sigh, Edward said, "I shall go with you."

"No." This came from Simon. "You're not well enough."

"The salt water will do just as much cleansing as your herbs, Simon. Isn't that what John always says?" insisted Edward.

"But you're just recovering from a stab wound. We do not know how cut up you are inside. To join John in this pursuit is suicide," Simon protested.

"The knife didn't penetrate that deep." Edward grabbed one end of the rope they had aboard. "Besides, I can be just as stubborn as your grandchild's father."

John shook his head. It would do no good to argue with Edward. The man was as pig-headed as his Lordship. "Very well then, we'll tie the line to both sides of the raft, near the bow."

When that task was accomplished, John said, "If we dive at precisely the right moment, we should be able to slip the rope over the shoulders of the manta and across its mouth. Men, as you're pulled, oar more diligently than you have strength for, otherwise . . ."

"Right," said Edward. "Over the shoulders and across the mouth. On your signal."

They stood in diving formation, waiting for the perfect moment when a large manta would swim into position. It did not take long, three or four minutes at the most. Soon a large Manta was directly below them, swimming southward. John yelled, "Dive!" and the two men slipped forward into the water with equal dexterity.

Grabbing onto the beautiful manta was no problem. But putting the rope over her shoulders proved an insurmountable feat. Together, John and Edward coaxed her gently to the surface where they took a big gulp of air and tried once again to get the rope over her shoulders. Failing a second time, John slipped between the rope and the Manta, letting the rope pull tight over his waist, while he hung onto the Manta's shoulder with all his strength.

Edward followed his lead. Soon they were both straining to keep their hands on the manta while forcing her up periodically for a big breath. The rope bit into their waists as they tugged the raft forward, but the current wanted to carry them northward, and was almost too strong for them.

After a while, the manta seemed to adjust to their presence, and follow their lead, coming up for air, then diving about ten feet and swimming forward toward the island, ever forward. They continued this maneuver for about an hour, while the men on the raft continued to row strenuously.

By this time, John noticed that Edward's strength was waning. He was about to order him back to the raft, when all of a sudden, the line went slack, even though the manta was not swimming any less vigorously. The raft was no longer being dragged in the opposite direction by the swift current. Coming up for air, John yelled, "Let her go. She's freed us from the northerly current."

Releasing the giant manta, they watched as she dived deep into the sea, away from them, perhaps very happy to be free again. Edward laughed aloud as they waited for the raft to catch up to them, but in doing so, John noticed that he'd clutched at his belly. Disregarding his pain, Edward gasped, "What a ride!"

"How are you doing?" John asked.

"If a ride like that does not kill me, nothing will," Edward said.

John noticed Edward's wound had started bleeding again when they were pulled aboard the raft by Red, Simon and the other men. John exhaled deeply. They may have saved the other men, but what of Edward?

"Just what did that accomplish?" Simon asked. "Edward's wound is bleeding again!"

Edward gave him a weak grin, his face pale as summer clouds, his body shaking with exhaustion. "Tell him, John, I'm too drained of strength," Edward gasped. And with those words, he rolled over and fell into a deep and peaceful sleep.

Red was laughing so hard he almost fell overboard as Simon pouted and fussed around Edward, swabbing the oozing blood from his stomach.

"Well, what did Edward want you to tell me?" asked Simon.

John smiled as he rolled over on his side and looked up at his son's grandfather. "Only that the manta pulled us out of the north current and now we will not have to do much rowing at all to reach the island."

"But we could have done the same ourselves in a while."

"No," disagreed Red. "The current was whipping us. We were too tired to row our way out of it. If they hadn't taken us on that wild ride, we'd be halfway to Florida by now."

"Hmm," said Simon. "Well, I suppose you're forgiven then."

John just curled into a cozy little ball and fell asleep.

When he awoke, surf was pouring over him. Big Mike and Elias were pulling him up onto the beach. It was already late at night.

"Is he here?" John asked. "Where's Thomas?"

"He's being held down by his grandfather. They were the first to shore," said Big Mike. "But you were still sleeping when the raft hung up on a rock, so they sent us out here to get you."

John was incredibly tired. He couldn't remember a time when he had physically ached for more sleep. Disregarding his lethargy, he asked, "Where is Edward?"

"Red and the others brought him ashore. Looks pretty sick to me," said Elias.

"He was wounded and whipped, but I never doubted that he would recover. Perhaps our ride with the manta today was too much for him," said John.

"Perhaps it was too much for you," said Big Mike.

By now they were walking up the beach, and Simon could apparently restrain Thomas no longer. The young man ran to him, wrapped his arms around his waist and cried, "Father! You're all right?"

"Yes, son. I'm just worn out, that's all," said John. "I will mend."

"I was so worried," said Thomas. "Grandfather told us that Edward will not make it through the night, and when you did not come ashore, I thought—"

"What?" John asked. He looked at Big Mike and Elias quickly. "Edward's not—?"

Simon reached them next, and wrapped John in a warm blanket as he walked wearily up the beach, his son plastered next to his side, not likely to leave him anytime soon.

"Edward's bleeding internally, John. It started while you were sleeping. I tried everything I could to get the bleeding to stop, but he's nearly gone."

John hurried over to Edward, who was stretched out upon the sand, cradled in a warm blanket by a fire. He sank to his knees beside him, took Edward's hand and rubbed the back of it for a moment. It was ice cold.

Edward's face was blue, and he struggled for every breath. He looked completely drained from apoplexy. "Thank you, John," whispered Edward.

"Edward, you shouldn't have gone in with me."

"You couldn't have done it alone, and the current would have carried us away from Thomas. I couldn't—" He coughed and blood gurgled up into his mouth and ran down the side of his chin. "I couldn't let that happen." Then, Edward released a long breath of air, and never took another one.

Tears flooded John's eyes as he realized his friend was gone. Just when Edward had stopped being his enemy and become his friend, John did not know. But this he did know: Edward's heroic act of bravery would not be forgotten. Without Edward's assistance, John knew he couldn't have wrestled that manta by himself. Even with Edward's help, it had taken every ounce of strength that John had. And now, Edward had crossed the veil, leaving seven men alive because of his heroism.

The rest of the night was a blur. Thomas snuggled up to him all night long. Men kept the fire going, some rested, some did not. Simon made tea and insisted John drink it several times.

When morning came, John felt so bereft over Edward's death he did not know how he could face himself in the looking glass, should he ever be so fortunate as to see himself there again.

He grieved not only for himself, but for Lord Blackwell, Edward's father. John knew the agony of losing your son, and it was almost impossible to bear. His Lordship would find comfort in knowing that Edward laid his life down so that John and Thomas could be together, so that seven other men would not be swept around the Great Circle of the Atlantic while suffering a horrendous death from starvation.

Such an act of heroism would surely soften God's heart toward Edward. An old scripture came into his mind and John remembered it with unquenchable hope.

> *"Greater love hath no man than this, that a man*
> *lay down his life for his friends."*
> ~John 15:13

It was the same scripture which John quoted the next morning when a grave-side service was held for Edward Blackwell III. When he was finished, each of the men, in turn, spoke a few words about Edward.

Last of all, Thomas stepped forward and put a handful of island blossoms upon the mound. "What I wanted to say about Edward was this: I didn't much like him to start with because he hurt Rebecca and her father. But I got to thinking about Joseph with the coat of many colors. His brothers sold him into slavery, and then they felt real bad about it, but they couldn't get him back. But if they hadn't sold him, he wouldn't have gotten close to Pharaoh, and saved the world, including those brothers that sold him, when the famine came. Edward was kind of like that. If he hadn't done what he did, I wouldn't have a mother or a sister. Since Joseph forgave his brothers, I decided I had to forgive Edward. That's what I did. Only problem was, when he died, then I couldn't be happy about it, because now he's my friend. And when a friend dies, it just feels awful inside. That's all I've got to say."

Thomas stepped back in line and wiped the tears from his eyes.

Simon was the concluding speaker because he could quote scriptures like no other man of the age. But all he could say after Thomas got through was, "Take him home, God, and forgive him like we have. He deserves a hero's welcome on the other side. In Jesus' name, Amen."

REBECCA LET SEVERAL weeks go by with Jane's words, *Papa. Thomas. Not come home. Must go get them*, echoing around in her mind. When she could stand it no longer, she knew she must speak with someone, but whom?

The twins spoke of God freely in their home. They read the Bible, and they attended Sunday meetings together at the Stepney Parish. Most of the time, Rebecca went with them. John had asked her not to mention her experience to anyone, and she knew that included their aunts.

Now that Jane had an even more astounding experience, was Rebecca also to retain that information in silence? She just couldn't, but to whom could she turn this time?

Praying diligently for answers both night and day, Rebecca did not know what to do. She couldn't sleep or eat, and she knew she would have to do something soon or have a complete nervous breakdown.

Asking Jane's advice was no good either. The dear child had completely forgotten their conversation. Whenever Rebecca brought it up, it was apparent by her expression that Jane did not know what her mother was talking about.

After several weeks of mental torment, Rebecca made the decision to go visit Lord Blackwell. He had always treated her as his own daughter, and he was more than generous in providing John with the means to find their son. Perhaps, he would understand her feelings, especially since he was a parent himself.

Rebecca sent his Lordship a letter first, by way of courier, and waited for his reply, which came by carriage and her special friend, Wilson. When she opened her front door the following week and found Wilson standing there, she gave him a fond embrace.

"Wilson, how good of you to come for me."

"How did you know, Mistress, that I had come for you?" he asked.

"Well, you came in the carriage, didn't you?"

"Yes, Mistress, but I always come in the carriage."

"Not the one with the trunk storage off the back," she said, teasing him.

"Nothing escapes your notice, does it, my lady? I assume you'll be bringing young Jane with you."

"Yes. She's still rather fond of her mother," said Rebecca. "And I wouldn't think of depriving his Lordship of visiting with her."

It only took a few minutes to pack a trunk and have Wilson carry it to the carriage. The moment he did, Rebecca's aunts were like bulldogs, barking at the side door.

Bursting inside without knocking, Naomi spoke first. "Where are you going?" she asked. Naomi had a rounded body style, and a cherub face with dimples and kind blue eyes. In her white-streaked hair, she wore a snug little bun.

"Yes, dear," added Ruth. "We saw Wilson come for you in his

Lordship's carriage. Has anything happened?" Ruth was thinner than her twin, with dimples and deep, green eyes. She wore her completely silver hair in a braided knot.

"Lord Blackwell has invited me to come visit for a few days," said Rebecca. She dared not tell them she had hinted that he do so in the letter she sent to him a week ago. It was probably too bold for women of her culture, but Rebecca was not known for her reticence. The fact that she had kept this secret from the twins weighed heavily upon her conscience.

"Oh," said Naomi. "And you're going just like that?" She sniffed.

Rebecca gave them both a hug. "I would have come to say goodbye before we left. And, we'll only be gone a few days."

"It's just that we've had you next door for so long, it feels terrible having to say goodbye at all," said Ruth, blowing her nose on her handkerchief.

Smiling brightly, Rebecca said, "Will you wake up Jane, and put her in a clean diaper and dress for me? Then, we shall say goodbye properly."

By the time she got away from the twins and was playing finger games in the carriage with Jane, Rebecca heaved a great sigh of relief.

The words, *Papa. Thomas. Not come home. Must go get them* still tortured Rebecca's mind. They drowned out the sound of the wheels on the dirt road and the horse's galloping hooves.

From the moment Jane had shared this experience with her, Rebecca was gripped with a burning desire to share the burden with someone. Surely, his Lordship had experience in such matters beyond her own.

After all, he had crossed the oceans many times, and if ever a man needed communication from God, it was during those times when he was most vulnerable.

With all her heart, Rebecca prayed his Lordship would understand, and advise her as to her best course of action.

Chapter Fourteen

The Work of Angels

*"For he shall give his angels charge over thee,
to keep thee in all thy ways."*
~Psalms 91:11

*A*rriving late in the night, Rebecca retired with Jane to one of the guest bedrooms, preferring not to disturb his Lordship until morning. Sleep came no easier for her at Blackwell Tower than it did at *John's Cottage*, and Rebecca was grateful when the morning sunrise began to spread warm ribbons of light throughout the stately old mansion.

Blackwell Tower in late September was a beautiful place to spend the fall season. The leaves on the trees ranged in colors from fiery red, deepest orange and pink-tinged yellows. The pumpkins in the gardens sprawled out across the lawns, their squat, orange globes would be made into pies, cakes and breads before winter passed. The ground, crisped with a thin layer of frost, lay sleeping, awaiting the sounds of songbirds who'd already departed for warmer climates.

After an early breakfast in the kitchen with Wilson and his sister,

Wilhelmina, Rebecca started to clean up after Jane, who'd had a fun morning smearing porridge all over the table, chair, and her arms, hands and face.

"Rebecca, let me do it," Wilhelmina encouraged. "It's been a long time since we had a baby around."

"Oh, but she's such a mess," Rebecca moaned. "I couldn't ask you to—"

"I believe his Lordship is already waiting for you in the drawing room," said Wilson. "We promise not to spoil Jane too much." He gave her a wink and a smile.

Rebecca returned his smile. Two dearer friends she'd never known than Wilson and Wilhelmina. "All right," she agreed, "but if she gets fussy, bring her to me."

"I will give her a bath and put a clean dress on her first," said Wilhelmina. "I do think it would have been better to have left Jane in her nightclothes for breakfast. We had to wash them, anyway."

Laughing, Rebecca said, "How right you are." Giving Jane a kiss on the top of her head, the only place there wasn't a smear of porridge, she said, "I shall see you in a little while, Jane. Be kind to Wilhelmina and Wilson, will you?"

"W'mina nice," cooed Jane, reaching out a grubby little hand to Wilhelmina.

Knowing the Wilsons had the situation well under control, Rebecca left them and went into the drawing room where thousands of books lined one wall, and alcove windows framed another. In the center of the spacious room stood a round maple table with two comfortable reading chairs. Rebecca had expected to find Lord

Blackwell sitting in one of them, reading the Bible, as was his custom each morning. But no, he was standing by the window, looking out onto the fall morning, his hands clasped behind his back.

Dressed in a handsome velvet doublet, navy blue with silver buttons, he also wore cream-colored breeches and tights, and knee-high, black top boots. For a man old enough to be her father, Lord Blackwell had aged well, and she suspected he had many years of useful service left in him.

"Good morning, your Lordship," Rebecca said as he turned to notice her entrance. Giving a small curtsy, she entered the drawing room and crossed over to Lord Blackwell, where she took his open hands in hers and kissed him tenderly on his cheek.

"Rebecca!" he exclaimed. "You get more beautiful, every day."

"Thank you, sire."

"I trust you brought Jane with you?"

"Of course," she smiled. "I knew you would never forgive me if I left her home."

"Come, sit down," he said, leading her to one of the comfortable arm chairs.

"Thank you." Rebecca sat upon the chair nearest the window. This would give her the greater advantage, since the early morning sun would be more upon his Lordship's countenance than hers, giving her an opportunity to assess his expressions as they discussed that which was most dear to her heart.

"Your letter has piqued my curiosity, Rebecca. Have you heard from John, yet?" Lord Blackwell asked.

"No, sire. I was hoping perhaps you had."

He shook his head as he sat in the chair opposite her. "I am getting worried. It's nearly October, and no one has heard anything regarding them since they left in May. That's five months, more than enough time to find Thomas, sail the Great Circle and arrive home with the fleet that came in last week."

"The Great Circle?" she asked.

"John and Edward both thought it best to sail the circle," he explained. "It's the way the currents and winds travel around the northern hemisphere in the Atlantic. West to east in the north, east to west in the south, north to south in the east, south to north in the west."

Rebecca gave him a curious expression. The truth was, she hadn't any idea what he was talking about.

"Let me show you." Patiently, Lord Blackwell pulled his chair near hers, pulled a piece of parchment from a drawer beneath the table and smoothed it out upon the table in front of her. He then drew a hasty map upon it. "Here's England, France, Spain, Portugal. The Strait of Gibralter, and below it, Morocco. Farther still is the equator. On the west side of the Atlantic, we have the Americas, North and South, and the islands. The Great Circle is the area the winds and currents make going in a clockwise direction around the Atlantic Ocean."

"So, you're saying that John planned to sail around this circle to get home, rather than sail up the coast of Portugal, Spain and France?" she questioned, tracing the circle route with her finger.

"Yes."

"Why, your Lordship? This other route is less than one-fourth the distance." She indicated the northerly course directly past Portugal, Spain and France.

"Because going back, it would be tediously slow. Our ships do not sail well up-wind nor up-current. Any pirate coming down the coast, would find them going up and they would likely be unable to escape being captured."

"Wasn't that risk just as great going south, with the current and the wind?"

"Yes, and I expect they would have been captured except for three factors. John and Edward had a numerous assortment of camouflage aboard, which would have aided them in slipping right past most any sailor's nose. They would have also hoisted a pirate's flag the moment they left sight of England. What pirate will attack another pirate? Eh?" Lord Blackwell raised an eyebrow and leaned his head toward her.

"And the third factor?" Rebecca asked.

"John had reconfigured the sails like those the pirates used, which makes the ship sail almost as fast as the wind that blows it."

"John told me about the camouflage. And I knew the sails were reconfigured, but I did not realize this changed the speed of the ship."

"My, yes. The *Warwick II* sailed wickedly fast. Going south down the European coastline, I doubt anyone could have caught them while they had the wind chasing them. But sailing north against the wind and the current would put them at a disadvantage. Neither John nor Edward would risk it."

"Suppose they have found Thomas, rescued him, and are sailing this Great Circle," she said. "When is the earliest we can expect them back?"

"I was hoping with the fleet that came in last week," he admitted. "Seven ships arrived, but not John's. That means they'll have to winter in Virginia, then head north to the Massachusetts Bay Colony come Spring, and sail with the next fleet coming east."

Rebecca moaned silently in her heart at this news. "And if something went wrong?"

"Everything could have gone wrong, my dear. Surely, John told you that much." He gave her hand a patronizing pat.

"He did," she agreed, "but I have been praying for a miracle, I suppose."

"With your faith, you'll surely get one," he encouraged with a smile. Apparently waiting for her response, Lord Blackwell returned to his chair.

Rebecca hesitated. Should she take the conversation one step nearer the heart of her worries? How would Lord Blackwell react to such a personal, inspirational message as she had received from Jeremiah Webster, himself, and through her own daughter, Jane? Would he think her insane and have her committed? If so, what would become of Jane? Dare she risk everything to tell his Lordship what was really on her mind? Could she word her thoughts in such a way that he would not doubt her sincerity?

Finally gathering courage, Rebecca said, "I can only pray that God will show us what to do to help our men, should they happen to need it."

"Yes, that would be a trick." He smiled kindly. "If only God would send an angel to speak with us about our loved ones, to tell us whether they are safe or in dire straits."

"Do you believe in angels?" Rebecca questioned, praying he would not misconstrue what she had asked.

He laughed. "Well, the Bible is filled with them, isn't it? To say that I did not believe in angels would be like saying I did not believe in the Bible."

Rebecca smiled in relief. "I firmly do believe in them, your Lordship."

"I never doubted that for a moment," he affirmed.

"If an angel were to appear to you, sire, what do you suppose he would look like?"

Lord Blackwell's mouth dropped open slightly, and an almost inaudible gasp escaped his lips. "Why—" He stopped himself.

"What were you going to ask?" Rebecca wondered.

He shook his head. "It was nothing, I suppose."

Rebecca heard the uncertainty in his voice, and decided she had better address the issue straight on., "I've given the matter a great deal of thought lately, your Lordship," she began. "Who would God send to me, if he were to send an angel to me? Would it be some beautiful woman with angel wings and perfect face and features? Or, would it be a strikingly handsome man dressed all in white to match those wings of his?"

Lord Blackwell smiled faintly. "I – I have no idea," he stammered.

That's when she knew he was lying. He had a very good idea what an angel may look like, but he was unwilling to share it with her. How could she persuade him to give it up? "Your Lordship, if a winged anything appeared in my home it would scare me half out of my skin. If God is a kind and wise God, as we both believe, wouldn't it make sense to send someone to us whom we already know? Someone who could never frighten us. Someone familiar, for whom we already have tender feelings."

Lord Blackwell fidgeted with the ruffles of his shirt poking outside his doublet, scratched his forehead, but did not look straight into her eyes.

Leaning forward, so that he had no choice but to look directly at her, she said, "You've seen an angel, haven't you, sire? I see it in your eyes. Why will you not share your experience with me? I would keep it confidential, even from John."

Lord Blackwell turned away, pushed his chair back and stood up, then walked over to the window and stared out into the courtyard.

Following him, Rebecca placed her hand upon his elbow. "Forgive me, sire. I did not intend to upset you."

He cleared his throat and turned to look down at her, as though he wanted to study her expression when he confessed. "You've not offended me, dear Rebecca," he said, his voice cracking. "It is only that I know your idea of an angel visitation is correct, for one appeared to me last week in a dream."

"That's nothing from which to be upset," she comforted. "Who was your guardian angel?"

"It was Edward," he admitted, his face pale and drawn as he said it.

Rebecca's eyes widened and her mouth dropped open. Stubbornly, she said, "I have long believed that when God sends His messengers, they are really our family, those who love us and are most concerned for our welfare."

"I believe the same, " he responded. "But if it was Edward who visited me in my dreams last night, if my son has become God's messenger, it can mean only one thing."

Rebecca's mind whirled round and round, pondering what his Lordship was getting at, but she couldn't believe it.

Lord Blackwell nodded and gave a grim expression, "Dear child, it means that Edward has died. He could not be an angel, otherwise."

"But you said that he visited you in your dream," she argued, unwilling to consider such a thing. "Perhaps, dreams of angels are different than visitations while we are fully awake. God may give dreams to us in the form we would be most likely to accept. It does not, necessarily, mean that the person in our dream is dead."

"It does when the person in our dreams gives us something tangible," he admitted. "Something important. And, when we awaken, we find the very thing he gave us . . . in our hand." Lord Blackwell took a scroll from his doublet, and gave it to her.

Rebecca unrolled the parchment and stared at the nautical map in her hands. It was a sailing chart of the Great Circle, similar to the one his Lordship had just drawn for her. Where the Spanish Colonies were listed on several islands in the lower left hand corner, on the eastern realm of the Caribbean Sea, a red "X" was drawn upon a remote island.

Rebecca staggered backward. She would have fainted had his

Lordship not helped her to a chair and called for Wilson to bring a glass of water for her, which he did.

Sipping slowly, Rebecca tried to calm herself. Astounded at what had happened to his Lordship, and the evidence which she held in the palm of her own hand, she trembled and took great gulps of air.

When Wilson was apparently satisfied that Rebecca would be all right, he left them alone. It was only then that Lord Blackwell spoke, "Forgive me, Rebecca, I did not mean to alarm you."

Trembling, Rebecca took from the pocket of her dress, a piece of paper upon which she had written,

> *And being warned of God in a dream that they*
> *should not return to Herod, they departed toward*
> *their own country another way.*
> ~St. Matthew 2:12

She gave the paper to his Lordship. "After a particularly bad dream, I turned to the Bible, and this is the verse that jumped out at me," she explained.

After Lord Blackwell read it, he nodded. "We have been presented with clear evidence that Edward and John have found Thomas and are sailing now in the Caribbean Sea, or perhaps, they are marooned there."

Tears slipped down Rebecca's cheeks, but she could not contain them. "Jane had a visitation, as well," she admitted. "A few weeks ago she said that my father told her Thomas and John would not come home, that we had to go find them."

"What?" he questioned, going down on one knee to face her more directly. "Jeremiah Webster appeared to Jane?"

222

"Yes. But she does not even remember it now, as I've asked her several times since then."

"How do you know it was your father?"

"She described him as her Grandpa with the curly hair, then she swirled her finger in her own curls just like my father, Jeremiah, used to do," she confessed. "Of course, her grandpa, Simon, has very little hair, so it couldn't have been him that she saw. I have worried about her experience ever since our conversation. I know that sometimes children are closer to God than we adults, and that is what scares me most, your Lordship. I have hardly slept or eaten since then."

"Do you suppose she might remember if I spoke with her about it?" he asked.

"You may certainly try, though I doubt you'll be successful," Rebecca answered. "She has never spoken of her grandfather since that day."

His Lordship stood, and called for Wilson once again. When he arrived, Lord Blackwell said, "Ask Wilhelmina to bring Jane in for a visit, will you?"

"She's just dressing her after her bath." Wilson said.

"If she has to bring her in a towel, Wilson, I must speak with her, at once."

"Yes, sire, Straight away." Wilson turned and hurried from the room.

While waiting for Jane to arrive, Lord Blackwell turned back to Rebecca. "I assume you agree with me, that Edward must have passed on."

Rebecca studied his sad, almost desperate expression, but she could offer him false hope no longer. Lowering her eyes to her lap, Rebecca nodded. "I'm so sorry, your Lordship, but I cannot imagine that Edward could have brought you a map without having permission from God. The only way he could have received that authority, in my estimation, is to have spent some time in God's presence, pleading his case with Him."

When she lifted her head, Lord Blackwell was back near the window again, looking out of it. Rebecca stood and walked over to him, placed her arms around his waist and held him close to her, comforting him like she had done her father when her mother had passed away. "We cannot understand all of God's ways," she consoled, "for there are many mysteries, but I do believe that we are not alone on the earth. Whether they have great and mighty wings, or whether they are still much like the simple people who lived here once before and now watch over us, angels may very well be our own family members. If Edward has taken his journey back to God, it only means that you cannot see him every moment, but I assure you, sire, he is not far from you."

Feeling his Lordship tremble, then sob against her, Rebecca rubbed his back until he was able to compose himself. Afterward, she stepped back and turned him to face the drawing room door.

Jane stood in the frame looking like a little angel, herself. She was dressed in a white silk and taffeta gown that almost touched the floor, with green velvet ribbons, and lots of ruffles and lace. Her curly blonde hair was still wet, but it had a lovely bow in it. As Jane stepped forward, Rebecca noticed that her feet were still bare. Apparently, Wilhelmina hadn't quite finished getting her dressed, though warm as Lord Blackwell kept the mansion, this was not a reason for concern. Besides, Jane's pink little toes sticking out as she walked made her sweet daughter seem even more angelic.

"Good morning, Jane," said his Lordship. "My, aren't you growing big?"

"Gwampa!" Jane squealed with delight, and ran quickly over to Lord Blackwell, where he scooped her up into his arms and hugged her. The dear child knew only three men with silver in their hair, so it seemed reasonable she would call his Lordship by the name, Grandpa.

"He's not—" Rebecca began to correct her.

"It's all right," his Lordship interrupted her. "She may call me by any name she chooses. In Simon's absence, I'm probably a welcome substitute."

He carried Jane over to his chair where he sat down and held her on his lap, laughing at her cute antics as she patted his face and straightened his collar. Rebecca joined them, sitting in the chair beside him.

"Well, what have you got to say for yourself, today, young lady?" Lord Blackwell asked Jane.

Jane looked seriously into his eyes. "Gwampa sad," she observed.

Indeed, his Lordship's eyes were red from crying, and his face was pale and drawn, though he tried to put on a happy smile for Jane.

"Grandpa missed you so much!" he exclaimed, snuggling her to his chest for a moment.

As soon as he released her, Jane took the time to show her

'grandfather' her toes, feet, knees, elbows, hands, fingers, eyes, and hair, enunciating each body part with an exacting memory as she did so. They made a game of it, and soon she was patting his Lordship's hair, saying, "Hair," to demonstrate her new skill.

"And do you know ship?" his Lordship asked, pointing to a small model of a bark upon the center of the table.

"Papa's ship," she said quickly, almost as if she recognized it as the *Warwick II*. "Papa lost. Thomas lost."

"What did you say?" he asked, apparently as perplexed as Rebecca at her daughter's comment.

"Edward sad," added Jane quickly, as though this was an ordinary, every day observation.

"Why is Edward sad?" his Lordship asked.

Jane stood up on his lap and held his face close to hers, her chubby little hands on both his cheeks. "Must find Papa," she begged. "Must find Thomas. Use map, Gwampa." Jane wrapped her tiny arms about his Lordship's neck and snuggled close against him. "Pwease, Gwampa," she pleaded in a tone that nearly broke her mother's heart.

Rebecca reached out and stroked Jane's curls. To her secret delight, she heard his Lordship whisper, "I will, Jane. I will find Thomas and Papa for you."

Now the tears slipped from her own eyes, and Rebecca could contain her joy no longer. "Thank you, sire. We shall be forever grateful for this act of kindness."

"Nonsense," he said, setting Jane down upon his knee again, and giving her the scroll to hold for a moment, apparently wanting to distract her. "I have another ship that was recently finished, Rebecca. Without your permission, I took the liberty of naming it the *Jeremiah Webster*. I hope you'll forgive me."

Gasping in surprise, Rebecca stammered, "Wh-Why, of course, sire. You may name your ships anything you choose. But I thank you for remembering my father in this manner."

"He's a stout and sturdy warship," Lord Blackwell added. "One-hundred twenty-eight feet in length, forty feet across the beam, and four-hundred tons burthen. Forty-five cannons to each side, capable of withstanding most pirate attacks all on his own. Oh, he's a fine ship, Rebecca. A handsome brute."

"I shall be greatly interested to see the *Jeremiah Webster*, your Lordship," she said, thrilled to see how proud he was of it.

"He shall be ready to sail by week's end," he confided. "I have a full crew, plenty of provisions, and loyal officers. However, this is not a job I will leave to my men alone. No, if my son has asked me to sail the circle and find your husband and son, I will do it in person. It's been a few years since I've sailed, having left that work to my hired seamen. But this is one mission I will not turn down."

"I'm going with you," Rebecca said quickly, while his mind was still on other things, hoping he hadn't really noticed and would agree before he'd had time to consider.

"Of course you will," he agreed, surprising her with a big smile. "There are two spare cabins across from the Captain's quarters. I will have these outfitted for you and your family. You will be bringing Simon's sisters, I presume."

"Your Lordship, I never dreamed you would take women with you."

"Why not?" he asked. "The *Jeremiah Webster* is a formidable ship, one that a pirate will think twice about before attacking. I am bringing a crew of two hundred able sailors. I dare say no pirate vessel travels the seas with a fourth that many men."

"Thank you, your Lordship. I shall leave at once and bring my aunts back with me by week's end." She stepped forward and kissed his cheek. "While we are voyaging, you will teach me all that you know about sailing. John shall be surprised to discover that his wife has learned well in his absence."

Lord Blackwell laughed aloud. "My son is gone to me, yet my daughter still fills my soul with laughter. Bless you, Rebecca, for making me feel a part of your family. You are all that I have left now."

"If you desire to consider me your daughter, *Father* Blackwell, I shall accept it willingly. A woman cannot have too many fathers in her life." She patted his cheek, kissed Jane quickly, then rushed upstairs to pack.

Rebecca had so much to do to prepare for this voyage. She would have to hire someone to watch over the houses and the animals in her absence. And, she would have to bring as many of her foodstuffs as possible. Of course, his Lordship might object, but Rebecca would pay her way on this voyage, one way or another. If he would not accept her winter's food storage, he would accept her hard labor. Surely, there was some usefulness a woman could serve aboard a warship.

By the time she had Wilson take her belongings to the carriage and had gathered her daughter, shoes upon her feet this time, his Lordship had one of his workers bring around a stout wagon to follow them.

A young man and his wife were standing by the carriage, waiting for her to arrive. Lord Blackwell introduced them. "Rebecca, this is Roger Henson, and his good wife, Virginia."

"Pleased to meet you," said Rebecca, shaking their hands and receiving a similar greeting from them.

His Lordship continued, "I have taken the liberty of assigning them the care and keeping of *John's Cottage* and the Harris' home in your absence. Henson is one of the Englishmen rescued by the Salé fleet last year. In appreciation for your husband's diligence in finding young Henson, and returning him to his wife, they have agreed to take care of your property without compensation. It will serve a dual purpose, giving them a place to stay while he finishes his apprenticeship with the ropery master here at Chatham, and repaying John's efforts with the Salé Fleet. You will find the Hensons are completely trustworthy, and entirely capable of caring for your property."

"It will, of necessity, mean that I will be taking care during the week," Virginia Henson qualified. "But I assure you, mistress, I was raised on a dairy farm over in Gillingham. I can handle all kinds of animals."

"I'm sure you'll do well," said Rebecca. "Thank you for your kindness."

"'Tis no kindness, Mistress," said Roger Henson. "I owe your husband my life. It was with great shame that I did not sail with him when he left Chatham last May, but I arrived a day late and he had already sailed. Perhaps, this will help me repay him a bit for his goodness."

"Thank you," said Rebecca. "What you are now doing for John will more than repay any debt for which you feel obligated."

Within minutes, Rebecca and her daughter were packed and in the carriage, heading back toward Stepney Parish. She hadn't told his Lordship about her father's visit to her, wherein he told her to trust those whom she was disinclined to trust. It was not the time, today, to do so. She vowed to save that memory in her heart, until such time that Lord Blackwell might need the telling of it for encouragement. A warm feeling spread through her unlike any she'd ever known, and she was pleased with Edward's willingness to continue his rescue of Thomas, perhaps from beyond the grave. Looking heavenward, Rebecca whispered, "Thank you, Edward. I shall never forget this kindness . . . and I . . . I forgive you for everything."

Rebecca would not turn back now. God was giving messages to her family through the son of one of her dearest friends. Somehow, God would help them find John and Thomas.

She fully believed that her husband and son were together now. Otherwise, why would Edward give his Lordship the map? And, why would Jane have said that John and Thomas could be found by using Edward's map?

Surely, these amazing messages from beyond the grave to Lord Blackwell, and through the heart of a little child, meant that John had rescued their son from captivity, but now, they were stranded, or in some other kind of trouble on an island in the Caribbean Sea.

Chapter Fifteen

Survival

*". . . Man shall not live by bread alone, but by every word
that proceedeth out of the mouth of God."*
~Matt. 4:4

"How long will it take the pirates to sail the *Warwick II* back to Algeria?" wondered Simon as they ate a meal of coconut, bananas and roasted crab, one night in September. Young Thomas sat beside him, and the other men sat around the fire, eating their share.

"They have thirty-five hundred nautical miles to reach the Strait of Gibralter, going against the wind and the current," said John calculating in his head. "Seventy days minimum. Ninety if the wind is strong against them."

"If the wind's as nasty as it was when we came through," squawked Red, "they'll be back on our shores before you know it."

"We'll have to make some plans," John suggested. "If the pirates return, we'll be outnumbered. We only have eight men."

"Eleven," said Thomas. "I'm a man, too! And so are Scotty and George."

John nodded. "And eighteen of them. Those are not bad odds. I could take out two of them, as could any of us here."

Thomas folded his legs under him. "I can kill at least one of them, if I have to. I've seen it done many times."

"With the right weapon and the element of surprise," John agreed, "I believe you could." He tousled Thomas' hair, then returned to the conversation. "There are other concerns as well. We will need shelter from the storms that come through, and a load of wood for a signal fire, stacked at the ready atop the mountain, with a clear trail going up to it. A man will have to be stationed up there throughout the day and night, just as though it was the crow's nest. If the *Warwick II* returns, we must be notified and ready to defend ourselves. If a Spanish galleon passes, or an English ship, we must be prepared to light a signal fire."

As the men listened intently, John continued, "We must prepare for the long haul. We could be marooned here for months."

"Years," Elias pointed out quickly. "Remember those three men we found off that island near the Florida colonies, John? They'd been there five years, and were half mad by then."

"Yes, it could be years," agreed John. "But we'll not be driven mad. We have water, tools, seeds. We will plant our seeds and grow whatever we can. Industry will be our motto, for it is the idleness of limb and mind that drives a man insane."

"It is also the lack of spiritual guidance," commented Simon quietly.

"Then, you shall be our spiritual advisor, Simon," John responded.

"How can I do that when I have no scriptures?" the older man asked.

"Simon, there are enough scriptures in your head to teach a lesson a day for ten years." He gave him an encouraging smile. "Not that we'll need a lesson a day, mind you."

"No," Simon agreed. "But we should at least say prayers over our meals, and a morning prayer to break the day."

"How about one at night, to end the day?" asked Thomas.

Red moaned squeakily, "I've got nothing against prayer, mind you. But I'd rather keep 'em between me and the Creator what made me."

John could see there would be heads rolling before long if he did not intervene. "Simon, we shall have Church services with public prayers on Sundays, and private prayers in our hearts continually. No one will be required to attend services. It will be their choice. You've said yourself, many times, that God will force no man to Heaven."

"B–But—" sputtered Simon.

John interrupted him. "God expects us to address him secretly. Wasn't it Matthew who wrote that God, who seeth in secret, will reward us openly?"

Simon clamped his mouth shut, making it apparent to everyone that he knew the subject was not negotiable.

"I'll attend your Sunday Services," said Red, his voice squeaking with sincerity.

"Hear! Hear!" said the others.

233

With that matter resolved, John said, "We'd best turn in. We've a long day ahead of us tomorrow."

That proved to be an understatement. The following day, they worked from the crack of dawn to the last rays of sunset, clearing the trail to the top of the mountain, which they named Zenith, after having determined that a readily-combustible pyre would be their first priority. Rotating in shifts, in teams of three, they switched every four hours, three times a day. One team was to clear the trail, the next team was to cut timber and bamboo for their housing, and the third team was to prepare and plant a field of wheat, and a paddy of rice. These rotations gave each man the chance to do something a little different three times each day, with exception of Elias, who remained in charge of the cooking, and George, who was still recovering. Thomas stayed by his father's side. On Sundays, the men put down their tools and attended Simon's Sunday School, as they came to call it. Afterwards, they rested or played games with Thomas, or went swimming.

Thomas became an excellent instructor, and the rest of the men learned to swim, knowing they may have to swim out to a ship someday, and would need such a skill. Besides, they did not want young Thomas outshining them. It was a pleasant time whenever they were with Thomas, or Scotland or George. The men felt protective and paternal toward the three lads, though they expected them to work as hard as they could.

John was surprised at Thomas' and Scotland's agility and stamina. Indeed, they often outworked the older men, with energy to spare, and they never complained. By the end of their first two weeks, George was feeling better and was given light duty, making baskets,

dinnerware and cutlery from palm wood and fronds.

It took nearly a month to put the island in order, with a clear trail to the top of Zenith, two separate houses made with bamboo, palm trunks and palm leaves for roofing and flooring. In one of the houses, they slept ten at a time, cozily. In the second house, they cooked their meals, stocked their stores, socialized in inclement weather, and held Sunday Services.

Bowls and cups were made from crab and coconut shells. Plates were made from young palm trunk slices that were sanded smooth over the coral and rocks. Wooden spoons and stabbing forks were whittled. Crab traps were made from bamboo and cord, sunhats from palm fronds.

John and his men did not lack food, and ate an abundance of bananas, papaya and mango, manta wings, crabs, turtles, turtle eggs, fish of several varieties, rice, split pea soup, and once in a while, they shared a wild boar.

Elias made various types of porridge . . . wheat with rice, and rice with wheat. Occasionally, not often, he'd grind up enough wheat, using two large stones on top of each other, to make a tasty batch of fried flat bread.

The crew was thankful, now, that John had been so kind to the pirates, for they had two pans with which to cook, a shovel with which to keep the latrine downwind and frequently covered, a saw and an axe with which to cut down timber for lumber and firewood. The men had hammers and nails, machetes, knives and pistols, fishhooks and several sizes of line and rope which they had brought aboard the raft, and which came in handy on more than one occasion.

One day in late September, when their island paradise was fairly well completed, they decided to follow the stream up the mountainside and see where it originated. To their amazement, they found a small waterfall shooting straight out of a rock out-cropping, and a deep pool of water below it, perfect for bathing and fresh-water swimming. They soon made an unencumbered trail to this area, and made use of the fresh water on a daily basis.

By the end of October, many of the men considered the entire island their own personal paradise and wondered among themselves, should a ship happen by, if they would still want to leave.

John did not share their sentiment. He longed keenly for his wife and daughter. Hope still lingered in his heart that he could introduce young Thomas to Jane. They were both missing out on Jane's toddler years, a time they could never recapture. Besides, John's physical and emotional aching for his wife could not be assuaged by all the paradisaical locations in the world. Right now, he would settle for nothing less than reuniting his family, and rekindling his love with Rebecca.

🌴 🌴 🌴 🌴 🌴

WHEN REBECCA FIRST saw the *Jeremiah Webster* she could hardly believe her eyes. It was more than twice as long as the *Warwick II* and almost twice as tall. It had four masts with three large square sails apiece, and several triangular sails forward and aft. The bowsprit was nearly ten feet long, making the ship seem longer than its one-hundred and twenty feet. She noticed that his Lordship addressed the ship as male, and decided she would have to do so at once. The *Warwick II* had always had a feminine gender, but she assumed because this ship was named after her father, Jeremiah Webster,

nothing less than male would be suitable.

Built as a warship, it had forty-five great guns to each side, twenty-five on the lower level and twenty on the next deck up, both port and starboard. The forecastle was more than twice the size of the *Warwick II's*, as was the aftercastle. Inside the aftercastle, was a hall that separated starboard rooms from port. The larger port side held the Captain's quarters, including a massive planning/dining table, a huge, four-poster bed with fine, velvet curtains in a rich, burgundy color, a desk and chart bins, as well as a wardrobe and chest, and a complete locker filled with the finest weapons of the age, including swords, daggers, and pistols.

Two cabins to starboard would be Rebecca's and her aunts' quarters. These were similar to the *Warwick's* she noticed, only much more elegantly appointed. A child's bed sat on one side of the room, while a larger four-poster awaited her on the other side. A large wardrobe with mirror and dressing stand separated the two beds, and would be more than adequate for storing the clothing Rebecca had brought along. Rebecca's room was the last door on the left. Her aunts' cabin, forward of hers, held two comfortable twin beds with adequate dressers and wardrobe.

Getting her aunts to agree to this voyage had not been difficult. The moment she told them she was going with Lord Blackwell in search of Thomas and John, even before she told them the circumstances that led to his decision to make the voyage, they both chimed in, "We're going with you." It was settled before Rebecca could even discuss the matter. Now, they were unpacking their trunks in their aftercastle cabins.

Meanwhile, Wilhelmina was unpacking Rebecca's and Jane's

belongings. To her surprise, Lord Blackwell insisted upon the Wilsons joining them on this voyage, to look after the female passengers. Rebecca, Jane, Naomi and Ruth were their sole concern, he'd told them, and they were eager to share their services.

Rebecca had brought everything she could possibly think she would need aboard the vessel, much of it stored in trunks in the hold of the ship. A few hundred pounds from Rebecca's stores would not even make a dent in the space available.

By the fifth of October, they were headed out of Chatham Bay, and south toward the English Channel. It seemed to Rebecca that the *Jeremiah Webster* had a much easier time going through the swells, and a kinder motion than the last ships she'd sailed. During those voyages, she had spent the first few days vomiting, and had worried this would be equally as lurching to her stomach. Fortunately, the seas were also kind and the *Jeremiah Webster* was well underway down the coast of Spain before she had any queasiness of stomach.

Later in the month, as they were entering Portugese waters, a sudden squall attended them. But by this time, Rebecca had her sea legs, and she and the ship handled the disturbance well.

Many times she'd pondered on the miraculous experiences both Jane and his Lordship had with their departed loved ones, and kept sacred her own familiarity with her departed father many months past, who had told her, ". . . Rebecca. Trust me."

Rebecca did trust the vision she had that day. How could she doubt it now, after Jeremiah's visit to Jane, and Edward's visit to both Jane and Lord Blackwell? She doubted his Lordship ever let the nautical chart Edward had given him out of his possession, and imagined he even slept with it at his bedside. Had it been given to

Rebecca by her son, Thomas, she would have kept it near her heart, forever.

IT WAS NEARING November when Thomas and John went swimming out in the lagoon together. Their days were not so strenuous as they had been at first. Two houses had been built, a wheat field and a rice paddy cultivated. Now, therefore, the main emphasis of the day was bathing, carrying water to the kitchen, fishing or hunting for food, and keeping their surroundings clean and orderly.

Today, Thomas wanted his father to teach him how to catch fish with his hands. Elias did it all the time, and the men had been learning how to spear the fish for supper, but Thomas knew he could learn how if his father taught him. He'd been asking for a while now. It just seemed there was so much to do, before.

Thomas was glad for this opportunity, the two of them, away from the other men. Not that he did not enjoy their company, but they tended to treat him as though he was still a child, whereas his father told him he considered him a man. That meant a lot to Thomas.

They were about waist deep, and there weren't too many fish around, but John turned to Thomas and said, "Watch how I lay on my belly, keep my eye on the ocean floor, and breathe at the same time."

"But how do you breathe, Father?"

"Just watch," said John, as he pulled forth a stem from a bulbous seaweed and broke off the bulb. He blew through the tube it left and then used a leather strap to tie the tube to his head. Keeping his mouth securely over one end, John used the tube for breathing, while he put his face down in the water.

Studying his father intensely, Thomas noticed how John made no movement, except for breathing through the tube as he lay flat down in the water. Another thing Thomas noticed was that John's legs were straight as he floated, but his arms hung down and his hands were in a cupping shape.

Without waiting for further instructions, Thomas grabbed a bulbous piece of seaweed, broke the bulb off, blew through the end, and was surprised at how much air he could get through it. Thomas tied the tube to his own head with a cord from his waist, took a deep breath, stuck one end of the tube in his mouth, and laid down upon the water like it was a cozy bed. He got water up his nose a number of times, until he learned to breathe properly through the seaweed tube. It took a great deal of sucking, but he soon found that he could breathe through his mouth with very deep inhalations, which made it a little easier. It wasn't long before his hands were dangling just like his father's as the two of them waited for some fish to find their fingers appetizing.

It did not take more than ten or fifteen minutes, but it required an enormous amount of patience. Waiting that long seemed like waiting forever, but Thomas was determined. If his father could be that patient, so could he.

Then, Thomas noticed something rather odd. Small fish, too small to eat really, were coming up around his hands and arms, usually below the elbow, and bumping him with their mouths, as though trying to see if he was edible. He held very still, breathing only when he absolutely had to, and watching his father, to see how to proceed.

Another ten minutes went by, and Thomas realized that it was a comfortable place to rest floating on the water, breathing through the seaweed tube, watching the marine life around him. Patience was the only tool a fisherman had, even if he used a handwoven, bamboo net or a line studded with fishhooks and bait.

All of a sudden a large fish, perhaps twenty inches long, came up to his father's arms and Thomas watched intently to see what John would do.

Disappointed, Thomas noticed immediately that his father did nothing. He just let the fish bump against him, same as the little fishes did, testing him for edibility. But the larger fish did not leave as quickly, it seemed to want to use John's body as a sun shelter. Soon the two were resting in their own water column, John on the surface, and the fish in the shade from John's body.

Frustrated, Thomas realized his father could have grabbed the fish at any moment. He wondered if he should disturb John long enough to ask him why he hadn't. Instead, Thomas waited and waited, and enjoyed watching the fish chum up to his father's shadow.

Suddenly, Thomas felt something touch his own arm. He almost jerked up when he felt it, then realized he'd been so intent on watching his father's fish he hadn't realized he had one of his own. It was at this moment that he realized what his father was waiting for . . . Thomas' fish.

But what should he do? The fish had sharp teeth, and was almost two feet long. How had Elias caught fish this way? He hadn't remembered, except he did remember that Elias always carried them to shore by their gills. Suddenly everything clicked inside his mind and he could visualize himself slipping both hands between the fish's gills and lifting him clear up out of the water in one clean sweep.

How would he tell his father he intended to do just that without disturbing the fish and scaring them away. Then, he saw his father's hand nearest him, and noticed for the first time the fist was closed, and one finger was still pointing down. One finger, then ever so slowly, two fingers. Thomas instinctively knew that his father would move on the count of three. A sudden image of them racing across the yard, back at *John's Cottage* came into his mind. They would start their race just after the count up, "One, two, three." Thomas knew he had perceived his father's intentions correctly. It would be like racing across the yard back home, but this time, they would be racing to get the fish out of the water before it realized what had happened. The only real difference was that this count up was in slow motion so the fish wouldn't know they were planning anything.

When John's third finger stretched out, Thomas' eyes were glued to his own fish, his hands ready to slide beneath the gills, his body taut and anxious for battle. He had no doubt it would be a battle, after all, he was half his father's size, and his fish was much larger than John's.

Moving his hands faster than he had ever seen them move before, Thomas thrust his fingertips into the gills of the fish and hauled it up out of the water in one clean swoop, attempting to stand straight up in the process. He would have had no problem if he'd still been waist-deep, but he hadn't noticed that they'd drifted farther out into the lagoon than when they had first started waiting for the fish, and he couldn't touch bottom.

All of a sudden, Thomas felt his father's hand on his forearm, lifting him and his fish out of the water. The fish squirmed its big tail back and forth, but Thomas would not relinquish his hold on it, no matter what. His hands were small, and they fit inside the gill plates so well, that he found he could hold hands with himself inside the fish's throat. Locking his fingers together, he yelled with excitement, "Just get me to where I can stand up, Father. This fish isn't going anywhere."

John laughed aloud and carried his son by the arm through the deep water back toward the beach until Thomas was neck level in the water. "That's a real beauty, son!"

By this time, the men ashore had noticed Thomas' big catch and had come out to cheer for him. The fish struggled for a while, but Thomas knew it would not get away. He looked back at his father, who was following him up to the beach. He had caught his fish, too, but it was much smaller than Thomas'. For a moment he wondered if his father would feel bad that Thomas had out-fished him. Then, he thought to himself how he would feel if the situation was reversed. He'd be so proud of his father for catching a whopper, it wouldn't matter at all if his was the smaller of the two. It was at this moment that Thomas realized what it must feel like to be a father. All you want for your son or your daughter is their health and happiness. He knew John was watching how happy his son really was, and somehow he knew this made his father happiest of all.

After the men had all patted him on the shoulder and exclaimed several times, "Great fish!" They ran out of compliments and both George and Scotty said, "Captain Dunton, will you teach us sometime?"

"No," said John. "I think Thomas would make a much better teacher than I would."

His father's words surprised him, but pleased Thomas at the same time. "I'd be glad to show you," he said to George and Scotty. "But I think I'll go one better than Father." He gave John a quick wink. "I'll tie cords to one of our ankles, and stake us onto the beach at the other end. That way, we won't drift out above our necks."

John smiled at him and Thomas beamed. His chest filled with happiness at the look in his father's eyes, for he saw pride within them, and it thrilled him to know that he had made his father proud.

Then, Thomas carried the fish to Elias. "For supper, sir." He gave a gracious bow.

To his surprise, Elias gave the fish right back. "I'm the cook!" he reminded with a snap of his jaw. "Whoever catches the fish, cleans the fish!"

"Oh." Thomas had completely forgotten that part of the task. He looked back and saw his father at the water's edge, blade in hand, gutting the fish he'd caught.

The other men laughed and teased Thomas until he went back to the beach, but George and Scotty went with him, to watch him and learn. By the time he arrived, his father had finished. John knelt behind him, and asked Thomas to kneel in front. Thomas held the knife, while his father guided him through his first cleaning. It was not pleasant, and at first made him a bit queasy. But gutting a fish was a real man's job, something Thomas knew he would have to do the rest of his life, if he planned to eat fresh fish. He buckled down and did the best he could, his father guiding him every step of the way.

When they were finished, and had put the entrails in a bucket to take to the crab traps, Thomas' stomach began to settle down, and he asked his father, "What kind of fish do you suppose it is, Father?"

"A good fish," John said. "There are many species, and I do not know all their names, but if you'd like, I might be able to find a book for you in London that will tell you all about them."

"It's not a cod, like you caught near Plymouth, is it?"

"No, and it's not a salmon like we caught up at Strawberry Bank," said John.

"It's an ugly fish," said Thomas, pouting to form his lip like the fish in hand. "And it's teeth are real sharp."

"That's why we do not handle fish through their mouths, son." His father gave him a smile. "I don't know that we've eaten one like it before. Mine is a common bass, just like we've been catching, but yours is definitely different. It looks something like a Portugese grouper, but it's rounder and it's lips protrude more."

"I think I'll call it a fat-lip fish, until I find out for sure," said Thomas.

"Well then, you are the first man to ever catch a fat-lip fish that I've ever known," John said with a handshake. "Congratulations, son."

They walked back to the kitchen house, George and Scotty accompanying them, and presented their fish to Elias, the cook, who smiled and said, "That's better, young Thomas. That's better."

As Thomas went to bed that night, which was really just a bunch of palm fronds stacked on the floor and a light blanket, he thought proudly, *I'm a man according to my father, and that's good enough for me.*

Chapter Sixteen

The Warship, Jeremiah Webster

"We did stand and looke upon them in our shippe as they
were in sight, and could not reach
them with our Ordnance . . ."

~John Dunton

"Planning to make our turn to the southwest toward the Canary Islands makes perfect sense to me," Rebecca told Lord Blackwell at breakfast one late October morning. "If I have made the correct calculations with the astrolabe, we should be able to make the turn about ten of the morning tomorrow."

"Yes, the butter is beginning to melt." Lord Blackwell nodded his head, indicating he expected her to puzzle out his response.

His words troubled her for only a moment, then understanding came immediately to Rebecca's thoughts. "Of course! Southern climate. Warmer weather. When the butter melts, we've come far enough South. Am I right, your Lordship?"

"Very good," he smiled. "You have a quick mind, Rebecca. By the time we reach the Caribbean Sea, I will not be surprised to find you at the helm giving orders."

"I intend to be welcome at the helm long before that, your Lordship."

"There'll be no arguing with her," Ruth told him. "Naomi and I learned long ago that Rebecca has a will of her own, and there's no way of bending it."

Lord Blackwell smiled. "Yes, I think she's proven that on many occasions. Now, Miss Harris, I believe you were planning a lesson for me in herbal toxicology today, weren't you?"

Ruth blushed under his watchful gaze, then said, "Of course, your Lordship. I—"

"And how many times must I ask you to call me Edward?" he asked, interrupting her. "Surely, we're mature enough to share first names together?"

Raising her shoulders in a cute little shrug, Ruth stood up and said sheepishly, "Yes, Edward. It's just so out of character for me."

"Ruth, Ruth, Ruth," he sighed, obviously infatuated with her. "It is exactly your character that has attracted me to you."

She blushed once again as Edward stood, took her hand in a gentleman's gesture, and said, "Come. I'm ready for your lesson."

As soon as they were out of earshot, Naomi cringed. "What am I to do with her, Rebecca? She's entirely smitten with him!"

"I would step out of the way, Aunt Naomi, and let nature take its proper course." Rebecca removed the napkin from her lap, stood up and began clearing the dishes.

Wilhelmina stepped quickly into the room, "No, you mustn't, Mistress. Lord Blackwell said this was to be a holiday for you, and that you mustn't be required to do anything, but nurse your little Jane when she wants you."

"At the rate I'm going, I will not have any usefulness left," Rebecca complained. "Jane has given up nursing entirely except for her bedtime."

"They grow up, Mistress. You cannot prevent that, even though you'd like to, I suppose."

Naomi stood. "Well, I can help with the clearing, Wilhelmina. Even if Rebecca cannot." Together the two women set to work, while Rebecca went out on the weather deck.

Standing beside the main mast were three older gentlemen who had made it their duty aboard ship to keep Rebecca entertained whenever their Captain, Lord Blackwell, was not available. It appeared that would be most of the voyage, since his Lordship had become so smitten with Ruth he could hardly contain his affection.

The three men were brothers, having served in his Majesty's Royal Navy all their lives, each with a wife and several older children still at home. Because they all had the same last name, it would have been difficult to converse with them all at once, but they had asked Rebecca to call them by their given names, and that is what she had done. They were Andrew, Allen and Avery, from oldest to youngest. Andrew seemed to watch over her a little more closely than the other two, but each was a true gentleman, and she was certain they would lay down their lives at a moment's notice, should it become necessary to protect her.

Never had Rebecca felt so safe at sea, for not only was the *Jeremiah Webster* a strong and sturdy warship, but there were two-hundred men standing at the ready to defend Rebecca and her family.

"Well, gentlemen," she said as she greeted them. "How do you plan to entertain me, today?"

"Today," said Andrew with a wry smile, his brown eyes dancing, "We will take you up to the crow's nest, so that you may see our world from a bird's point of view."

Rebecca smiled. "And how do you propose we do that?"

"With the Captain's permission," said Allen, scratching his balding head.

"And use of the boatswain's chair," said Andrew, holding up an odd-looking contraption consisting of a board notched at both ends, with a rope attached to it and knotted together fifteen inches up from the bosun's chair. Above the knot, the rope went all the way up to the top of the mast where it looped several times through a purchase made with pulleys, then went back to the gunwale where it was secured at a row of wooden bollards.

She laughed gleefully. "I"ve always wanted to go up to the crow's nest," she agreed. "When may I?"

Andrew answered first. "Captain said this morning, while it's still somewhat calm. The wind usually freshens later in the morning, after the sun's higher in the sky."

Since Naomi and Wilhelmina would have little Jane's interest for a while, Rebecca agreed eagerly. "Very well, gentlemen, tell me what to do."

"Slip this over your head," said Allen, handing her the boatswain's chair. "And slide it over your—"

"I get the picture," she said, interrupting him before he went three shades of purple. Doing as she was instructed, Rebecca asked, "Now what?"

"We'll manage the down lines," said Avery, who held a rope that was attached to a ring off the bottom of the chair on one side, while Allen held another rope attached to the other side of the chair.

Andrew took her hands and placed them on the two ropes in front of her, just below the knot. "Just hang on tight, and enjoy the ride," he said. "Wilson and Sampson Boone are waiting up yonder to bring you into the nest."

Rebecca sat down cautiously into the chair as tension was put on the line. Fortunately, the men were true gentlemen, and allowed her a moment to get accustomed to the swinging motion. When she gave them a nod, indicating she was ready, they hoisted her up through the air until her breath fairly caught in her throat. Allen and Avery kept the swinging chair as steady as possible by keeping tension on the two ropes hanging from the seat. Laughing with delight, she stared in wonder at the sea around them, relishing every single moment of her new adventure.

No wonder Thomas likes to spend his days aloft, she thought as she neared the topmost pulley. A hook on a wooden dowel was used to bring her nearer the mast, and soon Wilson and Boone had her safe and secure inside the crow's nest.

Rebecca understood now why they called it that. There was barely enough room to walk around the topmost portion of the mast. It seemed quite sturdy, though, and she leaned against the rail with her hand to test it for strength.

"It's not going nowhere, Goodwife Dunton," said Boone. "I've fallen asleep against the rail many a time."

"Oh," said Rebecca, feeling a bit dizzy from being so high above the deck. "It looks much higher from up here than it does from down there," she observed.

"Don't look down, Mistress," said Wilson. "Look out to the horizon. That's what a man in the crow's nest does. He's constantly on the alert for any ships that might be lurking on the horizon. We're still in pirate territory, and the most important job a man can have is to keep the men and ship safe from attack. The Captain's job is important, but it cannot match the man on first alert."

"Or the woman," she pointed out. "Now that I'm here, put me to work. What should I do?"

Boone handed her a spyglass. "You watch the horizon all day long, all directions, with this. It should always be flat and straight, with a slight arc to it, but there shouldn't be any bumps or distortions in the line whatsoever. If you do see something, watch it for only a minute or two, to make sure it's not a breaching whale or a log. As soon as you see something, you yell down to the Captain, and tell him what you see."

"Aye, Aye," she said, taking the spyglass from him.

"Wilson will stay with you, Goodwife Dunton. Captain says he thinks you can handle an hour or more of the confinement, so I will come back up top then, or whenever you wave to me." Boone tied the boatswain's chair to a bollard, climbed over the crow's nest railing and scampered down the ratlines as though it was child's play to him, leaving Rebecca with Wilson.

Putting the spyglass to her eyes, Rebecca scanned the horizon in a full circle around her, noticing immediately the fine arc-shape the earth made. "I do not know how any sailor ever thought the world was flat from this position," she remarked. "Imagine how crowded we'd all be today if Columbus had not gone exploring a hundred and forty-five years ago."

"Yes, and to think it only took five thousand years or so to figure it out," Wilson said, giving her a smile.

"You think the world's that old?" she asked.

"It says as much in the Bible now, doesn't it?" he asked.

"It certainly does," she agreed. "But Wilson, where do you suppose God got his materials when he was creating the earth?"

"I don't know," he said matter-of-factly. "But next time I see Him, I will ask Him for you, straight away."

She laughed. "And, if I see Him first, I shall ask Him myself."

"Oh, Mistress, I ask God every day to spare your life into old age. Yours, John Dunton's, Thomas' and Jane's," he said. "The old should never have to bury the young."

"I agree entirely, Wilson."

"It's time to make another round in the crow's nest," he said, pointing to a spot behind her.

Rebecca noticed, for the first time, a small hourglass that hung on a bronze gimbal. Since it had just run out of sand in its upper chamber, she said, "Thank you, Wilson."

As she turned the hourglass over, she wondered why they called it that, since it only took three minutes to run out. Shouldn't it have been called a three-minute-glass? To be certain, she counted out the seconds for herself. *One-London Tower, two-London Tower. . . .*

The hourglass was precisely three minutes, and she wondered how anyone knew how much sand to put into it, thinking it would be a tedious job, adding sand until it amounted to three minutes worth. How would one shut it off when there was enough sand added?

Beginning another three-minute watch, Rebecca scrutinized the horizon, but she couldn't see beyond the ocean's arc no matter how hard she tried. She did not see any bumps upon the earth's curve either. It seemed a very important job to her. The man on watch up here would be the first person to see a ship coming toward them, and the entire safety of the voyage rested solely on his, or her, shoulders. Rebecca took this responsibility very seriously.

About three-quarters through her hour, she began the spyglass vigilance once again, searching along the horizon in a circle all around her. When she reached the port side of the ship, not far from its nose, which she judged about ten of the clock in relationship to the ship's bow's position, as any good seaman would, she saw a speck on the horizon. At first, she thought it an anomaly, and went around her circle once more, then back to ten o'clock to study the spot more closely. To her dismay, it was still there. Worse, there was another dot almost beside the first one. "Wilson, Wilson, call the Captain. I may have spotted something at ten of the clock."

"What is it ?" he asked.

"It appears to be two ships, traveling together no doubt. It has to be ships because there is nothing else within a hundred nautical miles of us in any direction." She looked again, and was certain the dots were now a little larger than before, almost the size of a pinhead. "Quickly, Wilson. I think they're gaining on us."

Wilson cupped his hands around his mouth and yelled for all he was worth, "Two ships off the port bow!"

After that, everything happened so fast Rebecca hardly had time to catch her breath. Boone was in the crow's nest before she had time to turn the hourglass over. He helped her into the boatswain's chair, and while she was being lowered, he assessed the situation for himself, and made the same call that Wilson had just made. At first she was insulted, then she remembered that all sightings needed to be confirmed by a second party. Andrew helped her out of the chair, and sent it back up to Wilson, who came down, straight away.

Men were running all over the ship attending to their duties. Cannon doors were opened, cannons stuffed with balls and fodder. The entire ship's railing was lined with foot soldiers, standing on the weather deck, their scabbards and swords at their sides.

It was a ferocious time, and Rebecca thought it best to get herself out of the way. She went straight to her quarters, where Wilhelmina was playing with Jane upon the floor. They were piling up wooden blocks together, and as soon as they were three or so high, Jane would knock them over and laugh.

When Jane finally looked up and noticed her, she stood and ran over to Rebecca. "Mama!" she squealed in delight. "Miss-oo."

"I missed you, too, darling. What have you been doing?"

"Pway bwocks."

Rebecca laughed. "Playing with blocks, very good."

"Mama pway."

"That might be a good idea, Mistress," said Wilhelmina. "I heard Wilson's call from the crow's nest. It nearly scared the life out of me."

"Did it bother Jane?"

"No, she just laughed and said Wilson was funny."

"At least she has a good sense of humor," Rebecca admitted.

"Are they pirates, Mistress?"

"Pway, Mama," insisted Jane.

Rebecca sank to the floor and built the blocks with Jane while she talked with Wilhelmina. "I do not know. But we're in the pirates' territory, so they may be."

"Whatever shall we do, Mistress?" moaned Wilhelmina.

"We'll be safe enough, you'll see. But we mustn't show fear, not around Jane. We must pretend that everything is normal."

When she felt the ship turning toward the two ships she saw on the horizon, Rebecca couldn't figure it out. Why would his Lordship deliberately put them in harm's way? "Watch her until I return," she said to Wilhelmina. "Jane, darling. I will be back in a few minutes. Be a good girl and stay with Mina, all right?"

"Mina funny," said Jane as she knocked a pile of blocks over and laughed playfully.

Pulling herself up, Rebecca went outside, intending to go up to the helm. But she saw Lord Blackwell standing near the bow above the forecastle, with his spyglass in his hand, and joined him there. The moment he saw her coming, he said, "Good call, Rebecca. Boone said you have very good eyes for this sort of thing."

"Begging your pardon, sire, but aren't we now headed toward the two ships I saw?" she asked, a crease of worry wrinkling her brow.

"You are getting good at sensing the movement of the ship," he observed casually. Then, "Yes, the only way to meet pirates is head on, child. This way they'll know we've spotted them. I doubt they'll come any closer when they see us broadsides to them."

"You plan to attack them?" she questioned, trying to make her voice sound nonchalant and carefree.

"If they're pirates," he admitted. "If not, we'll let them pass."

I hope you know what you're doing, thought Rebecca, but she held the retort in check. It would not do to irritate his Lordship this early in the voyage, nor to insult him in front of his crew.

"One thing I noticed," she observed cautiously, "is that you never man the helm yourself, sire. Is that normal on a vessel?"

"It depends upon the Captain," he said, taking her by the elbow and directing her toward the steps and across the main deck to the aftercastle deck. "Some captains love the helm, and spend a good deal of their time there. Others share the post in equal times slots with their navigators, mates and masters. Then, there are men like me, who have done their share of sailing, and who prefer to leave the menial tasks to the crew. There is no hard and fast rule. Not yet. But I expect the day will come when each man will follow an exacting pattern, no more and no less, as mandated by law."

"I like the fact that there is more freedom at sea," she confessed.

"Ashore, we must all act according to royal decree or there will be severe consequences. John says that is one of the reasons why he wants to move to New England. There are some restrictions, to be sure, but they are less exacting."

"John is a very wise man. I used to think otherwise, but now I am of the persuasion that he is a wiser man than I," said his Lordship.

"He has always emulated you, sire. It seems odd that you should feel the same about him." She put her hands upon the stern rail and deeply inhaled the salt air because it felt so good inside her lungs.

He chuckled. "Except for my lack of compassion toward my crew," he agreed. "I try to follow his Majesty's royal decree in regards to the punishment of the crew. John always seemed to believe there was a better way. After what has befallen us these past three years, I am inclined to agree with him."

"He's a good man," she nodded. "I miss him so, sometimes I do not know what I will do with myself if we are not reunited, soon. I cannot thank you enough for what you are doing, your Lordship."

"It is Edward's doing, child. Even in death, his only thought was to spare you the misery of losing your son and your husband."

"I know that," she whispered. "I told him that I could not forgive him until he proved he could be trusted. How will I tell him, now that he's gone, that I have completely forgiven him?"

"I'm sure that he already knows," said Lord Blackwell.

"I whispered these words to him on my journey home from your house," she confessed.

"I'm sure he heard your prayer," comforted his Lordship.

"This will be my prayer for many years to come," she admitted sadly. "I am so sorry for your loss, sire."

"I can only imagine what must have happened to him," he admitted. "Each day I mull it over in my mind. It's obvious they made it as far as the Caribbean, and that they have Thomas. But what happened from that point, I cannot understand."

"We shall know soon enough, your Lordship."

"Speaking of which," he said slyly. "How you would feel about calling me Uncle?"

Rebecca's eyes widened. "Ruth?" she whispered.

When he nodded, her smile widened all the way across her face. "Have you spoken with Ruth about your feelings?"

"Somewhat," he admitted. "But I haven't announced my intentions. I suppose I will have to wait and ask Simon for permission."

"You will have it," she encouraged. "How wonderful, sire. After all these years."

"To have gone this long and not found anyone has been very difficult," he admitted. "Now, with Edward gone, I will need someone in my life, and Ruth has all the qualities I have been looking for in a wife. She may be six years older than I, but age does not seem to matter anymore. Besides, she makes me laugh."

"I will keep your secret until such time as you announce your intentions, sire. But my heart shall be singing for your happiness throughout the rest of our voyage."

"Within warning range," came a voice from the crow's nest. Another man climbed up quickly and confirmed the report.

"This shall prove interesting," said Lord Blackwell. "Do you want to watch, Rebecca? Or, like all women, shall you retreat to the comfort of your quarters?"

"I shall watch," she insisted. Her child was safe with Wilhelmina and Wilson, and her aunts were tucked safely in their cabin. "Show me how a true captain commands his ship."

As she stood upon the aftercastle, out of the way, but with a full view of the proceedings, she watched Lord Blackwell give the command. "One single shot from the starboard bow!" His call was passed down to the gunnery deck and a great blast was soon heard from the front of the ship. A cannon ball flew through the air and landed way short of the other ships.

Rebecca wondered why his Lordship should fire so early, but found the answer soon enough, when he yelled, "Show them our port petticoats!"

"Showing port petticoats," said the helmsman. The ship was steered to starboard, revealing all forty-five cannons on the port side to the two ships.

As Rebecca waited to see what was next, the two ships did an about face and fled before them as quickly as two pups with their tails between their knees. Unable to prevent herself, she burst out laughing. The crew followed her lead and did the same.

"Stay on them half an hour," ordered his Lordship. "That should give them something to think about."

"Aye, Captain," said the helmsman.

"That will teach them to fool with the *Jeremiah Webster*," said Rebecca, gleefully.

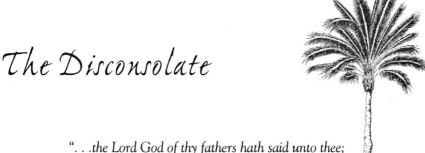

Chapter Seventeen

The Disconsolate

> "... the Lord God of thy fathers hath said unto thee;
> fear not, neither be discouraged."
> ~Deut. 1:21

By mid-November, fighting among the marooned seamen was at an all time high. Their bickering began as soon as the heavy work was done. *Idle minds make idle fools*, thought John as he heard Elias chasing someone from the kitchen house. He wasn't certain it was the lack of things to do, or the inclement weather on the horizon that had the men on edge. A storm was brewing, and it looked to be just as nasty as the one they had recently experienced, aboard the *Warwick II*. For the first time since the bark had been taken from them, John was glad they did not have a ship to worry about, now.

John stepped from the bed-house and walked across the path to the kitchen. Red was arguing with Elias while Big Mike was pushing Robert around. The cacophony was so loud he couldn't tell who was yelling what, or why.

"Storm's brewing!" he yelled above the din of raucous shouts.

Elias yelled back, "There sure is, Captain!"

"Outside!" John shouted. "There's a storm brewing outside!"

A calm came over the men that was beautiful to behold. They stopped their squabbling and went outdoors to see why John was yelling.

Dark gray clouds towered high above the horizon, almost as high as a man could see. There were no yellow streaks in the clouds this time, but it was definitely going to be bad blow. "We've got to secure everything we can."

Red squeaked, "It won't do no good, Captain. A storm like that'll bust all the cords we have and we'll lose everything."

"Then get the shovels and start digging," John said. "And make it deep enough to hold everything because we're only going to get one chance at saving ourselves on this island. If we lose what little we have, we may not survive."

The men who were not shoveling went to work bringing supplies for the hole: several barrels of wheat, peas and rice, a few bottles of wine, tools, swords, saws, hammers, and hand-made cord they'd been braiding together, one frying pan and one kettle, a soup spoon and a spatula, and their eating utensils. It took several hours to get the hole dug deep enough to suit John. Then, they cut some thin palms and used them as rollers for pulling the *Warwick II*'s stern-raft up the beach. They finally got it positioned over their stores in the hole, then took the mounds of sand they'd dug up and covered the raft and all their supplies with it, except for their blankets, knives, a few coconuts and two machetes.

Finding suitable shelter for themselves was the next project. The men decided they should move farther inland, away from their makeshift houses near the beach. Toward the lee of the island, where the fresh-water pool and waterfall were located, a large rock outcropping with a deep overhang would provide their refuge from the storm.

With the wind whistling around their ears, the men quickly carried their blankets up to the waterfall. Soon, they slipped beneath the outcropping and wrapped themselves up inside their blankets. The night would be long and hazardous for them all.

Thomas snuggled up to John, which always pleased them both. The lad was certainly a joy and a miracle, John thought, as he wrapped his arm around Thomas and pulled him closer. He noticed Big Mike had taken responsibility for Scotty, and both Miles and Daniel were watching over George. Great father figures, all of them.

When the storm hit, there wasn't much reason to make idle chatter, for the wind was so loud, it almost seemed deafening. They watched in horror as the trees below them swayed fiercely as they began to uproot. All their hard work would, no doubt, be swept away. Only the grace of God would spare their houses, now.

Fortunately, the outcropping beneath which the men were huddled, was somewhat sheltered from the storm by the mountainside. Without that protection, they would have been blown off the island, tossed to and fro, completely at the mercy of the wind.

"YOU KNOW WE are headed straight into hurricane season," Rebecca heard Allen telling Avery one afternoon, several days after they had made the turn past the Canary Islands.

"Sure, but this ship can handle almost anything," said Avery. "It's built just like the *Admiral* owned by Captain Rainsborough."

"Aye," agreed Allen. "Only bigger."

"It's been given full privateer status by the King," bragged Avery.

"Privateer status?" questioned Rebecca, coming up behind them unannounced. "You mean to say Lord Blackwell is authorized to attack any ship not aligned with Great Britain, and plunder its contents?"

"Naturally," said Allen. "Ahh, 'tis a fine ship with a great captain. Not many men get to sail under the command of a man like Captain Blackwell."

"One ship off the starboard bow," came a cry from the crow's nest. The sighting was affirmed a moment later by a second lookout.

"Another pirate's ship?" she asked.

Allen smiled, "If we're lucky, Mistress. It's high time we earned our privateer standing."

Rebecca went up to the aftercastle deck to see what Lord Blackwell intended to do about the newly spotted ship when it came within range of the *Jeremiah Webster*. Sailing at well over ten knots, they would be upon the ship within an hour or so. It wouldn't be a long wait. When she was within hearing distance, she spoke softly, so that the men at the helm and forward would not hear her. "What are your plans, Captain?"

His Lordship turned and smiled at her, "The usual maneuver, Rebecca. But for your own safety, and my peace of mind, you should go to your quarters."

At first, Rebecca was disappointed. Obeisance was not her strong suit. Considering his request, she decided that Captain Blackwell may have reasons beyond her own understanding. She swallowed her pride, and went below to check on Jane, Naomi and Ruth, who were all napping peacefully. As Wilhelmina stepped quickly from the Captain's quarters, where she had been cleaning, she suddenly noticed Rebecca.

"What is it, Mistress?" she asked. "More pirates?"

"Wilhelmina, you're pale as a sheet. Surely our last little encounter proved to you that we've little to fear from pirates when we are sailing a warship this size."

"Yes, Mistress, but it does bring some apprehension until we know what we're up against. What if the pirate ship is as large as the Captain's warship?"

"You cannot live your life around 'What if?' You'll never have any peace. We must learn to trust his Lordship's judgement. He proved his cunning last time, didn't he?" Rebecca gave her a gentle hug. "You know, it would make me very happy if you would lie down and take a nap. Perhaps a little sleep would settle your nerves."

"I haven't cleaned your cabin, Mistress. Lord Blackwell wouldn't like that very well."

"I will not tell him," she encouraged. "You deserve an afternoon off. Wilhelmina, I am ordering you to spend the rest of the day pampering yourself. Take a nap, a bath, whatever you would like. Just don't go up on deck for a while. Let the Captain and his crew deal with the ship they have spotted."

At first Wilhelmina's eyes got big as saucers. Then she nodded her head, apparently pleased with her new orders. "Thank you, Mistress. Thank you very much."

Rebecca went back into her cabin and stretched out beside Jane, who was sound asleep. Her precious daughter no longer took morning naps, but in the afternoon, she could sleep for two or three hours. As she looked down at Jane's rosy cheeks and her long eyelashes, Rebecca remembered how thrilled she was when first she saw her daughter. Her feelings for Jane were strongly maternal, warm and wonderful.

Yawning sleepily, she dozed off for only a short time, until she heard another call from the crow's nest. Sleeping, as she was, she hadn't quite understood it. Slipping from the bed, she left the room after pulling the door closed behind her, and went out onto the weather deck.

"It's the *Warwick II*," came a voice from the crow's nest. "She's flying gray sails."

"Can you see her flag?" asked Captain Blackwell.

"Not yet, sir."

Rebecca stumbled, then caught herself. The *Warwick II* was within a mile or two of them. She sank onto the aftercastle steps to wait for news from the crow's nest.

His Lordship paced back and forth, apparently waiting for an answer from the nest. When it came, Rebecca's stomach sank strangely, and her heart felt like it had jumped up into her throat.

"She's flying the pirate's flag, Captain."

"Steady at the helm," the Captain ordered. "Load the cannons, and stand by to fire."

"But sire," said Rebecca, racing up the steps to join him. "John and Thomas may be on that ship. What if they are flying the pirate's flag as a disguise?"

Lord Blackwell turned to her and smiled, "John would never fly a pirate's flag with one of his Majesty's ships approaching under full colors."

"Oh." Yes, it made perfect sense to Rebecca. Still. "But they could be captive in the hold, sire. What if they're injured?"

"Trust me, Rebecca," he said. "I have no intention of sinking the *Warwick II*."

"Of course not," she whispered, realizing that she did not have Lord Blackwell's experience or expertise. As her father had counseled, she must trust those she was inclined not to trust.

"Steady as she goes!" commanded his Lordship as he turned his attention back to the task at hand. His orders were relayed along, and once again, a hundred footmen stood around the railing upon the weather deck, their uniforms crisp, their hands on their sword handles, their expressions grim.

When they were within warning distance, Captain Blackwell called, "Prepare to fire from the starboard bow."

Just then they heard a faint bang, and watched in amazement as a cannonball flew through the air towards them, landing several hundred yards forward of them. The *Warwick II* then turned to port, giving the *Jeremiah Webster* a full view of her ordnance, twelve cannons per side.

His Lordship failed to restrain himself and burst out laughing. When he'd composed himself, he said to the helmsman, "Show the *Warwick II* our petticoats, will you my good man?"

The helmsman turned the boat to starboard, giving the pirates a full view of the firepower aboard the *Jeremiah Webster*. They heard some shouts and anxious movement aboard the *Warwick II*. Then, they saw the pirate's flag removed and draped over the side of the *Warwick II*, and a white flag went up the mast. They were giving up without a fight.

Rebecca sighed in relief, and waited anxiously for the two boats to come alongside. It seemed to take forever, though it could only have been fifteen to twenty minutes. When they did board the *Warwick II*, the seamen found the pirates on the aftercastle deck, on their knees with their hands stretched forward in front of them, and begging for mercy.

It was all Rebecca could do not to swing across the space between the two ships, using a long rope, and search for her son and her husband. But she restrained herself and waited, knowing there would likely be captives in the hold.

Within a few minutes, she heard a cheer from deep below the *Warwick II's* decks, and its crew and captives were brought forward and moved to the *Jeremiah Webster*. When Rebecca saw the rescued seamen and the stripes upon their backs, she was sickened. Raw memories flooded over her, for she knew what their punishment had felt like. For unknown reasons, there were several dozen additional Englishmen, who were all unharmed, though they looked as though they had not seen the light of day in quite a while.

Peter Bayland came forward, his tongue swollen, his eyes and face bruised and bleeding, his back oozing. "We thank God you came for us, sir," he said to Lord Blackwell. "But we must sail immediately for the Caribbean, Captain."

"At once," said his Lordship. "John Dunton and his son?"

"Alive, last I saw them, sir."

Relief swept so quickly through Rebecca's heart that she hardly heard the rest of the conversation.

"My son, Edward?" Lord Blackwell asked.

Peter winced at the name. "Wounded, but he, too, was alive when they rafted off the *Warwick II.*"

Lord Blackwell seemed to consider Peter's words, as Rebecca's heart sank back into her chest from her throat. Turning his attention to the rescued sailors, he said, "Gentlemen, tend to the wounds and the stomachs of these men. When they are refreshed, we will talk with them. Which of you know what happened to your Captain and my son, Edward."

"I do," said Peter.

"And I," voiced three or more others.

"As soon as you are cleaned and your wounds attended to, come to me in my quarters. I will have the cook prepare a special feast for you."

"We'll be able to eat it," Peter told him.

"Good."

LORD BLACKWELL SENT forty men over to the *Warwick II*, to crew it and follow *Jeremiah Webster* wherever he sailed. An inventory of the stores on board indicated there was more than adequate food to feed the crew for at least another month. Some supplies were shipped over to the smaller vessel, but there wasn't much need for a large quantity of staples.

The pirates were brought over to the *Jeremiah Webster* in irons, and were shackled to eye-bolts inside a holding cell that looked very much like a miniature prison with clanging steel bars for doors and walls. There was no hemp anywhere for them to pull free from their cage, a design his Lordship explained, he had built into the ship under his own pattern. There would be no more captive pirates sinking Lord Blackwell's ships, nor hiding in the hold to ambush his crewman.

Soon, the two ships were back underway, headed toward the Caribbean Sea until such time as they were told by Peter about the fate of the missing seamen.

By evening, Rebecca and her aunts had joined the Captain, Peter Bayland, Barnabus Martin, and several other crewmen for dinner in his Lordship's quarters.

At first, not a word was spoken, for the rescued crew was famished, and this was their first hearty meal in a long time. Their wounds had been tended and dressed, they were cleansed and shaved and were dressed now in his Majesty's Royal Navy uniforms. They appeared much relieved from their prior condition. When they finally pushed their plates back, protesting they had eaten more than enough, the conversation turned to the fate of the twenty-four missing seamen.

"Tell us, then, Peter, what happened to you, from the time you left Chatham, up to this evening. Leave nothing out."

Peter took another swig of wine and sighed, "Well, we had no difficulty getting down to Algiers, and were even accepted into port by the local authorities. While we were at anchor, Captain Dunton, Edward, me and some of the other seamen went into town, dressed like pirates, looking for clues regarding young Thomas."

"I cannot wait," said Rebecca, interrupting him. "Captain, I implore you. Please let him confirm to us whether or not they found Thomas well."

His Lordship squeezed her hand tenderly. "Yes, do, Peter. Start there."

"We found him well, all right. Rescued him off a pirate ship called *El Djazair*. He's in good health, and at that time, he was mighty glad to be with his father again." Peter smiled.

Rebecca sighed in relief, tears stinging at the back of her eyes. While she tried to compose herself once again, Peter continued, telling about the island upon which Thomas and three seamen were marooned, Edward's being wounded by Abu, and the whipping both Edward and John received from Abu without uttering a sound so as not to frighten young Thomas. He wrapped up the story at the point when John, with seven seamen, dropped the stern-raft off the ship and the *Warwick II* sailed eastward without them.

Then Peter said, "We hid the rescued slaves in the barrels, you see, so Captain Abu thought they'd all escaped or plunged themselves into the sea and drowned rather than remain slaves to him. He was furious, as you can see by the beatings we took. When they finally worked their way through our barriers, my men and I paid the ransom upon our backs for our Captain's escape, along with part of the crew and all of the rescued Englishmen. We made several attempts to mutiny against Abu, but some of the seamen were cut down in the attempt, and some of them was tortured for sport until they couldn't take no more."

"And every one of you refused to leave the *Warwick II*, forcing your captain to abandon his ship?" Lord Blackwell asked.

"Aye, sir. We did. If it makes a difference to you, Captain Dunton named me the Captain of the *Warwick II* until I could recapture her, or sink her. He didn't leave her without a man in command." Peter's chin jutted out in defiance, as though to say he was proud for the stand he had taken to protect John at all costs.

"You volunteered for this horrendous punishment so that your captain could be with his son?"questioned Blackwell.

"Aye, sir," said Peter. "It's what he did for us in Morocco, and it's what we did for him this time round."

"Do you suppose John and the other men on the raft made it back to the island?" Rebecca interrupted at this point.

Peter smiled and his eyes glinted in promise. "Yes, Goodwife Dunton. Nothing could stop the Captain from making it back. Nothing."

"Saying that John and the rest made it to the island. How many men are marooned there?" Lord Blackwell asked.

"Twelve, counting Thomas."

"And you're certain Edward was alive when the raft was released?"

"Aye, but just barely. Like I said, he'd been thrust through his gut with Captain Abu's sword, and then whipped like a rabid dog. He stood it well, though, and never let out a single complaint."

"Thank you, Peter. And thank you for allowing John to be the one to go with Edward. I'm sure it meant a lot to him."

"There ain't a one of us who wouldn't die for John Dunton, Captain, because he'd do the same for us."

Rebecca noticed Peter's eyes filling with tears, as did several of the other seamen, her two aunts and his Lordship's as well. She tried her best not to join them, but she couldn't help herself, and soon had to dab her eyes with her handkerchief.

"That will do," said Blackwell. "Now, I'd like to speak with Rebecca and Peter in private, if the rest of you would please go to your quarters and try to get some rest. We've an island to find and hurricane season will soon be upon us. Everyone will need their strength."

Rebecca remained at the table, giving Naomi and Ruth a smile and a nod. She was sure that they were wondering what this private discussion might be about, and since she had never told them why Lord Blackwell had volunteered to go after John and the crew of the *Warwick II*, she knew there would be questions for her once she was finished.

When all the dinner guests had departed, except herself and Peter, Lord Blackwell brought forth the parchment scroll from his pocket and spread it out upon the table. "I wonder, Peter, if you might tell me. Have you ever seen this map before?"

Peter gasped first, then answered, "Aye, sir. That map was on the Captain's table about an hour before the mutiny. John and I were going over it earlier that morning, before we went out on deck."

"Why does it alarm you that I should have it in my possession?"

"Captain Abu broke into the hold a couple of days after the stern raft was dropped," Peter explained. "He was furious, not only because John, Edward and some of the men had escaped, but because many of the rescued slaves he never found. We'd hidden them in barrels, see. But mostly, he was angry because John kept no chart around with the Caribbean Islands or the West Indies on it. Said he wanted to take the Great Circle back to Algiers, but couldn't navigate the islands without a chart. I told him he was mistaken, that John and I had been studying it earlier on. He dragged me up to the Captain's quarters and made me search everywhere for it, but I couldn't find it. That's why we were headed east when you found us. For my incompetence, Captain Abu punished me severely."

"Thank you, Peter," said his Lordship. "That will be all."

"Beg pardon, sir, but where did you find that map?" Peter asked, rising to his feet.

"From John's guardian angel, apparently," said Blackwell.

"His what?" asked Peter with surprise.

"Thank you, again, Peter. Your actions and devotion to Captain Dunton are to be commended. You have my highest praise for what you have done, sir. You will also receive my recommendation that you be advanced to the position of Captain in his Majesty's Royal Navy the moment we get back to England."

"Thank you, sir!" exclaimed Peter, apparently taken aback.

"Good evening, Peter. Thank you for sharing this information."

When Peter was gone, Rebecca stood and scraped the dishes. After a few moments, Lord Blackwell noticed and pulled her aside. "Rebecca, let Wilhelmina do this."

"I gave her the rest of the day off," admitted Rebecca. "She looked tired, your Lordship, and I did not want her to overdo. She's not used to looking after three people while learning to adjust to the motion and worries of a ship."

"Ah, well. I shall ask one of the cooks to do it. Tell her to take all the time she needs to recuperate. We cannot have our best servant getting ill because I insisted she come on this voyage."

"You really think of Edward as John's guardian angel?" she asked.

Lord Blackwell nodded. "It seems apparent that he has taken on that role, Rebecca. Yes!"

WITHIN A FEW days, the seas seemed somewhat confused to Rebecca. It certainly appeared as though they had recently missed running into some foul weather that had occurred earlier on, for the waves crashed into one another, and came from all directions for hours on end. Fortunately, they were in the trades, and the wind nearly always blew in a westerly direction. They could only pray that the wind behind them would be favorable.

Rebecca knew they were still at least two hundred miles or more from any landfall. But the wind was fresh, and the *Jeremiah Webster* was sailing a good ten knots easily. The pirates were brought up on deck that same morning, where they were huddled at the foot of the steps leading to the aftercastle deck. She had expected they would be hung for their crimes, but this was not his Lordship's plan.

While the rest of his Majesty's Royal Navy were gathering together in their ranks, Lord Blackwell spoke to Rebecca in a booming voice, apparently so the pirates could hear him, as well. "Do you know why very few Englishmen know how to swim, Rebecca?"

"They're afraid of the sea creatures, I suppose," she guessed.

"That's precisely right," said Blackwell. "But more than any other sea creature, sailors are afraid of sharks. You see, if a man falls overboard and he cannot swim, he drowns. It's usually a quick death and most Englishmen feel that drowning is preferable to being eaten alive."

Her stomach lurched as he continued loudly, "On the other hand, many pirates have learned to swim so they can stealthily sneak upon the ship they desire to plunder. When a pirate walks the plank, we know he can swim, therefore it is highly unlikely that he will drown. We also know that pirates are just as afraid of sharks as any other men."

"It all seems so barbaric to me," Rebecca whispered in his ear. "If the pirates wouldn't kill us, we wouldn't kill them. What's the purpose in all this bloodshed? Sometimes it makes me sad that we've brought children into the world, for it is turning into a horrible place in which to raise them."

"Someday, dear Rebecca, decency will prevail, and there will not be quite so many pirates to contend with," he suggested. "I hope that happens before young Thomas and Jane grow to adulthood."

"There are no guarantees of an easy road, sire," she agreed. "Not even the righteous are spared, but the Lord has a purpose to everything under heaven, and those who remain faithful to Him will surely receive their reward."

By this time, the crewmen had assembled, and Lord Blackwell turned back to his duties. "By royal decree," he said coldly, staring into the eyes of each and every pirate before him, "no pirate will be allowed to live long enough to plunder again. Unfortunately, these pirates received mercy and gave back death in return. I have no sympathy for them. Therefore, it is my duty to put it before a vote among my officers. I would like to also ask the rest of my men to vote in this, for it is you who shall be responsible for their care if they are to live. Shall we take them back to England, and risk them trying something so depraved once again, or shall we save England the trouble of a trial?"

"Hang the lot of them!" came the cry from all two hundred crewmen.

"Hanging is too easy," said Blackwell. "Royal decree does mandate that they can be forced to walk the plank. Do you want them hanged," he said with a pause. "Or eaten?"

"Eaten!" the men yelled with one accord.

"Then throw their worthless bodies overboard."

Immediately, the Englishmen surged upon the pirates, removed their shackles so they could, at least, try to survive the monstrous sea. Then, they forced the pirates off the plank, one at a time. Peter was responsible for sending Captain Abu to a watery grave, by special request of his men. Some of the pirates went willingly, apparently consigned to their fate. Others fought long enough to be thrown over the gunwale. But one by one, all of the pirates landed in the angry, hungry ocean.

Rebecca could hear their screams for a long ways afterward. She could only be glad that she was not the Captain and did not have to order the execution of fifteen men, pirates or not, for she doubted she could do it.

Chapter Eighteen

Adrift in Desperation

*"Then the mariners were afraid, and cried every
man unto his God, . . ."*

~Jonah 1:5

It had been a terrible night, one that John prayed would never be repeated. If he and his men had not been leeward to the wind they would have been blown away. To prevent that from happening, they had put Thomas, Scotland and George in the middle of them, then every man had held onto each other and onto the very rocks which protected them, hanging on with all their strength. At one point, one of the boulders dislodged and blew sideways down the mountain, nearly taking Robert and Big Mike with it.

All night the seamen could hear the waves pounding on the beach, roaring upon the land, washing away everything they touched. The pelting rain stung their skin and left round welts all over their bodies. Thomas was in agony and John could only throw his body over the boy, in an effort to protect him.

Once during the night, a strange blue light arced through the storm like a freak form of lightning, and everywhere the light touched, plants sizzled. John prayed silently, feverishly, for the Lord to remove the blue lightning from the storm, and within a few moments it subsided. He was not the only sailor who felt the immense relief when it ceased, leaving them unharmed.

By morning, the wind had died down. All eleven men were too weary to do anything more than to fall into a deep, exhausted sleep, thanking God that He had allowed them to survive.

When they awoke and left their stronghold, they were utterly dismayed. As they hiked down to the beach to inspect the damage, they found debris scattered everywhere. The landscape was worse than any battlefield they could have imagined. Trees were uprooted and many had vanished completely. Where there were ferns and lush foliage, now there was soil stripped bare of vegetation. The houses they'd built were not merely blown down, they were blown away. Even the water in the stream was filled with mud and debris.

The pit they'd dug and buried their supplies in had been unearthed. The raft was turned over at least twice and was now wedged between three stout palm trees whose fronds were shredded. The hole was empty of everything except two bottles of wine and one barrel of dried peas.

Even Edward's grave had been laid open by the wind and the waves. The first thing they did was remove the body then dig the grave out again with their bare hands, and bury him, once again. They scrounged around for several miles before they found enough dry wood to start a fire. For dinner that day they had rehydrated peas in boiled coconut milk, and a few smashed mangoes they had managed to salvage.

The next morning, Thomas, George and Scotty floated in the lagoon for hours, but the water was too cloudy for fishing, and the fish were apparently in hiding, unaware that the storm was already over.

Despair easily settled upon the men. John did not know which was more harmful, their constant bickering when there was not much left to do, or their morose faces and droopy countenances as they contemplated their food supply over the next six months. It was more than John could bear, and he sought a silent place where he knelt in prayer.

Pleading with God for direction, and thanking Him for sparing his son and his crewmen, John inquired of the Lord as to what he should do now that the island had become a desolate wasteland. John had heard that many people received answers to prayers, and he knew the Lord was mindful of him, but to actually receive a whispered answer to a question he had asked, had never been afforded him.

Remaining on his knees long into the day, he heard Thomas calling for him, but he paid the lad no heed. Sometimes a man must turn his heart to God regardless of the world around him. This was such a time.

When the answer came, John was astounded by it, but it came with such force he could not deny it. A voice sounded in his ears and in his heart and in his soul. He recognized the voice immediately, for it was Edward's voice. *Take the men and flee the island on the raft, for Masmuth approaches in the* Larache.

Astounded, John thanked the Lord eagerly, then stood up and ran back to the beach, where the men were gathering what little smashed fruit they could find, that it might be eaten before it was spoiled.

"We've got to get the raft out into the current and leave this place," he said to Thomas, who had been waiting for him. "Tell the men, quickly."

While Thomas went to find the rest of the men, John yelled to Big Mike and Elias, who were headed out to the lagoon to fish. "Come help me, hurry!" They quickly ran to him. John went straight to the three trees wherein the bulky raft was wedged.

"What is it?" Big Mike asked, the moment he reached him.

"We need to get off the island now," said John. "Otherwise, we will not survive."

Elias stroked his scraggly beard. "That's a fact," he agreed. "But just this minute, John? Shouldn't we at least try to provide some food for our voyage?"

"We will not have time," John said. "And what we need, God will provide."

The urgency with which he spoke must have sparked a fire within them, because they quickly turned their attention to the task of trying to dislodge the raft.

"If we only had our tools," moaned Elias, "it would be easy."

"We'll have our saw in a moment," said John. "Look, Robert has found it."

When the other men noticed what John, Elias and Big Mike were trying to do, they ran forward and began sawing the raft free. While they worked, taking turns the moment one man's arm tired, John told

Thomas, "Gather all our blankets. Take them to the stream and wash them as clean as you can. Simon and Red, help him with this job, for he must not wring the water out. Roll the blankets into loose balls. They will be heavy to carry, but they will provide the only water we will be able to bring with us. Hurry. We haven't much time."

Without complaint, the men seemed to sense the immediacy of John's request, and rushed to help Thomas with this important task.

"Scotty, George," said John. "You and Robert get the barrel of peas and the wine, and as many coconuts and food as you can find, while the rest of us work on freeing the raft." They complied immediately.

After a few more minutes of vigorous sawing, the men freed the raft and turned it right side up. They soon cut the other two palms down, and used them as rollers to get the raft back down to the beach, taking it to the outside skirt of the lagoon, so they wouldn't be trapped inside it, nor unable to break free. They had no oars, but took the saw, their knives and machetes, and the three palm trunks with them. The moment Thomas, Red and Simon arrived with the water-soaked blankets, the men pushed off. John and Elias remained in the water, paddling with their legs while pushing the raft forward. The other men used their arms for oars, and stroked vigorously, trading sides when one arm became too tired.

All of a sudden, they heard a big banging sound, and they looked back at the lagoon, now far in the distance. A large pirate ship was entering through the narrow channel that led into the lagoon, and had fired a cannonball at the beach, perhaps to warn anyone ashore that they were about to be captured.

"Everyone in the water," said John. "Hang onto the sides of the raft, keep your head low, and paddle with your feet deep in the water. Keep the raft headed north, toward the current." The men obeyed immediately.

"It's the *Larache*," said Red. "I'd recognize that ship anywhere."

"How did you know, John?" Simon asked. "She wasn't there when we were still ashore."

"She was probably on the lee side of the island," explained John, "waiting for a good weather break to come around to the lagoon."

"You saw her then, when you went on that long walk?" asked Red.

"No, I didn't go that far."

"Father was praying the whole time," said Thomas. "I think God must have told him what to do."

The men were silent for several minutes, and John wished Thomas hadn't said what he did. Some of the men weren't all that inclined toward spiritual matters, and these feelings were of a private nature to all of them, save Simon.

After a while, Elias broke the silence by saying, "Well, lad, if any man among us is good enough to talk to God, and have God talk right back to him, it'd be your father, wouldn't it?"

"Yes, sir," said Thomas.

"We'll have to stay in the water until dark," said John, changing the subject. "Or until they can no longer see us."

"Aye, Captain," said Big Mike. The others nodded their assent, and kept on paddling, keeping silent, yet persistent, in their efforts to escape a possible capture.

After a while, Miles Weatherby asked, "Do you think Masmuth

came looking for us, Captain?" It was apparent by his question that Miles had no personal experience with pirates before sailing with the *Warwick II.*

"Of course. Anything for sport," answered Elias before John could respond. "When we were in Morocco, they'd go tearing off after slaves for no reason. He's probably remembered who you are by now, John, and saw ten thousand ducats in his greedy mind."

"How could you tell it was the *Larache?*" asked Daniel. "You never saw its stern."

"Believe me," said Elias. "A man learns to identify pirate ships straight away. We used to see the tall English ships brought in at Salé, the masts topped and the sails cut and sewn to fit the pirate's style. It's like their signature, you see. That's one of the reasons why we were able to slip into Algiers without any trouble. Pirates know their own kind, and they thought we were pirates when we used their crafty sail plan. But more importantly, they have their own insignia sewn into the sail. *Larache* had a big 'L' sewn into that came all the way down the mast and across the foot, just like that one in the Lagoon does. A sailor learns to notice these things."

Sunset came, and John could hardly see the ship any longer. By morning, they would be out of sight completely. When John felt the current pulling him under the raft, he said, "Everyone out of the water, and lay flat. We're heading into that northwestern current, and our destination is now in God's hands."

Weary and waterlogged, John pulled himself up onto the raft and helped Simon in, who was having a difficult time. Scotty and Thomas, whose energy seemed boundless, helped pull the others onto the raft. George, who was shivering violently, needed assistance onto the raft.

"I know you won't like it, men," said Simon, "but we'd best curl up together before we all go into the shakes like young George here."

John took his spot nearest the water's edge to start the spoon, with Thomas curled up next to him, then Simon, Big Mike, George, Scotty, Red, Elias, Robert, Miles and Daniel. Eleven men snuggled up with one purpose in mind. Survival.

Although exhausted, John said, "I will take the first watch. The rest of you try to get some sleep. We have eleven men, so each should take a two-hour watch, and I shall take four." The men nodded their assent and dozed off, one at a time. Soon, the raft was filled with a chorus of snoring.

When the sky had darkened completely, John allowed himself to sit up. Staying awake and flat at the same time was almost impossible. Thomas sat up, too, and scooted over to him, curling up against him with his back to John's chest. "Can you not sleep, son?"

"No, Father. I was wondering why it is that God watches out for us so directly." He shivered, and John wrapped his arms around him to keep him warm.

"I suppose because we are eleven men who love the Lord, and pray often to Him, albeit in private, and He knows that."

"He rewards us openly, like you said," Thomas agreed philosophically. "I never told you, Father, but that day I found Edward and William Moore near dead on the road to the wheat farms, I had a notion to leave them there. In fact, I passed them right up the moment I noticed one of them was Edward. Then, I heard a man's voice that sounded very much like yours, and it said, *I will forgive whom I will forgive. But you are commanded to forgive every man.*"

Thomas shrugged, then continued, "I turned back to help them, and Edward grabbed hold of my hand and begged me to have mercy on his companion, and spare his life. He did not ask for his own life to be spared. I knew then that something had gone terribly wrong, something completely beyond his control, to make him do what he'd done to Mother."

"If you hadn't gone back to him, son, I may never have found you. The Lord taught you an eternal principle when He spoke to you that day." A lump formed in John's throat as he realized just how much he owed to Edward Blackwell, III. It pained him that they had left his body on the island, because he had supposed his Lordship would have liked to bring Edward home and bury him in England. For this purpose, John had given up his own blanket in order to bury Edward somewhat properly.

"Father, do you suppose we'll ever get home and be with Mother and my sister?" Thomas asked, changing the subject.

"Yes, I believe that with all my heart. I promised your mother I would bring you home, and I am a man who takes promises very seriously."

"Do you love her?" Thomas asked.

"With all my heart," John agreed. "With all that I am, and with every ounce of strength that I have. Although the love between a man and his wife are different than between a man and his son, the depth and intensity is the same. You will learn this when you get a little older and marry, and have children of your own."

"I will be a good father," mused Thomas.

"You think so?" smiled John.

"Yes," Thomas said. "I know that because I'll be just like you."

BY MID-NOVEMBER, Rebecca was becoming impatient spending her life at sea. She insisted that she be hoisted up to the crow's nest each morning so she could look for the island, and for pirate ships. It seemed an incredibly long time for a naval journey, and she now realized just how short her first voyage had been.

A strange tension had been in the air all around her yesterday, and today the atmosphere felt oppressively heavy. She realized the cause of it immediately upon arriving at the crow's nest, for huge dark clouds hung across the horizon, portending the threat of a terrible storm.

Disregarding the heaviness of the air, the first thing she looked for was the *Warwick II*, still trailing the *Jeremiah Webster* like a gosling chasing its mother. For some unknown reason, just seeing her husband's ship made him feel nearer to her. She may not completely understand the feeling, but she embraced it fully.

Breathing a sigh of relief at the tall, triangular sails that followed them, she then noticed that the storm was headed their way from the port side of the ship. It was far enough away that it wouldn't reach them for at least four or five hours. Then she realized that they were headed south and this knowledge quite dismayed her. This wouldn't do at all.

Knowing that the Captain was still eating breakfast with Ruth and Naomi, Rebecca called down to Andrew and his brothers, "Hoist me down, gentlemen."

Within minutes she was marching into the Captain's quarters, her head held high, her manner authoritative. She pushed open the door and noticed little Jane now sitting on his Lordship's knee, eating an apple he was peeling for her.

"Mama!" Jane exclaimed. "Jane eat appo."

Rebecca smiled. She couldn't confront his Lordship in front of Jane, now, could she? Instead, she pondered how she should approach the subject. Should she make light of the change in the ship's direction? Tousling Jane's golden curls, she smiled. "Jane loves apples, thank you." Giving a little curtsy, she sat down cheerily beside Lord Blackwell, unwilling to restrain herself any longer. "Correct me if I'm mistaken, your Lordship, but are we going south?"

"You know very well that we are," he smiled kindly. "Yes."

"But John's island is almost due west, isn't it?"

"Within a day or two or us, yes."

"Why—" she began.

Lord Blackwell cut her off. "While you were sleeping, my men began noticing a strange blue flashing almost beyond the horizon. I've seen that only a time or two, but I know that it often accompanies a hurricane. We turned directly south about midnight, and hope to outrun the storm before it reaches us."

"Oh." It was all she could say. Even Rebecca was wise enough to know that every life on board was dependent upon the safety of the ship. The *Jeremiah Webster* could probably weather a hurricane well. But the *Warwick II*? It had already been through one terrible storm, and had received some major damage from it. Although the mast had been repaired by the crew shortly afterward, Rebecca wasn't certain the forward mast could stand the strain if the ship were to encounter another hurricane. "Well, then," she said, standing up again. "I shall make certain that all our belongings are secured and strapped down, and help my aunts with their things, as well."

"I believe we'll miss most of it," advised his Lordship. "We can already see some clearing to the south of it, which indicates that we may have made the turn south just in time."

"Thank you, sire. Still, it will not hurt to take every precaution."

"You are right, of course."

"Shall I take Jane with me?" she asked.

"No, leave her with me," he implored. "I would like to play blocks with her for a while. She seems to know the exact spot to touch that brings them all down at once, and she astounds me with her astute mind. Jane is much like her mother and father, Rebecca. More so than I think you realize."

"Oh, I realize, sire. She's also got the ability to wrap her little hand around your heart, and when she does, there's no letting go."

"You're too late to warn me of that," he admitted. "I will bring her to you when we're done playing."

Rebecca kissed his cheek, and then Jane's curly head. "I shall be in my quarters, then."

"I shall join you," offered Naomi, standing up and giving Ruth an encouraging hand squeeze.

When Rebecca arrived in her cabin, she and Naomi set to work making sure all the clothing was packed neatly in the wardrobe and chest of drawers, then latched shut so they would not fly open and cause bodily injury. When they were finished, they took turns reading to one another from the Bible.

Apparently, Naomi could contain herself no longer, for when it was her turn to read again, she put the Bible aside and folded her hands in her lap. "Rebecca, what does it feel like to be in love?"

Rebecca smiled. "All consuming," she replied after thinking about it for a moment. "It feels as though your whole life, before that moment, was inconsequential, and that you were born to love the man you love. Naomi, it's difficult to explain, but once you feel it, and you know that he has similar feelings, there is no turning back. You sacrifice whatever you have to in order to be together. You work together as one unit to reach your common goals."

"Ruth was in love once before she met Lord Blackwell," Naomi confided.

"She was?" This information surprised Rebecca.

Naomi nodded. "She never got over it when he went to sea and never returned. Some said he got washed overboard, but no one ever really knew what happened to him."

"I didn't know that," said Rebecca, saddened to hear of Ruth's lost love.

"She didn't think she would ever love again, but last night she told me his Lordship and she were discussing marriage. He's waiting until he can ask Simon for permission."

"I wondered if that was the case," Rebecca said, refraining from revealing what more she knew about his Lordship's feelings.

"Do you think they're a good match?" Naomi asked.

"Yes, I do. They need each other, anyone can see that. Besides, haven't you noticed how much Ruth makes him laugh?"

"I have." Naomi twisted her handkerchief in her hand. "At first, I was dismayed about their affection for one another, but I wondered if you'd noticed Barnabus Martin?"

"Yes, a bookworm sort of man, isn't he?"

"There's nothing wrong with that!" Naomi exclaimed as though she'd been insulted.

"I did not say there was," Rebecca defended. "I think it's wonderful that he's as smart as he is, knowing so many languages, and teaching at the University."

"Oh," sighed Naomi. "I thought you didn't like him."

"I have nothing against him, and the few conversations I've had with him have been rather refreshing. Why? Is there something going on between the two of you?" As realization settled into her mind, Rebecca's mouth dropped open.

Naomi blushed. She put her hands up to her cheeks to hide the rosy color.

"Well, that explains a lot," said Rebecca, pretending she already knew. "I noticed you two were socializing quite a bit. I'm very happy for you. Has he mentioned his intentions?"

"No, he's quite shy. But the other day he asked me if there was someone to whom he should speak in order to court me," she snugged her shoulders up to her ears and giggled. "I told him to ask Simon."

"Your brother is going to be a very busy man when we finally find him."

"Simon is all that Ruth and I are worried about. We've always taken care of Simon. Who will do that if we are both blessed with husbands?"

"You do not need to worry about Simon," said Rebecca. "John and I will take care of him. The two of you deserve some happiness with the men you love."

"We're both beyond child-bearing, of course," said Naomi. "But we've never given up hope that some day we'd find someone to snuggle up with at night."

"It's just too wonderful." Rebecca could not restrain herself from smiling at Naomi's comment. "I cannot tell you how happy this makes me."

"Rebecca, there's something else." Naomi hedged.

"What is it, dear?"

"When John's first wife, Mary, died, we were all devastated. And, we were afraid John would leave us and go back to London where his family originates. When he decided to stay, we couldn't have been more happy. We hoped he'd remarry someday, but we never dreamed he would love again."

"Yes, love is a strange and wonderful gift, Naomi," agreed Rebecca.

"Which is why I wanted you to know," said Naomi. "If I had gone all about England to find John another wife, I could never have found someone I love more than you." Tears filled her eyes and she started to cry. "Oh, I'm no good at preventing my feelings from surfacing," she admitted. "I think my heart is connected to my tears."

Rebecca gave her a generous hug. "I love you, too. Both of you.

From the moment you first met me, you've treated me like I was your own daughter."

Naomi sniffed and wiped her nose on her handkerchief. "I just wanted you to know. We have this hurricane bearing down on us, and if something happened without my telling you, I couldn't bear it."

Smiling, Rebecca said, "Nothing will happen to us, Naomi."

"I wish I had your confidence," she responded.

"My father told me that I must learn to trust those who watch over me," Rebecca confessed.

"Your father?" she questioned. "How did he know to tell you this before he died?"

"I had a visitation," Rebecca whispered. "No one knows, but John. I was afraid to share it, for fear of what you might think."

"You're not insane, child," said Naomi. "I know this for a fact. Shortly before you found John, Mary appeared to Simon and told him all about you. We did not believe him, at first. When Simon went off with John on the bark *Warwick,* we did not think anymore about it. But when your notice went up all over London, about John being taken by the pirates and all, and then we found you at your father's tinsmith shop, you were exactly as Mary had described you. Long, curly blonde hair and eyes the color of the sea."

"Simon's daughter played a role in bringing us together?" Rebecca asked.

Naomi shrugged, tears brimming once again. "I do not know about that, but she knew you were coming and that you would fill the emptiness in John's life."

Rebecca could hold back her tears no longer. She threw her arms around Naomi's neck and the two women hugged and cried for a very long time.

Chapter Nineteen

Island of Hope

> *". . . With men it is impossible, but not with God:*
> *for with God all things are possible."*
> ~Mark 10:27

uring the storm, which seemed insignificant to the *Jeremiah Webster*, though of some small consequence to the *Warwick II*, Rebecca reflected over and over again about the many miracles afforded her in the rescue of her family. Trusting her father's words more than ever before, she realized that God had His hand in all her affairs. As she looked back upon the last three years, everything that happened had been another great step in the miraculous journey upon which God set her.

Edward Blackwell III had played his role in God's plan as well, and she wondered if they would ever know why Edward had gone mad and beat her. But if he hadn't, she would never have sought safety aboard the bark *Warwick*. Oh, the possibilities . . . the list of *what if?* scenarios was so long it seemed impossible to count all the entries.

The one constant that Rebecca knew with all the fervor of her being was that God was mindful of her plight, and the difficulties still facing her family, and He was ready to help her whenever she was willing to ask. It gave her calm in the storm to kneel before her creator, acknowledge her weaknesses, and plead for more strength and divine intervention on her behalf. This she did with all the fervor of her heart.

Is anything too difficult for the Lord? she wondered. A resounding "*No,*" filled her soul with peace.

Now, if the storm would pass soon, they could resume their voyage toward John's Island. She stood, once again, and carried her prayer with her, silently, in the deep recesses of her heart where only God could hear it.

It took nearly twenty hours for the storm to abate, and when it did, Rebecca went out to the helm station, where Captain Blackwell, upon seeing her come toward him, ordered, "I think we can turn the ship back toward the Caribbean Sea, Peter."

"Aye, sir," said Peter. "Good morning Mistress Dunton."

"A good morning it is," Rebecca agreed. To Lord Blackwell, she asked, "Are we out of the worst of it?"

"Yes, although we may have to backtrack a little. If we had stayed on course, we would have lost both ships, my dear. As it is, the *Warwick II* nearly lost her foremast through the night when the lashings broke under strain. When we stop at the island where John and Thomas are marooned, we will need to build another mast from a tall, sturdy palm."

"How long before we'll sight the island?" she asked, pleased that

they were once again heading in the right direction.

"I cannot say until I take the next reading with the astrolabe. Perhaps a day or two." He gave her a tender smile.

Rebecca sighed. "I do not know if I can tolerate being so close, and yet so far away, sire. My patience is wearing thin. I pray you will forgive me."

"Yes, I am most anxious to learn news of my son, as well," he commented.

Feeling duly rebuked, Rebecca said, "Your Lordship, please accept my apologies. What you must be going through is more terrible than any parent should have to endure, and my heart aches for you. Truly it does."

"I did not mention Edward to chasten you, my child. I merely wanted you to remember that there are those of us aboard who share your anxiety."

She nodded in understanding. "Please have Wilson tell me the moment the island is spotted," she requested, changing the subject. "And if it is possible, when you're finished with the astrolabe, I would like to borrow it once again."

He smiled. "Of course."

Near nightfall the next day, a speck on the horizon indicated a solitary land mass. It was interesting to Rebecca that she could see a faint green tint to the clouds above the island, and his Lordship explained that it was a reflection of the vegetation upon the water particles in the clouds.

As a precaution, the Captain ordered that all ship's lanterns were to remain darkened through the night, and signaled the *Warwick II* to follow suit. They did not know, with any certainty, that John and his crewman would still be alone on the island.

Rebecca prepared Jane for bed, then spent the next half hour nursing her. When Jane was sound asleep, she left her in the cabin and went on deck, where she watched the island loom larger from an advantageous position at the bow.

Around ten of the clock, a man from the crow's nest called down, "We've got company. One ship is lying at anchor in the lagoon."

Peter scrambled up the ratlines to see the ship for himself. "Confirmed," he called down to the Captain.

Lord Blackwell paced back and forth until Peter came back down. When he reached the weather deck, his Lordship asked, "Well, Peter? Is it another blasted pirate ship?"

"Aye, sir. Triangular sails. It's looks very much like the *Larache*, a ship we saw in Algiers. It was flying a black flag, sir, but I couldn't make out the skull because it's too dark to see it."

"Any chance she's seen us?" questioned Blackwell.

"It's hard to say. If I was in command of it, I would have left the lanterns cold for the first few hours, just to make sure no one was headed my way. She's lit up from nearly every gun port."

"How big?"

"About the size of the *Warwick II*. Seven guns to a side."

"How deep is the entrance into the lagoon?"

"The crew and I lead-lined it all the way in when we were sailing under Captain Dunton's command, and the most shallow point was four fathoms. The *Jeremiah Webster* should have no trouble crossing."

"Good. I have a surprise for our enemies they will not forget."

"Planning a fore and aft attack?" asked Peter.

When his Lordship nodded, Peter said, "I'll get the men ready, sir. It shouldn't be much of a struggle. We've got the ship outgunned more than six to one."

"Excellent," said his Lordship. "Proceed, Peter, and wake me the moment we reach the lagoon. Keep it dark and silent, and send a shallop back to the *Warwick II,* to tell them about our plans."

"Straight away," said Peter.

As Rebecca walked with his Lordship back to the Captain's quarters, she said, "Thank you, sire, for all that you have done."

"Do not thank me, yet," said Blackwell. "We must deal with these pirates at dawn, then see what terrors they've wrought upon our countrymen. It does not look good, and we must pray for your family's safe deliverance."

"Had it not been for Edward's giving you the chart, we may never have found this particular island," she said. "Because Edward is, as you say, John's guardian angel, I choose to believe that my husband and son are safe," she told him. "I have to trust God that He has somehow protected them."

"Yes, we both do," he admitted. "Without God sending Edward to me, or Jeremiah to Jane. I shudder to think what would have happened to the crew of the *Warwick II* if we hadn't rescued those that remained alive. Yes, I believe God is protecting us on this voyage, as is Edward."

"Goodnight, sire," said Rebecca, kissing him on the cheek. "Please send someone to notify me the moment you awaken."

"I will, child. Now, get some rest." He turned and went into the Captain's quarters.

If that's even possible. Rebecca knew there would be no sleeping tonight. After entering her cabin, she stretched out upon the bed, and held her sleeping daughter close.

Tomorrow she may be reunited with John and Thomas. How she had longed to hold them both. Her heart sang with maternal pleasure, knowing that Thomas and Jane would soon be introduced to one another.

Refusing to allow any doubts into her mind, Rebecca hoped that John and his crew were hiding in a cave, away from the pirates and completely safe. She feared that if she doubted, the Lord would not continue to bless her as He had already.

By the time Wilson tapped at Rebecca's door, it was four of the morning. "It's time, Mistress," he said through the door.

Slipping from the bed, Rebecca opened it and found Wilhelmina and Wilson together. "We'll both take care of Jane today," said Wilhelmina. "We'll bring her to you the moment you send for her."

"You're both such dears," said Rebecca. "Will my aunts be coming?"

"No, Mistress. They are both worried about the pirates and prefer to remain in their quarters."

"Tell them everything will be all right," encouraged Rebecca. "You'll see."

She left them with Jane, then hurried to the aftercastle deck, where Lord Blackwell was in full command. He motioned for her to be quiet, and handed her his spyglass the moment she arrived. Smiling, his Lordship whispered, "Look what we have in store for these pirates."

It was still dark, so Rebecca could scarcely see what was happening, even with the spyglass, but as she studied the terrain around the lagoon, she noticed his Majesty's Royal Footmen clambering from several small pinnaces onto the beach. They gathered at the water's edge in a complete arc, and stood at the ready should any pirates try to escape by land.

Along the lagoon reef, and just inside it, the men who remained in the pinnaces brought them to anchor, then waited for dawn. The *Warwick II* stood majestically behind them and the *Jeremiah Webster* blocked the entrance to the lagoon completely, anchored fore and aft across the channel opening, inside the lagoon, it's cannon doors open and ready to send forty-five cannonballs in one volley directly at the pirate's ship. Rebecca was amazed to discover that they were not more than two hundred feet away from the ship. How the men had managed to bring the warship in that close without being discovered was beyond her comprehension. But she knew the vision would strike fear in the heart of any pirate the moment he saw it.

Then, she remembered John telling her that the pirates were a lazy lot. When he was held captive in Morocco, they drank rum and brawled all night, then slept until noon. John said he'd often found them asleep in the crow's nest long past dawn. Rebecca was certain that Lord Blackwell also had this knowledge, hence his eagerness to present such a grand, visual display. She was interested to see what would happen aboard the surrounded ship when the pirates woke up.

Steadying the spyglass, she studied the stern until the sky

lightened just enough for her to read the name. "*Larache*," she whispered. "The ship is called *Larache*."

'I've seen her before," said Peter quietly. "When we were in Algiers, this one came sailing in one day. Her lines are as smooth as fine silk and she slips through the water in a grand, comely manner. A beautiful ship, this one. John turned to me that day and whispered, 'Someday I'm going to own a ship just like the *Larache*.' Maybe he'll get his wish?"

Lord Blackwell nodded. "If the Captain is wise enough to let us take her without having to sink her, I would be happy to present John with a second ship for his upcoming merchant's endeavor. It will be a good addition, especially since the *Warwick II* is in need of a couple new masts and a rebuilt stern."

Rebecca's heart soared with the happiness it would give John. She couldn't imagine anyone wanting to fight off the English when they were completely surrounded. Her flight was grounded when Peter said, "Captain Masmuth may not go down without a fight, Sir. There's a price on John's head in Algeria and Morocco, after his leading the British to Salé last year. Ten thousand ducats."

"Ten thousand ducats?" asked Rebecca, startled at the amount.

Peter nodded. "They blame John Dunton entirely for the raid on Salé. We only got away without his being arrested by the skin of our teeth."

Rebecca refused to be frightened by Peter's information. "Well, they didn't get him then, and they will not have him now."

"They may already have him," suggested Peter. "I was thinking that they may want to ransom his life for theirs."

"Perhaps," agreed his Lordship. "But for now, we shall wait for dawn and see what, if anything, they have done with Rebecca's husband and son. If I were a betting man, my money would be on John, and that he has already taken over the *Larache*."

As the sky lightened more and more, Rebecca was amazed that the cry of alarm had not sounded from the *Larache*. Was every pirate asleep?

The moment the sun reached the eastern horizon, Captain Blackwell said, "Fire one warning shot."

The message was relayed down to the gunnery deck, and one cannon blasted loudly with a burst of smoke. A cannonball went well over the tallest mast of the *Larache* and landed just on the other side, where its splash into the lagoon doused the pirate's weather deck.

It only took a few minutes, after that, for mass confusion to take place aboard the *Larache*, and Rebecca did her best not to burst out laughing. The pirates ran from port to starboard, trying to decide just how to escape. Some of them dove into the water in an attempt to swim over the coral reefs circling the lagoon, but they were soon scraped and bleeding from the sharp shards of coral, and were rounded up by the pinnaces waiting there for them. Others tried to retreat inland, some of them perhaps not noticing the hundred footmen who waited ashore for them.

Soon the Captain of the *Larache* came forward with a knife at the throat of a young Englishwoman. "You leave," he yelled loudly. "Or she will die! All the English slaves aboard will die!"

"It's Masmuth. Let me take care of this one," Peter said quietly.

Captain Blackwell nodded his consent as the pirate, Masmuth, continued to threaten the woman boldly.

Peter slipped past the men and climbed up a ratline to the first yard spar. Positioning himself so that the spar stabilized his hand, he carefully looked down the barrel of his long-pistol, took an exact aim and steadily squeezed the trigger. A flame burst from the end of his pistol and the pirate fell dead instantly upon the deck, a bullet through his forehead. The woman screamed and jumped overboard. One of the his Lordship's men dove into the lagoon to rescue her, then brought her aboard the *Jeremiah Webster*.

Twenty-seven pirates stood up and raised their hands high into the air, their swords extended. Upon the tips of all twenty-seven hung white scraps of cloth or handkerchiefs. The English cheered and the battle ended. His Majesty's Royal Navy sailed into the lagoon, and took all the pirates prisoner, locking them into the cell built especially for this purpose in the hold of the *Jeremiah Webster*. To their great dismay, and yet to their great relief, thirty-one emaciated English captives, who had been snatched from their homes six months previous, were rescued.

When Rebecca could stand the suspense no longer, she asked Captain Blackwell, "Sire, please. Allow me to go search for my family."

"We'll go together," he suggested. "Come along."

A shallop was brought alongside the ship, and Rebecca and Lord Blackwell, accompanied by Peter, Andrew and Barnabus Martin, were taken ashore.

The Royal Footmen were combing every inch of the mountain, looking for any sign that John, Thomas or the others had been there. As Rebecca walked along the beach she saw, for the first time, the devastation that the storm had caused. Trees were uprooted, palm fronds were shredded. If they had ever been on the island, she saw no sign of it.

Halfway around the lagoon, Rebecca saw a burial mound. "Dear Father in Heaven," she whispered. "Don't let it be John." She raced around the inner beach. Reaching the mound, Rebecca sunk to her knees. She did not know what to do. How would they know without digging up the body? Then, she saw a flat stone at the head of the mound. Someone had scratched it into a memorial headstone. It read:

> *Sir Edward Blackwell III*
> *June 5, 1609*
> *Sept. 18, 1637*
> *He gave his life for his friends.*

Finding her heart filled with emotions, Rebecca strived not to cry, but she couldn't help it. Lord Blackwell knew before they ever arrived that Edward was gone, otherwise how could Edward have given his Lordship the map? But now, his death was starkly final. She stood up and leaned against Edward's father to support him, and let him weep against her. Crying with him, she realized it was not only relief that had brought tears to her eyes, but genuine sorrow for this elderly gentleman who had welcomed her into his home and heart with open arms.

Finally, he nudged her away, as though composing himself and said, "I want his body exhumed and taken back to England, where he will have a proper church burial. And, a locket of his hair, as a remembrance. Will you ask Peter?"

"Straight away," she answered, leading him away from the mound and back toward the shallop that stood waiting for them.

"They won't find any of the men," Peter told her, joining them at the shallop. "They took off northwesterly sometime after the storm. I found their tracks in the beach."

"I will be all right," Lord Blackwell told her. "Peter, show Rebecca what you have discovered, for she will not be able to rest now until we find her family. That's why Edward wanted us to come, and I will not fail him."

Peter led her to a spot farther around the lagoon, where marks in the sand showed evidence of something heavy being moved to the seaside of the lagoon. "It has to be the raft," said Peter. "They either left because the island was destroyed, or because the pirates arrived."

Rebecca agreed with his assessment. "Would they be able to row the raft?"

"Not well," admitted Peter. "When he left the *Warwick II* that night, John hoped they would pick up the west current and ride it back to the island before it turned northward."

"Which boat will be caught up into the current fastest?" she asked.

"Any of them, but perhaps the shallop. She has a narrow under-body with a full-length keel."

"Quickly," she gasped, praying they would not be too late. "Set two men with provisions in the shallop and put them out into the current. We will follow the shallop and keep it in our sight at all times. We shall find John and Thomas, somehow. With tracks as fresh as these, they could only have a couple days head start."

"Aye, Goodwife Dunton." Peter left her long enough to hail two footmen and give them directions, then he joined her once again.

"Let me take you back to the ship. Lord Blackwell will want to be in on the search." Peter escorted Rebecca down to one of the pinnaces and she boarded quickly, eager to begin. As Peter rowed back to the *Jeremiah Webster*, Rebecca asked him to arrange for the men to build a box in which to take Edward's remains home to England, and to clean and clothe Edward's body in full military uniform. Rebecca also gave him specific instructions about cutting and saving a locket of Edward's hair.

After discussing the situation with her, his Lordship decided that the *Warwick II* would remain in the lagoon until another foremast could be made from a tall palm trunk. Then, the *Warwick II* would follow the current and join them.

In the meantime, the *Jeremiah Webster* and the *Larache* would follow the shallop, sailing ahead of her as far as they dared. They would search any and all islands they may encounter along the way. Both ships were flying the flag of England as they sailed, hoping they would only encounter Spanish Conquistadores from this point forward.

FOR THE FIRST several days aboard the raft, the men were able to catch turtles and eat them raw. John did not think they would taste so good, but by the third day, when the men's bellies were aching, raw turtle suited them fine. They were careful to consume all the animal's drinkable fluids, but after the fifth day out, they had to think of other methods of survival because the turtles and water supplies were becoming sparse. They saved the turtle shells to catch rainwater, should it rain anytime soon.

One day they were dive-bombed by an albatross, which apparently did not want them in its territory, but it made a cold, raw supper after one spectacular swoop of Elias' machete met it on its way by the men.

Twice, they were able to catch bass by hand, but now they were seeing huge dolphinfish, which were sometimes called mahi-mahi by the islanders. This species was often found around the Florida colonies, the Caribbean, and in the Pacific islands. It took much more patience to catch these beautiful fish with their flat faces and green, yellow and blue coloring. John and Elias would lay off the back of the raft, their shoulders and arms dangling over the edge, waiting for a fish to get curious about their fingers. Sometimes it took all day and long into the night to convince a dolphinfish that your fingers were just tasty little morsels on the end of your hands. Often, they were able to share a raw, green and yellow dolphinfish, which they found as tasty as the bass.

One morning, John was still waiting, arms and shoulders over the end of the raft, hoping to catch another fish. He'd been in that position, off and on, since around four in the afternoon the previous day, and his joints were so stiff, he doubted that he could move at all, let alone move fast enough to catch any fish.

Suddenly, something bumped his elbow. Out of the corner of his eye, he saw the swish of a tail under the raft, and he put his head down into the water, only to see a blue shark coming back for another bump. Not willing to see if the creature would open it's mouth this time, he lifted himself up with more agility than he thought he had, and dragged Elias up at the same moment.

The shark circled the men for the rest of the day. They could not catch anything to eat because the other fish refused to come near the raft with the shark nearby. The shark was about five feet long, with black-tipped fins, a silvery blue colored back and a white belly.

By the following morning, John's stomach growled hungrily and a keen thirst parched his throat. He looked at his son, suffering equally as much as the men, and he made a desperate decision.

"Elias, grab your machete. When I bring the shark on board, sever it's spinal column immediately. Use the saw, if you must, but cut off the head at the same time. Be careful, though. Even with its head removed, the shark's reflexes will keep going for quite a while."

"Can you eat shark?" asked Elias.

"Yes, and you can drink its blood for fluid."

"Father, no," said Thomas weakly. "We'll be all right without it."

"Son," said John. "When you are the father, you will understand why I am doing this. The rest of you, be prepared to get out of harm's way."

Slipping over the edge of the raft and into the warm tropical water, John paid close attention to every movement the shark made. Each time it came closer, John would reach out and bump it away from him. Soon the shark was getting a little more aggressive, coming in faster toward John. When it turned its head as if to clamp onto John's forearm, John moved out of its way, and used the shark's head angle to assist him as he flipped the shark over, belly side up. Holding it still with one hand, John stroked its belly with his other hand. The shark soon became docile and complacent.

"You've mesmerized it," said Elias. "When did you learn how to do that?"

"When I was ten, my father used to let me play with the shark babies that came out of their mothers when they were accidentally netted from his fishing vessel. I used to put them in a barrel full of sea water, and using a stick, tempt them to bite it. One day I turned one over and it became as gentle as a sleeping lamb."

"Really?" Thomas gave an enthusiastic query. "Did you eat the sharks?"

John nodded. "Yes, but my father often gave the flesh to his poorer neighbors, since no one would pay so much as a farthing to purchase shark meat. But he used the skins for smoothing wood free of splinters. He often sold quite a bit of shark skin."

"Father, what will you do if it wakes up?" asked Thomas, his voice fearful.

"That's the trick, son. Just scoot back, all of you, and give Elias a chance to do what he does best. Ready, Elias?"

Nodding, Elias gripped the machete and gritted his teeth.

"On three then," John instructed. He put his hand beneath the shark and took hold of the dorsal fin, while stroking the shark's belly with his other hand. "One. Two. Three." In one quick movement, he lifted and rolled the shark up onto the end of the raft, then pressed it down against the beams with all his strength. Elias sliced quickly down through the cartilage above the shark's shoulders, severing the head from the body. While John held the thrashing body down upon the raft with the weight of his body, his arms strapped over the shark, the men grabbed his hands and arms, and held him from going back overboard. Elias stuck the saw blade through the shark's throat and out through its mouth, keeping the teeth away from everyone on board until the mouth stopped thrashing completely, about the same time as the shark's body. Then, the men used their hands to cup away the blood in turns and drank it eagerly, even Thomas, who gave his father some while John prevented the shark from thrashing off the raft. Fortunately, John's tattered doublet protected his arms from receiving any damage from the shark's sandpaper skin.

Soon, there was plenty of raw shark to go around, and it wasn't too bad tasting, except for a tinge of the uric acid savor common in sharks. John felt that his seamen, in their starving condition, had no right to complain about the flavor. He remembered his father using cider vinegar and water in a bucket to soak the meat overnight before his mother cooked it. Since they hadn't a bucket, vinegar or the means to cook anything, the raw method of eating shark flesh would do well enough.

"Will you teach me to do that someday, Father?" asked Thomas, eating a healthy portion of shark.

"In about ten years," said John. "I know you're a man, son, but you haven't enough meat on your bones to take on a five-foot shark yet. By the time you're twenty or so, you will have."

Chapter Twenty

The Search Intensifies

". . . and a little child shall lead them."
~Isaiah 11:6

or two weeks, the *Jeremiah Webster* and the *Larache* sailed circles around the shallop, going as far around it as they could, while keeping it within their sight. But they did not find any raft, and Rebecca was growing more worried every day.

Jane had become quite irritable and would often tell Rebecca, "See Papa. See Thomas. Look, Mama." Rebecca had no idea how to calm her at times, and she wondered how the child could really understand, at her tender age of twenty-two months, what was really happening aboard the ship, and why her mother was so anxious and distraught.

The *Warwick II* joined the *Jeremiah Webster* and the *Larache* on the eighteenth day, and now they had three ships searching for the raft, to no avail.

"How wide is the northwest current?" Rebecca asked Lord

Blackwell at breakfast on the following morning.

"I have no idea," he said with a grim expression. "It could be a hundred miles wide."

"So, you're saying that we could sail past them and not even see them?" It was a blunt question, but Rebecca was determined to get a straight answer.

"Yes, it's possible," he agreed.

"Then, I say that we are searching for them in the wrong manner. We should spread out, all four vessels, and with as many pinnaces as we can spare, in a straight line the width of the current, for as far as we can see one another. It will give us more range of distance." Rebecca pulled the Caribbean sea chart from its bin and spread it out upon the table, while those at breakfast moved the dishes out of the way. "Look," she said. "We know that the current runs in this direction, but the area is what? A million square miles? If they're caught in the current, they may not even see one of the islands. And, if they reach the Carib tribes before we do, they'll be served up for breakfast, as we all know the Caribs are cannibals."

"You're getting yourself worked up, child," comforted Lord Blackwell. "Please, try to be patient. The Caribbean Sea is fourteen hundred nautical miles long, and six hundred nautical miles wide. We're only averaging sixty to seventy knots in any twenty-four hour period. In nineteen days, that's less than a third of the shortest length."

"But we've only had one rain squall. How will they survive without water? And how do we know that they have enough food?"

"We know that they are clever. John was able to keep the men alive through his knowledge of sea life when they were held captive in Morocco all those months. Do you think those instincts of survival have now vanished?"

Rebecca rolled her eyes and pushed her long, golden curls off her face. "All I'm saying, your Lordship, is that we should spread out, and make our range of vision more advantageous. That's all."

"If it will make you happy," Lord Blackwell nodded. "We will spread out today, using the pinnaces and shallop between us. But I want one of the other two ships to go forward, for it seems more likely they are ahead of us."

"It's just that we're going in circles," Rebecca tried to explain. "When we know that they are not. They could be directly to port of us, twenty miles to port, and we would never see them."

"Yes," he agreed. "But the *Warwick II* just barely joined us, so we couldn't have done a spread-out naval plan until now. We've had to go forward, ahead of the shallop. It's still the most logical point of sail."

"But we do not know that the shallop is in the current in the same position of width that they are. They could be at the edge of the current, to starboard or port of us."

He sighed. "Which is why we've sailed in circles, hoping to spot them to the sides of our ships."

Rebecca shrugged and great tears filled her eyes. She couldn't help crying, it just seemed so frustrating, sailing day after day, with no end in sight. Naomi came to her side and held her, but soon she was crying, as well. Then, Ruth started crying, and his Lordship held her tenderly while she spent her tears. Rebecca was grateful that Jane ate breakfast with Wilson and Wilhelmina in the morning, for if her daughter had been there, seeing all of them crying, she would have joined them, and her fussing could be far more vociferous.

After a while, all three women were able to compose themselves. Rebecca blew her nose on her handkerchief, while Naomi and Ruth busied themselves with the breakfast dishes.

His Lordship took Rebecca's hand. "Edward would not have sent us here to fail, child. We must believe that God sent him to me because God wants us to find your family. Without hope, trust and faith, what have we left?"

Rebecca gave him a faint smile. "Forgive me," your Lordship. "My strength wanes from worrying."

"I will gather the ships together straight away, and we will proceed with a more spread out naval plan. Perhaps you are right, the raft could pass us by without our noticing if the current is wider than we think it is. It's a big sea, and we've several hundred nautical miles of water between us and any sign of land."

"Thank you, your Lordship." She sniffed and blew her nose once again. "Perhaps I should retire to my quarters and try to sleep. I haven't been able to do so for the past several nights, and I am weary."

He nodded. "When you awaken, you will see ships to port and starboard of the shallop. With prayer and perseverance, we will find your family."

Inhaling deeply, Rebecca nodded, then retired to her cabin. Jane was already there with Wilhelmina. "Did she eat well?" she asked, taking Jane in her arms.

"No, Mistress. She threw her bowl at Barnabus and refused."

"She hardly slept at all last night," Rebecca confided. "I think she senses that I am not myself, and it worries her."

"Perhaps she will nurse, Mistress, for she must have some nourishment."

Rebecca nodded. "Perhaps we will both relax enough to sleep for a while."

Wilhelmina left them alone, and Rebecca carried Jane over to the big bed, where she stretched out upon it and snuggled her daughter close. "Must find Papa," whispered Jane tiredly.

"I know, my darling. I know." Rebecca stroked Jane's cheek and enjoyed the closeness she felt with her daughter. It was one of the few times when Jane was quiet, and she soon fell asleep in her mother's arms.

🌴 🌴 🌴 🌴

ALTHOUGH THE SEAMEN were adrift, they were not idle. The three palm tree trunks they'd brought with them had been carefully stripped of bark so that the thin wood could be opened up and used as a funnel for rainfall, to fill up the coconut shells, turtle shells, and the one barrel they had brought with them. The palm tree logs were then sawed lengthwise, and carved into eight crude oars and two bully sticks for subduing larger fish. They'd also made four sharp spears, each tipped with a shark's razor-edged tooth. All these wooden tools were sanded with shark skin until they were smooth and less likely to splinter.

Their water supply was not so plentiful, and they had used up the water in their blankets by sucking upon the fabric until they had drained it of every drop of moisture. Since John had wrapped Edward's body in his blanket, he was short of water. Although the men had shared their water blankets with him and Thomas, John deliberately prevented himself from drinking more than a swallow or two each time, so that he could preserve the lives of his son and his men. It had not rained the first two weeks they were adrift, and though they had sea life for food, their thirst was keen and terrible.

The men had been sucking upon the dried peas, ten each day per man, to keep up their nourishment, but now the barrel was half empty, or half full, depending upon one's point of view, and the ration was cut in half.

Robert developed sea fever, and had started drinking the salt water the night before. It took all John's strength, and that of his men, to restrain him. Now the poor man was delirious and pyretic.

Soon, all his men would succumb to sea fever if they did not get water. Fish blood and eyeballs could not provide enough moisture to keep them alive much longer. John looked upon the horizon and saw a few clouds, but nothing that would indicate a rain storm heading toward them.

He always took his four-hour watch from dusk to around midnight. The other men took a two-hour watch daily. It made life adrift a little less challenging on any one person, and even Thomas stood watch, usually first thing in the morning. Now, they couldn't depend on Robert to fill his two hours, and Simon was growing more weary each day, so John had been taking Simon's watch on occasion when he felt Thomas' grandfather needed extra rest.

Their sixteenth night out, his thirst was so severe that John spent the entire four hours in supplication to the Lord, for He knew it was only the Lord who could save them now. At midnight, he awakened

Red, turned the watch over to him, and quickly fell asleep.

It seemed only minutes that John was asleep, but he awoke suddenly to something falling onto his face. He opened his eyes and noticed, first, that it was already dawn, and second, that it was starting to rain. Robert was awake, sitting up on his watch, and was smiling from ear to ear. "Do you think we should wake the men, Captain?"

John laughed aloud and a big rumble of thunder echoed all around him. "I do not think we shall have to," said John.

Within minutes, the heads started bobbing up to see what the noise was, as the men felt the drops of moisture on their swarthy faces. The joy and excitement that came alive in their voices was music to John's ears. Soon, they were holding the bark strips open, letting the rain run down the wood and into coconut and turtle shells. A crack of lightening streaked across the sky and John realized they were in for a good squall.

John looked at his son, who was smiling broadly, holding his mouth open as he held his bark and coconut shell. "Thomas, spread your blanket out and pour the barrel of peas into it. Fold it up carefully and lay your body over it so that the peas will not get too wet. Stay there until the rain has passed. You can catch more rain once you lie down."

"Yes, Father," said Thomas, obeying John directly.

"Men, when we get all the containers full, let the moisture flow into your mouths for only a few minutes, then we'll form a cone with our opened bark pieces around the empty barrel, and fill that up, too. If we still have more rain when the barrel is full, you may drink and bathe until it's over."

It did not take long for the tropical cloudburst to drench them. Soon they had every available container aboard the raft filled to the brim with water, including the barrel, and were laughing and drinking water as it flowed down the bark pieces into their mouths.

John had never tasted such delicious water as this, and he knew his prayers had been answered. When he heard Red comment, "I prayed for rain, you know," every single man admitted that they, too, had prayed, many of them continuously. It was then that John knew God had answered their prayers.

When his belly was so full of water he doubted he could drink anymore, he helped Thomas and Simon force the water down Robert's throat, helping him drink a cup or two, until he vomited all of it overboard. They let him rest for only a few moments, and tried again. This time he was able to keep a cup of the fresh water down. They waited another twenty minutes or so, then helped him drink again. After this third cup of water, he started rousing a little more, and they were able to give him another cup every half hour for the next three hours as the rain pelted them with life giving sustenance.

By noon, the squall was over, the men were completely satisfied, and they had hope that they would now survive until they could find land. Steam seeped all around them as the sun warmed the sea, and they drifted for almost the entire day in a gentle fog, but they found no fish to spear or capture. The following morning, the fog had lifted, and the sky was clear, the sun, bright and warm.

John spotted a manta several hundred feet from them. The men were ordered to maintain motionless silence as they waited patiently until the manta came over to inspect the raft. Elias and John dove into the water and wrestled the manta aboard. The men had fresh, raw, manta wings for brunch that day, along with their ration of peas.

On Sunday, Simon gave them a pleasant sermon on keeping God always in their hearts, for He was always mindful of them, and they ought always return the favor. Thomas then offered a prayer of thanksgiving, without asking for a single blessing, which seemed to touch the men more than any sermon could. Among all God's many creatures, they had been richly blessed.

Later in the day John listened to a conversation between Thomas and Robert, who was recovering well from dehydration and sea fever.

"Are you a Christian?" Thomas asked.

Robert smiled. "I am, laddie. Which is one of the reasons why the pirates treated your father, me and my fellow sailors with such terrible disregard when we were captives aboard the bark *Warwick*. They believe that all Christians are heathens, and they will not listen to a word about the Savior or His Gospel."

"I never told them I'm a Christian," said Thomas. "Do you think that was wrong?"

Robert shook his head. "Not if they didn't ask, I'd wager."

"No, they didn't. But one time they beat one of the new slaves because he told them they were not treating him in a proper, Christian manner. I happened to agree with him, but after that, I figured I'd better keep my opinions about Christians to myself. I'm a Christian, too," added Thomas. "While I was a slave, I figured out that being a Christian meant that you believe in Jesus Christ. If you know that Jesus Christ is the Savior of the world, and you believe in Him, you're one of his disciples."

"But his disciples were only in the Bible, lad," Robert protested.

"No," argued Thomas. "Grandfather had a dictionary in his quarters aboard the bark *Warwick*, that we used for word challenges all the time. He'd give me a word and I would define it, or if he thought I knew the word, he'd give me a definition and I would have to give him the word. It was part of my schooling. I thought disciple meant only the men who were with Jesus at Jerusalem. But it means something far more personal. A disciple is someone who follows the teachings of another. Since I follow the ways of Jesus, like my father does, I'm one of His disciples."

Robert shook his head, "I didn't know that, lad. I guess that means I'm a disciple, too."

Simon had apparently been listening in on the conversation. "However," he added politely, "Jesus didn't write the dictionary, Thomas. I believe if He were here, he would tell us that a disciple of Jesus Christ is anyone who will bear record of Him, who testifies that He is the Son of the living God, and that He was and is to come."

"What do you mean, is to come?" asked Thomas.

"The Bible teaches that Jesus will come again in the clouds, with power and great glory, and that all those who love Him will look forward to that day."

"Will it happen in my lifetime?" asked Thomas.

John smiled and added to the conversation. "No man knows when that day will come, we are only told that it will. What makes you so curious over these matters, son?"

"You live your life as though you are a disciple of Christ," said Thomas. "But you keep your feelings about the Savior private from me."

John felt duly chastened. "I'm sorry," he said. "Will you forgive me?"

Thomas grinned. "Only if you promise to share the spiritual points of life with me more freely."

"You're a man, son. A man asks what he wants to know. When you ask, I will answer to the best of my knowledge," John answered.

"What if you don't know the answer?" Thomas questioned.

"Then we will search the Bible together to find the answers."

Thomas snuggled up to him. "I would like that very much, Father."

Apparently the other men had been listening, too, for Red asked, "Will you tell us what happened that day you made us leave the island, John?"

It was the first time Red had called him John, rather than Master, Captain or Sir, and it pleased John to hear it.

"Aye," said Elias. "I been puzzled about that, too."

John shook his head in bewilderment. There would be no getting out of it this time. "It was Edward," he said simply. "Our guardian angel. I had been praying all day, as Thomas told you. Then I heard Edward's voice, clear as you hear my voice now. He said to leave the island at once for the *Larache* was on its way. I suspect Masmuth is after his ten thousand ducats."

"Edward's voice, was it?" squeaked Red. "He was a better man than I thought."

For the rest of the afternoon, the men spent their Sabbath day sharing inspirational stories that had happened to them at some point in their life, that had uplifted them or brought them closer to God.

When night fell upon them, John was standing his watch once again. He spent the time in prayer, thanking God for the most glorious Sabbath he had ever witnessed, spent on a wooden raft in the middle of the Caribbean Sea.

ON WEDNESDAY, REBECCA felt completely frustrated with Jane. She would not eat, she was fretful and obstinate. All she would say was her sing-song insistence that Rebecca must look for Papa and Thomas. Unable to calm her daughter, Rebecca finally took her to Lord Blackwell, with whom Jane shared an unusually strong bond, especially since they began their voyage together.

It was a warm afternoon, so clear and hot that the sun blistered her skin when she stayed out in it too long. A gentle breeze kept the *Jeremiah Webster* sailing in a northwesterly direction, but less than a nautical mile per hour. The entire fleet, spread out over forty miles, was still pressing forward in a wide assembly, the shallot in the middle, still floating along on the current. To port and starboard, as far as they could go, yet still maintain sight of the shallop, were two pinnaces, then two more pinnaces staying within vision of the first ones. The last ship to port of the row of ships was the *Jeremiah Webster*, sailing just far enough away to observe the last pinnace. The *Larache* was in the same position to starboard of the shallop and two pinnaces.

Ahead of them, and out of sight completely, was the *Warwick II*, sailing back and forth in a forty-mile track, striving to locate any sign of the raft on which John, Thomas and its former crew must slowly be starving to death.

In Rebecca's arms, Jane tossed her head from side to side and whimpered. She knocked on the Captain's cabin.

Lord Blackwell opened the door. Rebecca stepped forward as he held his hands out to Jane, who went into the fold of his arms, immediately.

"What is it?" he asked, concern wrinkling his brow.

Rebecca complained, "Jane is beside herself, whimpering that I must look for her papa and Thomas. I do not know what to do with her."

"I suspect you are still in the throes of despair, child. It is no wonder Jane wearies you."

"See Papa," Jane said, snuggled against his neck. She lifted her head and pointed to Rebecca. "See Thomas. Look, Mama. Look!" She said it with such urgency for the twentieth time in as many minutes that Rebecca just sighed in resignation.

"Where shall I look, Jane? Show Mama where to look, and I will look there."

"See Papa! Look!" insisted Jane, whining now. "Look!" She held her little hand out toward her mother.

Rebecca caressed the chubby fingers and sighed, "Where, darling? We're searching everywhere for them."

"No!" Jane scolded. "Look!" It was more demand than anything else.

Suddenly, Lord Blackwell gasped and nearly fell backwards. He caught himself quickly and said, "Go up to the crow's nest, Rebecca. You have more eagle in your eyes than anyone aboard this ship. Go now!"

Rebecca stepped toward the door. "Is that where you want me to go, Jane? Up the mast?"

Lord Blackwell answered, "Yes, child. For I've just heard Edward's voice, telling me that you must." Tears filled his eyes, and he followed her quickly from the Captain's cabin.

Jane squealed delightedly. "Hurry Mama! Find Papa! Find Thomas!"

"Andrew," Rebecca cried out, rushing to the weather deck. "Prepare the boatswain's chair immediately."

Within minutes, Rebecca was being hoisted up to the crow's nest, the Captain's spyglass held tightly in her hands. If this is what Edward wanted her to do, she would not argue. She would trust him completely. And, it would also involve her going up the mast to settle Jane's anxious pleadings, as well. A scripture floated through her mind, something about a little child leading, but the reference escaped her. Perhaps Jane knew more than she could tell her mother.

As soon as she was inside the crow's nest, Rebecca searched the horizon all around her with the Captain's spyglass, but she saw nothing but sea and sky. For about ten minutes, Rebecca went in circles looking until she was dizzy. When she passed up a little line of thickening on the horizon, she stopped and focused on it. It did not seem to be a bump, really. Not like the mast of a ship would look. Rather it seemed to be a faint thick spot, almost indiscernible.

Her heart started to swell inside her chest and her eyes gathered moisture so quickly she almost couldn't see. She dropped the spyglass, picked it up again, and asked the man with her, "Do you see that?"

"No, Mistress," he said, "I don't see anything at all."

Rebecca looked one more time, gasped, then called down to his Lordship. "Straight off the stern to port, at eight of the clock. Turn quickly! Quickly!"

The Captain gave the order and the ship came about sharply, dipping into the sea, causing the ship to tilt to port momentarily. The top of the mast swayed precariously, making her feel as though it might drop her down into the sea, and dump her out of the nest altogether. In a few moments, the ship righted properly and she looked again through the spyglass.

The thickening that had been there moments before had vanished. Still, she knew what she saw, and she kept a vigil along the horizon. When she saw the same thickening once again, she called out, "Take the ship to one of the clock and keep her straight and steady!"

Both she and the seaman eyeballed the horizon for a full ten minutes before the seaman stood up and yelled, "That's affirmative, Captain. I believe she's found them!"

How he would know that, she had no idea, for she still couldn't see more than a flat lump on the surface, a faint small arc that seemed to be getting bigger. A roar went up from the men on deck, and the Captain called below, "Fire one cannon."

Rebecca knew that would tell the other ships they were veering off course to investigate something. Three cannon blasts would tell them they had found the raft.

Within seconds, a blast of fire and flame belched from a lead cannon, the sound echoing through the air for miles.

Suddenly, it seemed, Rebecca started to see a little taller formation, on the horizon. She studied it for several long minutes, the shape getting closer and a little more distinct.

"QUICKLY, MEN!" JOHN yelled. By this time, they had Big Mike standing in the center of the raft, with Miles and Daniel Weatherby on either side of him. Simon and Elias stood on their shoulders, while John climbed up and stood on their shoulders. They were now three men tall. "Get Thomas up here with that white shirt. Hurry, now."

Thomas scrambled up the men like a monkey swinging from branch to branch. "On my shoulders," John said. "It's a long shot that they've seen us, but we have to try."

"I'll get their attention," said Thomas as he climbed atop his father's shoulders. They were all in a precarious position, and if the ocean had been swelling much they wouldn't have attempted their athletic pyramid at all. Thomas waved the white shirt back and forth, back and forth. The men yelled with all the strength they had, but John knew the ship couldn't possibly hear them from this distance. He could only pray they would see them.

"What if they think we're a pirate ship? They can't tell from this distance, can they?" asked Thomas.

"Keep waving the white shirt, son. They'll soon know we're not."

"What if it's a pirate's ship, Father?"

"Not with square sails, son. English or Spanish, they'll be, but not pirates."

Thomas kept up his waving for a full fifteen minutes as the ship approached. When they'd first spotted it, John knew the man in the crow's nest would never be able to see them. Making a pyramid might help, but it was a long shot. As the ship went from east to west, they were certain they'd been missed. Heartache felt keenly heavy, and he was just about to order them all down, when suddenly he heard a sound, like a faint pop or bang. John knew instantly what it was. "Have they seen us?" he asked. "Did you hear that?

He heard the whispers of the men, asking God for the answers to John's questions, but no one spoke. They just listened.

Still, they waited in pyramid formation until they were certain that the ship was headed toward them. Thomas continued his waving, ever vigilant in his task.

"As soon as we know for sure," said John. "Thomas, I want you to dive overboard. I shall follow you. It'll make it easier for everyone to get down."

"I will dive off, too," offered Elias.

"I shall expect some help getting down from here," said Simon. "I may enjoy the water, but not when I'm in it!"

Chapter Twenty One

Heart-ward Bound

*"All these good Shippes with the Captives are in
Safety. . . , We give God thankes."*
~John Dunton

R ebecca watched from the crow's nest for another half hour, until she could see the human pyramid more clearly. At first it seemed like stick people, and she couldn't tell for sure. The man on top was definitely moving, so she knew someone was alive aboard the raft.

"It's them!" called down the seaman.

"Affirmative," she yelled, her heart singing, her soul rejoicing.

Then she heard the Captain's next order. "Fire off three cannons."

Almost immediately, three cannon blasts went out to starboard. She looked through the spyglass again, this time able to discern the men a little more clearly, though she couldn't identify who they were. Suddenly, the man on top dove off the third man's shoulders, straight into the water. The cannon blasts must have told them they had been spotted. *The man who dove must have been John,* she thought. No one dives like that, but John. Just as the thought formed in her head, the third man, who was now on top, dove off the human pyramid. *Now that was John!* Her heart sang inside her chest. But who was the first man? One of the seamen, no doubt. That only left two more to get down. One of them jumped into the water, and she knew that this one wouldn't have been John. He loved diving. The other, who she saw had a either a bald head or some shocking white hair, was helped down by the three below him. Then she realized that this one was Simon.

"Ruth! Naomi!" she called. "I can see Simon!"

Rebecca watched only for a moment as the twin sisters hugged one another, then turned her attention towards the raft again. The closer they came, the more that she recognized their features.

Through the spyglass, she saw a man stand up, and a shorter man beside him. When they put their arms around each other, she knew it was John and Thomas. Until their faces were clearer, she wasn't going to announce it. But she knew. Rebecca knew it was Father and son. When she could finally see their faces clearly, she memorized every line, every freckle. Thomas looked so good. He'd grown about a foot, but he seemed well and happy to be with his father.

"Mistress, isn't Captain Dunton among them?" asked the seaman.

"Yes, he is," she said, tears dripping down her face, her vision glued to the men she loved through the spyglass.

The man seemed to sigh in relief. "You had me worried, Mistress. You were crying, but hadn't announced anything yet."

"Oh, you do it," she said. "I cannot take my eyes off them."

"Captain Dunton and Thomas are aboard the raft!" the seaman yelled.

Another cheer went up from the men aboard.

"And nine other men," she said, reminding him.

When the cheering had died down, the seaman yelled the new number down, then said, "Whenever you're ready to go below, Mistress, I'll help you."

"Not yet," she said, still staring at her husband and her son. "I'm afraid if I was down below I would want to run to the front of the bow and jump off, as though I could swim there faster."

"You'd be run over," he observed casually.

"Which is precisely why I'm staying right here."

BY THE TIME the ship reached the raft, it was nearly sunset. The men looked half-starved, but well enough to climb up ratlines and come aboard of their own accord. Rebecca hugged Simon immediately, then motioned for him to be silent. She wanted to surprise John and Thomas, but she could scarcely wait for them to arrive. They seemed to have waited for all the other men to go first. *Isn't that just like John? Always the Captain, always a gentleman.*

When Thomas came up tenth, Rebecca stood before him, wondering if he would even recognize her. When he did, she could restrain herself no longer.

"Mother?" he questioned. "Is it really you?"

She grabbed him and pulled him into her arms, holding him as though she would never be able to get enough of him. "It is I, Thomas. Oh, Thomas, I've missed you so!"

John came over the gunwale just then, and when he saw her, tears filled his eyes. "Rebecca!" he exclaimed, pulling both her and Thomas into his embrace. For several long moments he held her as she wept against him, Thomas by her side.

"Now would be a good time, son," said John.

"You're too late, Father, I'm already crying," said Thomas, holding them close to him. When he had finally composed himself, he said, "Mother, Father told me I have a little sister."

"Jane's been waiting for you all day, son. She's with your grandfather and aunts," answered Rebecca.

"May I go see her?" he asked.

"A true gentleman, just like your father," she cried and laughed at the same time, never feeling more proud of her son than at that moment. "Yes, you certainly may."

He left them then, and Rebecca watched him approach Simon, who was standing a few feet away, holding Jane in his arms. She looked up at John, only for a moment, and saw the tears on his face as he watched this first interaction between his son and his daughter. Thrilled to see such love on his face, Rebecca turned her attention back to Thomas.

Holding out his hands, Thomas said, "Hello, Jane. I'm your brother, Thomas."

Jane clapped her hands excitedly. "Thomas!" she squealed in delight. Then she jumped into his arms as if she had known him all

her life and held him tight, just as he did her.

Satisfied that Thomas and Jane were going to get along splendidly, Rebecca looked up at John, pleased to be safe and snug against him, with his arm around her once again.

"How did you know?" he asked, looking down at her tenderly.

"We had a lot of help," she answered. "And a lot of miracles."

He stared into her eyes as though mesmerized by her, and Rebecca instantly felt the flames of true love sweep through her. John's lips sought hers and he kissed her eagerly, longingly.

A roar of cheer went up from the crowd of men, and John withdrew, blushed ever so slightly, then bent his head for another kiss.

🌴 🌴 🌴 🌴 🌴

"AND THIS IS a bollard," said Thomas, taking Jane for a stroll the following afternoon. He held her hand and walked beside her, proud to see all the progress she had made. In truth, he was expecting more baby than child, but she had grown beyond his expectations.

Jane reached her hand out and tried to touch the row of wooden dowels upon which ropes and hawsers were hung. Thomas lifted her up just enough so that she could grab hold. "Boward," she said.

"Hmm," said Thomas. "I've been noticing, Jane, that your language skills need a little work. Will you be offended if I offer my services? I'm sure Mother and Father are far too busy catching up on lost time to worry about that just now."

Thomas grinned and lifted Jane the rest of the way up into his arms. She squeezed him tightly. Sometimes his little sister acted as though she would never let go of him, and this pleased him for the moment. Mother warned him not to keep Jane out too long, for she was almost ready for her nap, but Thomas couldn't let Jane sleep. He had to take every opportunity to be with her, to show her he loved her, to let her know he would be around for a very long time to take care of her. As she rested her head upon his shoulder, Thomas started talking to her.

"Father says we're going to Virginia. Lord Blackwell is giving him the *Larache* and we'll be spending the winter there. In the spring, we'll head up to Massachusetts. Father's cousin, the one I was named after, lives in a little town called Billerica.

"Father's going to get mother settled in her own home, while Lord Blackwell goes back to England. Grandfather, Aunt Naomi and Aunt Ruth are going to England with him. Aunt Ruth is going to marry Lord Blackwell, and they're going to adopt the orphans, George and Scotty, who Father rescued in Algeria. Then, Barnabus Martin has been given permission to court Aunt Naomi, so they won't have to worry about Grandfather anymore. We'll get to do that now. While he's in England, Grandfather is going to sell the houses at Stepney Parish and settle his affairs. Then, he'll pack up our most prized possessions, and bring what he can back to Massachusetts."

Thomas glanced at his little sister's eyes, now closed in slumber, and felt a surge of pride deep within himself to know that he had been able to lull her to sleep. Continuing the conversation, regardless that she no longer heard him, he said, "I hope Grandfather remembers to bring my three clear rocks and my slingshot."

Jane stirred, lifted her head momentarily, then rested it once again, falling sound asleep. Thomas couldn't take her back to his parents quarters. Not yet. After all, he had so much to tell her. As he continued walking around the ship, he talked to Jane with all the pent-up emotions he had kept within for such a long, long time.

"Father's starting his own merchant business, trading goods between Virginia and Massachusetts. He'll have two ships to get the enterprise started. He's going to give the *Warwick II* to me, when I get older, if I tell him that I want it. He knows I want it, but he likes me to make my own decisions, because I'm a man now.

"Of course, I'll have to stick around for a long while. I've got to help Mother and Father raise you and the rest of our brothers and sisters. I hope we have a large family. It's great that you've come along, Jane, and I love you with all my heart, but I'd really like a brother, too. No offense intended, you understand. Right now, you're number one in my life.

"It was great last night, listening to Mother's and Lord Blackwell's stories about how you led mother to find us, and how his Lordship got that nautical chart from Edward. It's going to feel funny, calling Lord Blackwell, Uncle Edward.

"Did I tell you that Wilson and Wilhelmina are going to stay with us in America? They want to take care of Mother, instead of going back to Blackwell Tower. His Lordship gave them his permission, for he knew another young couple who would happily take their place. I guess they're living in our house right now.

"Anyway, when we get to Virginia, Father's going to change the name of the *Larache*. At first I wasn't sure I'd like it, but the more I think about it, the more I believe Father is doing something really inspired. He'll only deny it, so don't pester him about it."

Thomas smiled to himself, remembering the special man who not only got his family together, but saved them, too. Then, he shared the news with sleeping Jane.

"Father's going to name his new ship the *Edward III*."

Author Notes:

Astrolabe is a medieval instrument consisting of a graduated vertical circle with a movable arm, used to determine the altitude of the sun or other celestial bodies for navigational purposes.

Bollard is a thick post on a ship or wharf, used for securing ropes and hawsers.

Burthen tonnage was an official figure, used not only for commercial purposes, but also to calculate port dues. It was originally a measure of the number of tons of wine that could be carried.

A True Journall of the Sally Fleet was published in London, 1637, by John Dunton, and details his experiences as a Master aboard the ship, *Admiral*, called *Leopard* for King Charles' raid on Salé, Morocco. John's capture by pirates is detailed in other accounts of the Winchester Court record system, and in the Mariner's Mirror. It is believed that **A *True Journall of the Sally Fleet*** was printed with the intent that the world would know John Dunton's story, and the story of his only son, who were both captured by pirates sometime between 1632 and 1635.

Search for the Bark Warwick, contains the fictionalized account of John's capture and mutinous escape, and the English Armada's successful raid on Salé, Morocco, to free their countrymen and other Christians.

Search for the Warwick II is completely fictional. Only the name, John Dunton, is taken from actual historical records.

Other Books by Sherry Ann Miller

Search for the Bark Warwick

Beginning with the stowaway who interrupts and changes John's life forever, and concluding with John's desperate search for his captive son, *Search for the Bark Warwick* is a stirring tale of surprise, compassion, love and tenacious devotion to family. The story of a true hero in 1630's England, *Search for the Bark Warwick* will keep you on the edge of your seat, and leave you begging for more. Now available from your favorite bookstore. If they don't have it, please ask them to order directly from Granite Publishing & Distribution (800) 574-5779). ISBN# 1-932280-33-2 The Warwick saga is a two-volume series.

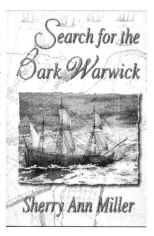

One Last Gift

First in the five-book Gift Series, *One Last Gift* revolves around Kayla, who gave up religion ten years earlier to pursue a lifestyle completely foreign to her upbringing. When she receives a disturbing telephone call from her father, Mont, she reluctantly leaves her fiancée, her sailboat, and her challenging career in San Diego, and hastens to her childhood home high in the Uinta Mountains. Her return stirs up questions from her past she thought she'd buried years before: Why does Mont tenaciously cling to his faith, regardless of his daughter's rejection of it? Isn't God just a crutch people use when they don't understand science? Does

her mother really live in the Spirit World, as Mont insists? Kayla conquers one issue after another until she faces the greatest obstacle of her life in a desperate race for survival. Will tragedy turn Kayla's analytical heart back to God, or will it take a miracle? *One Last Gift* placed third in the national "Beacon Awards" (2000) for published authors. Now available from your favorite bookstore. If they don't have it, please ask them to order directly from Granite Publishing & Distribution (800) 574-5779. ISBN# 1-930980-01-9

An Angel's Gift

An award willing novel!

While *One Last Gift* dwelt on Kayla's conversion, *An Angel's Gift* answers the question she left behind: What about Ed? When Alyssa drops in at the Bar M Ranch (literally!), she disrupts the life of the ranch foreman, Ed Sparkleman, and keeps him jumping hoops almost beyond what he can endure . . . *what a hero!* Along the way, Alyssa's confidence is shaken, and she must learn to trust God once again, but not until after a desperate sacrifice and the miraculous trial of her faith.

An Angel's Gift placed first in the Write Touch Readers' Competition (2004); tied for first place in the national *Beacon Awards* (2004); and placed fourth in the Utah *Heart of the West* competition (2002); *An Angel's Gift* is installment two in the five-book **Gift Series**. Now available from your favorite bookstore. If they don't have it, please ask them to order directly from Granite Publishing & Distribution (800) 574-5779). ISBN# 1-930980-98-1.

The Tyee's Gift

What about Abbot? Where did he go and what happened to him after Alyssa broke their engagement in *An Angel's Gift?* You will find all the answers to these questions when Abbot becomes Tyee (pronounced *tie-yee*, it means Chief or Great Leader) to a little boy and his trusting Aunt. Escape to the Northwest with Abbot, meet beautiful Bekah, go on an archaeological expedition, sail the Pacific Ocean in a terrific gale, and watch the miracle of *The Tyee's Gift* unfold. *The Tyee's Gift* is installment three in the five-book Gift Series. Coming in the fall of 2004. Ask your bookseller to inform you when it arrives.

Charity's Gift

When Hans and Tom sail to Cocos Island off the coast of Costa Rica, Hans meets and falls in love with Charity Blake. But winning Charity's trust will be difficult. She hates rich Americans, especially those who have no real goals in life. In order to change her heart, Hans' will need a miracle. *Charity's Gift*, the fourth book in the Gift series, is in progress.

The Refiner's Gift

Tom gets his miracle in this final installment of the Gift Series, in development.

Gardenia Sunrise

Frightened by the drastic measures it will take to provide even the remotest hope for a cure to her cancer, Brandje flees to her villa on the west coast of France where she hopes to prepare herself emotionally and spiritually to meet God. Her plans are interrupted when Nathan, an American with a hot temper, arrives for his annual holiday at the villa, unaware that his reservation has been canceled. Brandje's remarkable journey of spiritual and romantic discovery touches the soul with enlightenment, hope and inspiration. *Gardenia Sunrise* is a powerful conversion story that will linger in your heart forever. Now available from your favorite bookstore. If they don't have it, please ask them to order directly from Granite Publishing & Distribution (800) 574-5779). ISBN# 1-930980-33-7

Readers' Comments

Sherry Ann Miller loves to hear from her readers.
Please write to her at Sherry@sherryannmiller.com
Read what others are saying about her novels:

"I wanted to send along my thoughts and feelings about **One Last Gift** and **An Angel's Gift**. I read both of them really fast, ignoring almost everything but work. The stories were both wonderful. The feelings from the books were wonderful. I felt such a strong spirit within the stories that I had a hard time forgetting and moving on to another book after finishing them. I do believe in miracles and I am so glad for them in my life and in my heart. Thank you for sharing your strength and your spirit as you write your stories and pass them along"
~Robyn Cox

"Just finished reading your super *Search for the Warwick II* and the book is a great read."
~Ann Bradshaw, author

"Thank you so much for sending me a copy of *Search for the Bark Warwick*. I have been reading it during periods of "down time" in my office. It's great. You write beautifully and with a love of things nautical which I share."
~Daniel Paull, Cardiac Surgeon VMMC

"I have read *The Tyee's Gift* and thoroughly enjoyed it . . . you gave me so much pleasure reading it."
~Ivy Spencer

"*Search for the Bark Warwick* was absolutely my favorite of all your books but it left me on tenterhooks—what happened to Thomas?? I was so eager to read the sequel, *Search for the Warwick II* I did it in one weekend! Once again you combined history and adventure and suspense in a very human setting that left me satisfied. That is not to say I wouldn't just as eagerly anticipate a third novel in the series as well!
~Irma Furman

"I finished *The Tyee's Gift* today. It was Great as usual, but I didn't want it to end."

~Jackie Arnold

"*The Tyee's Gift* was amazing and an inspiration to me."

~Jennifer Manlove

YOU can receive a FREE book!

Participate in Sherry Ann's *Readers' Comments* and receive a free, autographed copy of the book in which your comment appears. All those people whose comments appear in this copy of **Search for the Warwick II** will, and you can, too. Simply e-mail Sherry@sherryannmiller.com, putting the title of the book in the subject line, and your comments in the body. If your comments are selected for inclusion in one of Sherry's books, you'll get your own autographed copy of that book! Permission to use your comments must be included, as well as your full name, and current e-mail and postal addresses. Thanks!

About the Author

Sherry Ann Miller
"writer of miracles"

Sherry Ann is the mother of seven and grandmother of twenty-five. She lives in Port Ludlow, WA, where she spends her life sailing, exploring marine life, researching her family history and writing miracles into her inspirational novels. Sherry Ann is the author of six published novels, several poems, short articles, one-act plays, and road-shows, and two full-scale musical productions. By writing miracles that foster hope and belief in a loving and kind Father in Heaven, Sherry hopes to convince her readers that " . . . with God, nothing shall be impossible." (Luke 1:37)